SONG OF THE SEA GOD

CHRIS HILL

First published in Great Britain in 2012 by Skylight Press,
210 Brooklyn Road, Cheltenham, Glos GL51 8EA

Designed and typeset by Rebsie Fairholm
Publisher: Daniel Staniforth

Cover photography:
Phil Murray, Cascade Photography, Cockermouth: phone 01900 828667

www.skylightpress.co.uk

Printed and bound in Great Britain by Lightning Source, Milton Keynes.

British Library Cataloguing in Publication Data.
A catalogue record for this book is available from the British Library.

ISBN 978-1-908011-55-8

For Claire, Joseph and Matthew

"The Ethiopians say that their gods are snub-nosed and black, the Thracians that theirs have light blue eyes and red hair."
Xenophanes (560 BC – 476 BC)

I

I remember the moment I died.

The end came subdued, like a doctor on call. There was no sensation. Feelings belonged to a different world – one which had finished with me.

Having a piss after eating asparagus. Getting a face full of sleet. The surprise of cold coffee. All gone.

I had been taken extravagantly ill. Pancreatitis thumped me in the offal like a cruiserweight and left me marinating in fevered slow motion. Either I would make it to the infirmary or I would not. Apparently I arrived.

I was laid out late at night, dozing and delirious yet no longer in pain thanks to the drugs they gave me. Comfortable they like to call it. Even if you fall a hundred feet down a mountainside and land on your rump they call you comfortable.

Then, in a moment, the lights went out. Everything was gone. The baleful glow of the night lamps, the red pinpricks on the glum machines. No sound, not even my own breathing. And I knew then that I had ceased to be.

So this is how it goes. No tunnel of brilliant white light or Aunt Maud mugging and beckoning. Just me on my own in silent darkness.

And my main feeling was anger.

I was unprepared – with no will or last words. There were things I had still expected to do. Books I was half way through reading, an episode of Eastenders I'd taped. It might not seem much to you but it's life. What would you worry about then? Global Warming?

I felt no fear but I tell you I was pissed off. What was I supposed to do now? There was nobody to give me instructions. I expected some sort of guide, a package holiday rep. I was baffled and, frankly, I was disappointed. It seemed to me that the whole afterlife experience had been poorly thought out.

You are ready for anything when you die. Except a sense of bathos.

Then suddenly, a sound. The rich melodic grumbling of the plump black panel nurse on her way down the ward.

"Power's gone – third time today – they should get this cable fixed soon – there's people lying sick in here…"

And with a florid rush of belonging I was alive again. There in the dark, swaddled in my NHS blanket.

So I sobbed soundlessly for whatever I had lost and whatever I had won and at fate's fat joke which had me as its butt.

It was my most profound spiritual experience. The only moment when I had ever felt in tune with the orchestra of the universe. Yet it turned out to have been a cock-up.

She came closer, the nurse, drawn somehow to my pain, and felt with delicate fingers my pregnant tears.

And overcome by my hot emotion she cradled my head, saying: "Don't cry baby. We'll do our best for you now. You're going to be all right my little sweetheart. Everything will work out just as it should, you'll see."

They gave me antibiotics and a lecture about drinking. When I was better I went home. To my island.

That was my only visit to the rest of the world and, no offence, but you can keep it.

At any given moment across the slender surface of the earth there are two hundred and thirty seven thunderstorms fizzing and popping. I don't know where the other 236 were the night John Love came to our island, but the one over us was special.

Early that evening I witnessed the dumb beauty of it as it came in across the ocean heading for our chilly lump of shale and pebbledash like a flock of crows.

In Florida they have a fish which grunts when a storm's coming and is said to be more reliable than the weathermen. We don't have that fish here, but maybe I'll do.

I sensed it was on its way and hunkered down on top of the geriatric concrete look out post left over from the last war. A redundant sentry which guards the golf links from sea borne attack.

I wasn't technically supposed to be on the course, given that I'm not a playing member, but usually no-one noticed me. And if they did I was tolerated, same way one suffers a stray dog: sometimes fed, sometimes kicked, accepted as an obstacle of the course.

So I watched the weather billow in under its dark awning. And I thought: let us have it. Give it to us now.

For I do like a good storm – the drama queen carnival of it all, the way those who stand too tall can end up blackened and ripped.

As it came, echoing and winking over the birth-black ocean, each moment expanding, it was comfortable to watch. Like it was on its way but would never arrive.

I sat exposed on the bleak concrete, sniffing the changing quality of the air, and felt the thrill of impending newness as the bruised night flooded in from the sea.

The rain arrived and the last of the twilight golfers cursed their way to the clubhouse.

Since childhood I have loved to be out in the rain.

The sky was weighed down like a fat man slumbering on a top bunk. Grey shafts railed towards the sea where water met with other water.

A camera click of lightning left a river tributary on my retina.

In that flick of brightness I saw something else too. A familiar shape which should not be there. A mote in the trashed ocean. And I thought 'fine weather for fishing.' Laughing silently to myself as the thunder came.

I knew as the rain melted me, there was a chance I hadn't made it up. The boat I thought I had glimpsed truly existed out there, bounced and harried like a cat toy.

The lightning blinked again – and there it was, the boat. Closer to the shore maybe. Or further away.

Roosting on the roof of the lookout post gave me the best view I could expect of the sea. But there's something in human nature compels us to crowd close as we can to an interesting thing. And I'm human, so I scrambled into the drenched heavy rough then slid a sopping path down the banking from the links to the pebble shore. Clutching gracelessly at glossy hanks of Marin grass and grunting with fear as my feet rucked on the sandy slip.

Last ten feet or so I rolled like a lager keg.

Paused before getting up, to check I wasn't injured, and make sure no one had seen me. A rich, daft rush of embarrassment at the thought of it.

Then the wallowing trot of one who wishes to move swiftly across wet stones. I have seen elderly fishermen do this jig, children with day-glo buckets and spades, women walking their dogs. It links all of us who live within reach of the sea.

Was it there? I strained to see. What with the wind, the spray, the desperate insistence of the rain, it was hard to make much out. Another blue fork of current and there it was. By the grace of the swell it approached the shore.

The seat of my jeans was wet where I fell down the bank. Everything about me was soaked, it's true, but my backside was wetter somehow – with a cold cloying dampness all of its own.

Maybe I had just seen driftwood?

All sorts blows up here: packing crates, dead whales, baffled lumps of obscure vegetation. We're on the Gulf Stream, though admittedly at its least fashionable address.

But I knew what this was.

A wet boat which ploughed in through the wet towards the wet stones as I peered through the wet and watched it wetly.

I felt strangely dry.

Not on the outside, clearly, where it was a harvest festival of dampness, but inside where I suddenly found my mouth parched and my head vague and dizzy. I had neither eaten nor taken on water since early morning, and here it was dark.

Fruitlessly I pointed my face at the heavens and opened my gob wide as it would go.

When I pointed it back towards the sea the boat had arrived.

Cabin cruiser. It was grey, but then so was everything else which wasn't black. It was also hilariously small. What was this Captain Pugwash thinking – that he was immortal? Out there on the evil ocean.

The whole enterprise was an invitation to a drowning. A blasé disregard for the mid-range forecast followed by bouncing and puking, drenched flares which fail to light and a last will and testament on the short-wave. Then fish-gnawed corpses, washed up some weeks later, a few leagues down the coast.

Yet here it was, this craft, who knew from where? It was with us on the island for the space of three waves, then out again for the next three bigger breakers, then back again, but closer so I heard its hull grumble on the stones.

A so what? tossed in from the vast wherever on this foulest of all possible whens.

Usually the only people to land here are those who left us some hours previously. They might be richer in fish, or experience, they may have scared or bored themselves yet we still know who they are. But this was not that. This was someone who did not know that ours is a place to leave from, not arrive at.

Feeling I ought to be of use, I hustled into the frothing brine which flashed past my face and dragged at my dancing heels. I grabbed a line hanging off the bow of the boat. I don't know what I thought I was going to do – drag the whole hulking weight a few feet further inland perhaps. The more likely outcome was that a big wave would lollop away and slurp the boat back out to sea, with me on the end of it. Storm wracked and bullied by the chill, I was about to drop the line. But I looked up to see a figure on the tiny deck. He'd popped out of the cabin like a rabbit out of a magician's sooty top hat, and was scrabbling at the other end of the rope, ready to drop over the side.

He tumbled ankle deep into the tide, then suddenly waist deep. I was a good way nearer the shore but more or less up to my neck so I had to wallow back across the slick stones to safety.

It was heart haltingly cold. Not just the sea but the air, the night, everything around me and inside me. Fucking cold. As cold as fuck.

The boat lay stashed on the shale. Waves heaved round it like they were going to drag it back out there and crush it. Post it back to us again in pieces.

My man struggled towards me against all the weight of the water. In the muscle of the wind he waited for the ebb and slipped the last desperate steps onto wet land.

He stumbled straight for me as I crouched on the stones. I felt bad.

Then he was yelling at me. Something diffused by the night.

"You've been expecting me," the words came. "It's all right now. I'm here."

Whether it was the weather, the unexpected arrival, the frailty of my flesh I don't know, but I felt myself drifting away there on the shore. I looked up into the unlit face above me and saw nothing, felt nothing, except giddy, and a bit sick. Then I was gone.

PUB CHORUS

Who is he?

Don't know.

He's got the wee man, the body of the wee man.

He's not dead surely? We'll have to find someone else to be wee.

Who goes out in this? Little fucker must be tapped.

What's he doing, the big guy?

I don't fucking know, who am I Russell Grant?

Watch and you'll likely see.

He's got the wee man on a table.

Mind my pint. Hey, my crisps. Fucking hell.

He's blowing in the wee man's mouth.

He's touching the wee man's ugly snot encrusted little face with his lips.

I'd not touch him with yours.

Why bother? Who wants him back anyway, he can be a narky little fucker.

D'you hear? I'd not touch him with yours.

Hey steady on love, that's not nice, with him dead and all.

He can be a narky little fucker is all I'm saying that's all.

Is it working d'you think? Is he breathing?

Pump his chest mate – to get his heart going and that.

He's pumping it. Ugh, he's kissing him again.

I said, I'd not touch him with…

I didn't really want them fucking crisps now anyhow.

How can he be narky when he doesn't talk?

He just is. You know. He just gives you a glare is all.

He's coming round! He's moving!
The big guy's brought him back!
Three cheers for the big guy and all that.
His name is Love.
He's called John Love.
That's what he says.
Yeah great, he brought back an ugly, silent, short-arse we didn't like much anyway.
He can fucking keep him.
He can have him as a pet monkey.
He can stick him on a chain round his neck as the start of an ugly charm bracelet.
A charmless bracelet.
Sorry?
A charmless bracelet.
No, don't like that. It's a bit brainy is that.
Sorry.

I was coughing up brine when I came back to life on the pub table. Who knew why? I'd not fallen into the sea. I'd barely got my wellies wet and, to my knowledge, I'd passed out on the stones a good ten feet from the tide. Something smelled fishy, and it wasn't just me puking up seawater and bits of bladderwrack all over the side of the poker beaten penny round copper-top table in The Ferry where they had me laid out ready for an autopsy.

"It is 'okay' child. You will prosper."

I looked up into the face of my saviour.

He was a handsome man. And you know when you've seen one. Which you seldom do.

Most people when they're young and fresh look okay – though not to each other funnily enough – only to older people to whom all youth appears beautiful.

You lose it though. It drifts. People swell like potatoes. This character, one glance told me, he hadn't stumbled into his thirties by the same self-tortured, poisoned route the rest of us had.

The light was dim. It appeared I had interrupted the karaoke, but not the traffic lights which accompanied it. The only illumination, they were still blinking. Red, yellow, green. Rage, jealousy, envy. Warning, sunshine, go.

There he was. Concerned and focused. That movie star face trained on me. Not made for TV either. A multi-million dollar Hollywood production. I wondered how much of him was real.

"How are you?" he asked, sounding as though he meant it. "Truly. Inside yourself?"

He leant in, stroked my straggly dog hair. He was bending over me with a crowd round but they clung to him rather than the event. As though they were bees and he had the right type of pollen to make honey. They were swaying towards him, even just to touch him was a start.

His hands licked me and moved off to conduct an unseen orchestra, then caress his hair, and his grin dimmed the karaoke lights.

They gawped at every tick like it was ballet. His beauty, his grace and balance. They brought him a glass of tap water. No-one gets tap water, only still or sparkling, it's house policy. He dabbed a napkin and anointed me, delicate butterfly wings and his lips ticking away like he was kissing me each time.

I wanted to hug him. I think we all did. I needed to cling to him and cry, as though he could protect me from whatever.

Then he reached down and laid his hand on my cheek, the way lovers do when they are about to kiss. Eye contact. That was for me, who else could it be for?

"Is that better?" he wanted to know. "Is there anything I can get for you?"

"He can't talk," one of the barflies chipped in.

"Well, you know," emolliated our man. "He's had a shock – he might have died. Technically, he probably was dead."

"No – he's never talked, so I can't see him starting now," said the fly, whose big red beery head had poked over Love's shoulder to peer at me. "But you did save him though – that's a fact. You're a hero. He'll be fine I reckon, and the ambillyance is on its way over the bridge right about now."

I gargoyle grimaced and shook my head like a mutt with a rag, scrabbling to get off the table. Not going back in there again. Never liked hospitals. I've seen too many friends go in and never come out.

"That good looking guy saved him," a girl at the bar was telling her boyfriend, presumably fresh back from the bogs. "He kissed him right on his ugly little mouth and saved his life. The wee man's fucking off now look."

I scuttled across the dance floor of the Ferry, past baffled punters and headed for the door. More or less made it before I felt myself levitating, feet flapping at the fag smoke tainted air.

Craning round to see who had picked me up – and what d'you know, it's your man. Carrying me back the way I'd run, cradling me in his arms like an infant as folk stared at us from their tables. He took me into a corner booth, plonked me down, on a stool this time thankfully.

"I know how you feel," his soft insistence with all the emphasis on *know*. "I sense how people are. I don't relish too much attention from authority myself in fact. But look – you've had a shock, a gutful of brine. At least sit here a while and compose yourself – get warm and dry."

It felt as though he was offering me his hospitality, rather than that of Little Shepherdess Pub Company Limited.

"Have a whiskey? Maybe there's some local quack round here who could have a poke at you, for form's sake – though if you want to know the truth I see that you are healthy."

He had these smoked brown eyes; seemed concerned. He stood up to get me a drink. He was tall, even I could see that, and as far as I'm concerned pretty much everybody is tall.

Barbara Taylor appeared to cluck over me. She's one of the middle aged dolls who consider me their chosen charity, faff around me saying: "Bless him," and "It's a shame," would doubtless dress me up like their bedroom teddy bears if I would sit still for it.

Babs lives in the terraces up Prospect Street. She drinks a lot and lets men have sex with her – pretty much anyone who wants to. They don't even have to be kind to her or grateful particularly.

She had a fag on the go and a pint of lager and lime.

"Bless his heart – he must have had a turn. You alright my little love? You okay?" She'd pressed her powdered head close to mine and subjected me to a matt smack of leather lipstick. Then she turned her attention to my rescuer, who was back with the double Bells.

I felt released for a moment to observe him.

It's not like we don't get new people on the Island. There's a bridge, a factory beyond, then the rest of the world. We're not ever so hard to get to; it's just that, mostly, there's no reason to come. We're that joke about a woman in her sixties being like Antarctica – everyone knows where it is but no one wants to go there.

That is the only thing which can leave you truly isolated in these magical times when you can travel anywhere on earth. You stay lonely if you aren't attractive.

People could come here. They simply choose not to. So what was this man doing on our thin strip of wind-licked limestone? Frankly he looked too good to be here.

Now he'd shed his outer layer of boating waterproofs he was a well made figure in a pearl grey jumper and dark denim jeans. He suited those simple clothes – the clothes looked special on him – so that you'd want to buy them if you saw him in a catalogue wearing them.

He had thick, dark hair shoved back off his forehead, those eyes: pale and brown and steady like a pint of bitter with a lamp behind.

Hey – I'm no judge of masculine beauty but you didn't have to be. Something you couldn't argue with told you that here was a special thing. An element beyond just the sum of his features.

If a woman saw him in the crowd on her mate's wedding photos she'd say he was a bit of all right and giggle. Even if she was married she'd say it anyway and what the hell and still giggle. She couldn't help herself from saying it right there out loud as if that meant she'd staked some sort of a claim, like it made her closer to him.

I wanted Barbara to ask him what he was doing here – he could have been anywhere. Somewhere good.

But she was just wheedling round trying to pull him – like she had a chance. But then I don't know – men are funny aren't they?

She wanted to buy him a drink, but she didn't want to get up and go to the bar – creating a vacuum into which a brace of her fat mates were ready to tumble.

Quite a crew of them had formed a loose huddle round us and some of the bar blokes beyond them – kind of half-interested to see who the stranger was and what he was about saving the dummy like that.

The karaoke had gone to hell in a handcart. Billy Mac who does it was still mucking about with his microphone, performing a stilted dad dance to the glucose background music – as if him shuffling about self-consciously would convince everyone that the fun to be had from howling half formed inanities into the smoke was preferable to watching something really happening.

Tracy Etherington who had been half way through Titanic was still up there, crying 'cos no one was listening.

Barbara finally got around to it.

"So what brings you to these parts then Lovely?"

She tried to make it sound like: 'Come back to my place and shag me.' She tries to make everything sound like that, even: 'A return to the Town Hall please Pet.'

"How did you land up here in all this foul weather? In that gear? Surely you can't have come by boat. Mind it's a good job you did arrive for the sake of our little Bes."

She ruffled my hair – as if I was a young lad caught scrumping apples. Grabbed a gobful of lager and lime to sustain her, then: "Who are you?"

All tinsel-toothed and twinkly.

He said nothing. Just stared at her with an eighth of a grin on his face. She was on the point of leaping in with a whole heap more words to fill the vacuum but, changing his mind, he spoke.

"I could ask you the same question. I've been wondering who you are. Would you mind?"

He seemed bashful suddenly. It was, endearing and stuff – you know.

"Would you allow me to see what I can tell you about yourself?"

Ooh! Ooh! Barbara wouldn't mind would she girls? Barbara wouldn't mind at all.

II

"What can I tell you?" John Love asked Barbara. Soft as if he hadn't said it at all. "What do I know? Very little. It's late, I'm tired and cold. This storm – it stirs things up beyond the world we can see."

He reached out and clasped Barbara's hands in his, which were surprisingly small and delicate for a seafaring man. He held her trembling mitts out in front of him as if to pray with her.

"Truth is," he admitted folksily, "I'm not very good at this. You'll need to help me to make it work. Will you help me?"

Barbara nodded, rapt and solemn. "Oh yeah love – what do I have to do – to help you?"

The pub was quiet. Someone had turned off the karaoke machine at the wall. And, over by the bar, the old by the bar boys were watching, by the bar.

Even the laughing lads on the pool table left the balls where they lay. Too far away they were to hear quite what was going on but still they sensed an entertainment was in progress.

I sat quiet in my covert corner, though no more silent than usual. I was engulfed in a Black Watch tartan blanket borrowed from Alfred the pub rottweiler who lived behind the bar. It reeked of damp hound and prickled with hair but I was glad of it.

Love was breathing – that's all. Breathing deep and slow like it meant more than just oxygen in, carbon-dioxide out.

"I see something," he almost said. "Someone's anxious to speak to you."

He paused, as if drained by the effort of even this much.

"Someone who was precious to you. Remains so. Is still important. Vital."

Bunny-eyed Barbara wanted to know "Who is it? What are they telling you?"

There's a little mumbled speculation from the cheap seats and a few 'sshhh' sounds like the movie's about to start.

"It isn't a voice," wafted Love, all sing-song and ululant. "It is a feeling, which guides me towards certain things. And it is telling me – that you should understand – you are too guarded about yourself. You have firm opinions on many matters, yet you have learned from hard experience in your life that it is best to keep them hidden from view."

Barbara was nodding: "Yes, that's right, yes."

"I'm sorry," said Love, with candour. "I'm sorry to raise these personal things here in public – he wafted a theatrical hand toward the watchers. "Even among friends. For I sense, I know, that you are a private person."

"No, it's all right," Barbara insisted. "You're right, I am, but it's best to know. Go on, please, what else?"

Love smiled. "I don't know. I can't ever know. But understand that the spirit seeking you wishes you to hear that your talents will be recognised – that the frustration you feel at not being properly appreciated won't go on forever. How could it with someone who has all you have to offer?"

"You know me," she cried. "You see inside of me."

She pulled her hands away from his gentle grip as if shocked.

Noises off again. Him holding out his hands beseechingly.

"There's more. There's more. I'm getting a name. Don't you wish to hear who is communicating with you?"

"No," she said, firmer than usual. "I know who it is and I don't want to speak with him."

Jack, I thought to myself. Dead boyfriend. Got pissed as a little beetle and mowed his Fiasco through the railing of the bridge to the mainland five years back. Police frog team from Liverpool had to fish him out of the channel.

Love still and sentient.

Then: "I sense the letter J."

A shriek from the crowd. The gaps in Barbara's fake tan flashed ivory. Even under the crass pub lighting you could see it, the absence of blood.

"Jack!" she cried. "Is it you Jack? Why did you leave me?"

She broke down, all messed up.

She was drunk, poor cow. It was a shame.

Love scooped her head and shoulders in his sirloin arms,

whispered into her ear.

"It's all right. It's okay. He says he loves you. He says he is waiting for you. Understand that he has known how keen your pain has been. He has been with you."

It was as if he was saying this all for her. But it was a stage whisper in truth and I expect they caught the gist of it as far back as the bandit.

There were some "Aws" and "Shames" and so-forth.

He held her a little longer, gently tapping her back like winding a baby – so she did eventually let out a gentle burp of satisfaction. Then, caressingly, he let her go. Her face was red, crumpled and wet, like a restaurant napkin on which someone's blown their nose.

She's still not a bad looking woman I'd say. That's her curse. She has that sunbed tan and salon blonde, the dental implants, the gym tum. Sure, she hangs around with the topers, but that's just so's she can lay hands on the endless and willing supply of blokes she needs. They feed off her for a few days at a time – though she dines on them too. They suckle her. She requires whatever it is they have to give in the way of warmth and, well, let's not use the 'L' word shall we? It gets thrown around far too much as it is these days.

Funnily enough there's one person who I would never hear say it. And that person was sitting next to me at the table surrounded by an eager crew of willing punters all on for having various parts of their anatomy read, dead pets contacted, fortunes enquired into.

We all need miracles I know, and even a little shabby one will do if it serves us. We drift through our lost lives, shoeless and alone, looking for something, as if hunting was, in itself, enough.

We, on this island, are like something vague the tide shifts. Something which moves despite itself. Like old newspapers maybe, bowling along the drafty canyon of Central Drive. All speed and flurry, going nowhere. That's how we feel Barbara. Used and once was.

And I heard her in the toilets out in the yard as I headed out in the dark to relieve myself, heard her blubbing an empty prayer into the weather over the gasping idol of the pot bog. Asking for help to do the right thing. Whatever the right thing was. Whoever she was asking.

"I'm tired," Love announced later, voice caramel with sleep. "It's been a long day. Longer than you know."

Boyish yawn.

"Where are you staying love?" asked Barbara hopefully through the fag end of her snot and tears.

"That," admitted Love, "has yet to be established. Normally I would rely on my craft to provide a bed but it's not the weather for it – I could end up anywhere."

Bloke in the crowd: "Where d'you say you came from this evening?"

"Out on the ocean. I suppose you'd call me a fisherman."

"You've been fishing? In this?"

Love nodded, knocking back his orange squash.

"Easier to catch fish when something has stirred them up. Still, I can't stay on the boat. Not tonight."

Barbara practically leapt across the table at him.

"Stay at mine!" Coquettishly: "In the spare room."

Frank the landlord shrugged as he collected our glasses.

"I'll find you a room upstairs if you like – we've a couple not let to contractors tonight – and it's the least we can do after what you did for the wee man."

Love made a panto out of weighing up the offers – but it wasn't believable somehow. Forced. A little hammy. Funny thing was, in all the time I knew him, despite being a man of many roles, when it came to straightforward drama he was always a terrible actor. Yet even that can be endearing. It can make one seem incapable of deceit.

He am-dram mugged an indication that he was licking his lips over two equally tasty offers. A few extra vaguely-formed ones were tossed in by the rabble round the table as he cogitated.

"He could stay at ours Alan."

"Nan's got a spare room."

Briskly, Love rose to his feet – as if to propose a toast. Looking down, he took my hand.

"I think, if you are willing," he announced staring into my sleepy eyes, "I would very much like to stay with you this evening."

I nodded.

I was curiously proud as we headed across the deserted dance square for the door watched by the fascinated, the somewhat jealous, clientele of the Ferry. I felt like a child lifting my arm up to hold his hand. But that was nothing, I knew, I spent a lot of my life feeling like a child.

Well, we all do don't we?

I also felt something new. I felt flushed with success, a little apprehensive, worried maybe about what others would think and what I had let myself in for. I have no experience of this but I would have to say: I felt as though I had pulled.

'Don't do it,' I wanted to tell John Love. 'If you're too weird round here the locals tie you to a pig and set fire to you.' And sleeping in my van rather than tucked up in an economy single at the Ferry or testing the springs with the still pneumatic Barbara would count as being weirder than a two headed flatfish.

But I didn't tell him anything. Since I am one who has always believed that silence is a language in itself. My pauses have their own grammar; my sullen stares their syntax. I am the Shakespeare of saying sod all.

We fight our way out of the front porch and into the brawling wind and rain.

"Which way?" he says, glancing down at me, clad in my dog blanket. "I'm hoping that it's not too far."

I point in the direction of the site. It will take me fifteen minutes, him five. A few yards make that much clear.

Without speaking he scoops me up and onto his back and carries me that way, like a pack.

As we head off into the leaping dark, into the spin-cycle of nature's washing machine, I peer over my shoulder to the pub. Its diamond doors and windows thronged with faces peering into the gloom to track our peculiar progress. A big man with a small man on his back, fighting their way through what fortune has for them.

Time varies widely depending on where you watch it from. So it either didn't take long for us to reach my chalet park, or it did – depending on whether or not you had a surprisingly dense and hefty small adult draped about your shoulders.

My journey, swaddled under the thick and pungent blanket, was mindlessly brief. Bit bumpy, windswept and black to be sure, yet relatively snug. A stepped and undulant voyage by camel through the imagined Sahara at midnight.

The scrape and snap of gravel at the chalet park entrance was a time machine to my childhood, made me think of the one time dad let me ride his shoulders like an elephant.

My father kept me at arms length. He was getting on when I was conceived by mischance and I suspect he didn't want to get close to me so I wouldn't be too disappointed when he died. It would have been like showing a kid tickets for Disneyland then telling them they couldn't go. Far better not to get my expectations up.

He died when I was 13 after contracting cancer of the oesophagus.

"You can beat it – you can win," I remember mum telling him in the through lounge of our chalet home. "Just be strong."

But he gassed himself in our Othello 1.3 hatchback with a hosepipe threaded from the exhaust through the nearside window. Perhaps that was being strong. So often weakness is doing nothing. We're told we have to hang around here on the planet as though it was some kind of endurance competition like one of those depression era dance 'til you drop contests. Expected to keep our heads in a tank full of scorpions like a Japanese gameshow.

But for what?

Who wins?

What if my dad had gone through months of agony and then died? Or recovered after a fashion and spectred on for another few years like a burst crisp bag tumbling in a gutter?

Who exactly would that have served?

If I learned one thing from that time in my life it's that static caravans provide a cheap and serviceable living environment. The ground rents are reasonable and they hold their residual value surprisingly well even in a bear property market. I've stuck with them ever since.

By the time we reached the door of the van Love was huffing heavily. He was gasping so loudly I could hear him over all the clangings and cursings of chalet park nights. We stood a while listening to the baleful rattle of aluminium walls, the soulful hollering of disparate dogs.

Theatre of the lost keys then a grateful scramble into my cave. Love said 'Where's the lights?' then barked his shiteing shin on something solid and oblong: volumes *Squ* to *Toc* of Britannica fecklessly left in an unruly pile not far inside the front door.

I don't get many visitors.

This tower of learning had been a perch from which to feed the card meter. I'd scaled the summit before realising I had no cards to satiate it. Then gone to get some, warm pub beckoned, stepped out later for a breath of air on the golf course – you know the rest.

Tragically I could explain none of this to Love as the gift of mime is pretty thin gruel with the lights out.

As far as he was concerned I was just some maladjusted numbnut who lived in dark and dung as a mushroom does, creeping out only to faint on beaches, get half-pissed and have to be carried home in a dog blanket.

Only half tonight alas, only half.

"Perhaps," Love enquired gently, "you could point me in the general direction of somewhere I can have a kip?"

He groped for my hand in the blackness and on the short scramble towards the bedroom it was unclear who was the father and who the child.

I deposited him there like a warm envelope and foetused up on the bench seat in the living area – lounge and kitchen with shower room off – very practical; admirably compact. Familiar to me as all my island. Light or dark. Drunk or sober.

Love slurred through some good-natured pleasantries about what a top sort I was and how I ought to snare myself a good night's snooze. I humoured him with a silent snigger which pulled me up short. Affection? How could I feel for him when I did not know him? He was as strange as any stranger who had landed on our bladder-wracked shores in a lifetime.

III

The place where I live is a small place to be.

What do I think of my fellow inhabitants? Well, they're people: what do you think of people?

Then that's what you'd think about the ones on my island.

If there's a common fault to be snuffled out among them I expect it's that, if you are one of us, there's a kind of unseen behaviour boundary. You're not allowed to swim too far from the shoal. Some kinds of odd they tolerate. It's okay to be extraordinarily stupid for example. Others are more or less encouraged – it's okay to be as much of a drunk as you like – or mean, that's a good one. A combination of both of these: 'It's never Fatty's round' is more or less idolised.

But try being too clever – sounding as though you know too much. That never goes down well. Don't worry. They won't tar and feather you, take you into the town square and break your joints with an iron rod. You won't be hung by the neck from a tree or have your house burned down by men with hoods.

But they'll notice, and they won't approve. They'll mug and grimace, they'll know they're superior because they are in the net of what is tolerated, while you are outside of it.

It's only a small matter – but it's there. And the quality of people's lives can often be weighed out in tiny things, like shale on the beach. A bucket full of small bad things can weigh you down if you have to carry it with you all your mornings, evenings, afternoons.

Me of course – I'd be isolated in most places where you could find a crowd. I'm everyone's idea of the far side of strange. Yet that, in a sense, has proved to be my salvation. Because, once you get beyond the reef then the waves stop crashing.

People tend to welcome freaks like me warmly to prove they're not the sort of person who would exclude someone for the sin of being not like them.

When John Love first landed here I feared for him. Imagine that. Knowing what I do now I find I can't. I feared he would cross the line at some point and find himself marooned in the unacceptable.

If you are one of 'us' the border is a simple thing. We know where it is at all times, like the tide, and sense where we are in relation to it same as a bird finding its way from one hemisphere to the other or a bat plucking insects from the night.

For those who lack that extra perspective, the border of behaviour can be as deft and baffling as a wolf spider's lair. Snag it once and you are damned to contempt.

I saw Love as a ready victim for the island's lounge bar bullyboys and WI wags. When I watched the way he dealt with people – up square and direct eyed, confiding in them things about themselves.

I thought: 'This is never going to play. Not in the provinces. This just won't test well.'

I mean I've been wrong before, about all sorts, me. Not just about people: sums, the weather – I once spent a hazy late afternoon convinced that the sun was the moon. If I had – never mind a pound – just fifty pee, I'm not greedy.

Morning has broken, like the first morning.

CHORUS OUTSIDE THE MOBILE HOME.
He's in there – it's where the dwarf lives.
Why did he go off with the dwarf?
Felt sorry for the little fella, bless him.
Bless the dwarf or the hunk?
The hunk, Well, both really. Dwarf for being diddy, hunk for being fit – by all accounts.
Though we've only Bar's word for that yet.
She sez she'd lick the sweat out the crack of his arse.
But that's not the main thing about him.
Aye, right.
No. She sez he has the gift.
Big n'all. Can't be bad.
Laughter.
The gift, the gift, he has the gift.
He can tell you all about yourself.

More than even you know about yourself.
And messages.
Like Royal Mail.
He can bring you messages.
From the other side.
Side by side.
This side, that side.
The other side.
Where the grass…
The grass is always greener.
On the other side.

I awake at the appropriate hour.

Whatever else nature has endowed me with she's graced me with an impeccable sense of timing. I could have been a drummer. If I could reach the bass pedal.

The correct time to rise is 7.30 am. Usually all I hear outside at that hour is the dissonant prickle and rattle of the milk float, swamped by history, persevering.

This morning I hear women. Many of them. Grown women in a group, like Bingo, or aerobics.

Aching in my spine and neck, my musculature, my skeleton, I squeeze my fucking grumpy arse up sideways off the bench seat, topple cluelessly to the floor, which somehow bites a hangover in. Legacy of the booze I drank before I met John Love. And I twitch my garish polyester curtains a thou of an inch west. And there they are. Like a tribe of Red Indians.

There's more oestrogen in the air outside my van than sloshing around the pool at swim-to-get-slim.

Where'd they come from? Why are they all here? Have they not got stuff to do?

But I know the why, and I know the what they want.

So I let the flame and green print curtain drop back and hurl myself around my place in a hysteria of tidying up.

When you live alone, just try it, when you solo-habit, there is a tendency to ignore the small-print set by the hygiene standards department, and instead drift towards your own basic mean.

If you're an anal retentive with a tendency towards psychosis then your living space will look like a mortuary slab.

Otherwise your place will look like you have inhabited every last millimetre of it. Lived it. Loved it.

I had cleaning up to do.

I'm not a messy eater. I scoff out of the saucepan mopping it up with toast to save on the washing up. I'm not much of a clothes horse – the youth section of C & A not exactly providing the cornucopia of delights you might expect.

My indulgence is books and I have tomes on every surface, pointy or flat. I store slim volumes on every speck of floor. As I now desperately scramble my ramshackle library out of view. Querulously scrabbling, banging and fumbling books into footlockers and cubby-holes until, eventually, here's John Love to lend a hand.

Emerging, skinny in his undercrackers, from the bedroom with barely a greeting glance, scooping up chestfuls of paperbacks, decanting them into his sanctuary.

Bang. Bang. Bang.

They want in. They want him.

Proust and Tolstoy, medical manuals, sociology texts, bound volumes of *New Scientist*, historical analysis. All are hidden from scrutiny.

Scramble and effort, sloughing and bundling, ramming home books where no books will fit until suddenly, unexpectedly, it's done.

We stand breathless for a moment in the fresh made emptiness of my curiously larger room.

Love catches my gaze, half-serious he seems, then giggling the way sudden shared effort will tend to make you laugh.

I cackle back soundlessly and we crouch for a moment there hobbled by mirth.

"Okay," says Love. "We have customers."

He positions me by the door.

"One at a time please. Hey – have you got some kind of hat? Not a baseball cap. Bigger?"

Hats? I have no hats. I am not a hat person. Then I remember the sou'wester I wear the odd time I take myself out with the trawlers.

My hat for when things get too much on land. For eight day holidays with five other taciturn souls, deep in the forlorn, colourless wilderness of the Atlantic. None of the others wear a sou'wester, which is considered old fashioned and quaint. I like the fact my colleagues on these trips think I am odd for that reason rather than any of the other boundless material they have at their disposal.

They call me their fisherman's friend.

I scramble about in a locker full of novels and produce, at length, my garish ochre headwear. Love chortles again, he's in good spirits this morning.

"Stick it on," he commands playfully. "I want to see it on."

I comply, glumly.

"Like a novelty condom," he guffaws. "Wave it at 'em on the way out. Think on now – no more than one at a time."

Hat still swamping my head I open the door. There's a damp cheer: whoop and a chortle of rich, bubbling, female fun.

"Aw, he's like a little cake ornament," says one.

And they laugh again, coarse and good humoured.

There's maybe twenty of them, all shapes and sizes, a card shop full of ages. I wonder again why they are here. Not just for the fun of it surely? Though that is what they would claim – a good craic, a giggle, just game for a laugh.

There must be more depth to it than I have wit for. I step back and let the first seeker after truth in the jostling queue pass into my domain.

Audrey Lemon. Aged maybe thirty-five, ought to be fifty. Lives alone, unless you count cats, in a Victorian semi up Paradise Mount.

I cleave to her for the same reasons no one else seems to. Her isolation, her socially autistic belligerence, the way she has aerobicised her body into a spiky machine for repelling sieges.

I find I often like people who can endure their own company. I am surprised to see her here. She joins in with the laughter billowing up from the others, but in a restrained, worry-lined way, as if fearing that at any moment the wind might blow the flames in her direction.

She elbows past me with barely a nod, though she's making use of my home.

She can be a fistful can Audrey, it's true, her personality brusque and angular with disuse, bristling with sharp edges. No nubs worn shiny by human caress.

Love is making himself comfy on the bench seat at the end of my van. He has the occasional table folded down and my pouffe pulled up opposite for the convenience of visitors. He looks like a one-man interview panel.

Audrey more or less storms up to him – wagging a metaphorical finger.

"You can't help me," she challenges him bluntly.

He surveys her silently, weighing her up, waiting for more – who knows?

She's sharply dressed. Marks and Sparks, very tidy, very businesslike. She's quite high up at one of the banks on the mainland. She has one of those careers which does for a life, thriving in the gap left by nothing better, like the peculiar scraps of existence which live on the deep ocean bed.

I expect she must be quite well off financially: mortgage all but paid, snug with her shares and her Isas, her Peps and her bonds. She has none of the cash distractions most people have what with lovers and kids. Nobody to have to share with. So she'll have built that money turret to protect her.

Yet here she is anyway. Seeking the help she is convinced Love cannot possibly give her. Angry with him over it. Determined to make him admit he is no use to her.

"There's nothing you can do," and her knees twitch like she's about to leave.

"Good. Then go," says Love without emphasis. He's found something interesting to look at on his trousers. "If you could leave a contribution with my friend on your way out to help support our work then that would be accepted with grace."

She hesitates. Perhaps struck by the impudence of the request.

Then slowly she lowers herself onto the pouffe, perches there birdlike and alert.

Next she says nothing. She just lets him stare at her.

I stare at him, staring at her.

Then she says, her voice grating down a gear in a self-conscious search for conversational: "There was a fair bit of lightning last night."

"I wouldn't worry," Love confides. "Statistically 80 per cent of people hit by lightning are men."

He's not shaved. It suits him that gesture towards stubble – makes him seem more like he lives with the rest of us.

"Is that right?" she ruminates.

It's not right. The figure is 83 per cent – but it was near enough in essence I suppose.

"I can tell you things about yourself," Love assures her, flattering her with his full attention. "I can tell you what you need to know. But you have to help me – commit to me. We're a team you see?"

She's smirking, like she's too smart for all of this, she's shaking her head.

"I know," Love staring at her. "I know there's something down inside you which is a torment to you. But it's not clear to me. You're not making it clear enough. It isn't simply the spirits who help me you know. It's your spirit."

He pauses, as if listening to a faint sound far away.

"I can't tell whether it's money…" Nothing from her, blank smirk, maybe slightly embarrassed. "Career…" same again. "Travel…" less than nothing. "Love."

He sees something maybe – perhaps a twitch outside of her control.

He melts towards her.

"You have so much tenderness within you, so much love that it is overflowing." And she's nodding now, despite herself.

He holds her gaze, his voice dropping lower and more personal.

"I am feeling something about you. They don't tell me, nothing tells me, it's just a sense of something like a Polaroid slowly developing. But I'm getting something… I believe… I'm sorry," he drops his head.

The caravan is quiet, the faint chatter outside fading.

"I'm sorry to get emotional. It's just that I sense you are so very *lonely*."

Nothing from Audrey for a moment. Then a snorting noise, which I assume, from my vantage point by the door, is a mocking bark of derision. But it turns out to be a sob.

By George he's got it. He's scored another hit. Just that one word is all it took. A code, a key to Audrey, an Open Sesame.

Yet what can he know of loneliness? I do not identify him as one who has ever shared a bunk with it before. Wherever he was living last Christmas, I'd see it strewn with cards – papered with them.

I had one. It read: "To all our customers. Wishing you a happy Christmas and a prosperous New Year. The China Palace."

I don't suppose Audrey Lemon got quite so many. She cooks her own tea.

By the time I'm paying attention again Audrey's rattling away as if she was in charge of dispersing the European word mountain.

One minute she's saying she didn't have very many chums as a young lass at school, the next she's on about how frequently she masturbates.

"I miss sex I suppose. I know I do. But it's always seemed to me such a strange thing, so destructive. It's what makes men kill little girls – defile them and kill them and chop their bodies up like they were carcasses. Just because of sex, that one little thing, like scratching an itch. It's over-rated, it seems to me."

Love breaks in, all puppy eager and attentive.

"I can heal you. I can heal your suffering."

He leaps up, flinging my fold down table sideways so it snaps back into its socket in the wall.

It makes me jump. I'm still wishing she hadn't gone on about how she likes to crack one out. It's an image I'm struggling to get out of my head.

Love takes three purposeful steps forward towards an alarmed Miss Lemon who's leaning so far back on the pouffe she seems in danger of toppling off.

Then Love reaches out and slaps his palm onto her forehead, grasping the top of her scalp with his meaty fingers like a mountaineer teasing out a grip in a crevice of rock.

Love closes his eyes, his body is tense but his head lolls suddenly as though he's nodded off. He's emitting a low hum like some kind of test signal.

It's alarming. I'd be alarmed if I was Lemon. I'm alarmed sitting here and it's not my brow he's clasping.

"What are you doing?" squeaks an alarmed Lemon.

"Communicating with the Akashic record," booms Love, an octave lower than usual. "It is a vessel which contains all that has been, all that will be. It can advise me what ails you, can indicate a cure."

He's grave and preoccupied as a doctor with his ears in a stethoscope. Then he breaks free, uncupping his hand and falling back. Shaking, sweat standing out on his chiselled chops as he sinks back down on the bench.

Gasping, Lemon gives him time to recover his poise before demanding: "What did they say? What do the records show?"

Love's back to holding her hand, stroking her hand. His voice is at its usual pitch again and soft, slow.

"You are suffering from a form of depression brought on by being too much alone."

He pauses to mop his face with one of my white tee shirts.

"I can cure you. There's no doubt. You'll be well and a whole person again. The free lively, loving person I know you are. You've had to shut yourself off from people; you have found it better, because of their unkindness, to hide your true self. It is a tragedy. A terrible tragedy."

And listening to him, seeing how sad it seemed, I believed it was a tragedy too.

"I will treat you with the essence of fresh green plants which I will gather from the edge of the seashore, and I will manipulate your aura."

"My aura?"

"Of course. But I must warn you, tender soul, this will not be a cheap process. It will not be cheap spiritually, physically, or financially. It is crucial you feel the impact of the treatment in the sacrifice you make. You must feel it in the core of your existence. It must be made to matter to you. In a very real sense. It has to cost."

She's nodding, I can only see the back of her head, it's wagging. She's trying to say something but it won't come out somehow. She's composing herself, and eventually finds a tiny voice.

"How much?"

"That," says Love, hands open in forgiveness, "is a matter for you to decide."

It went on. They came, they went. Mostly it seemed he was able to provide them with whatever they were after: comfort, confidence, hope.

He spoke to them gently of their untapped worth and the self-belief stolen from them by their exposure to the petty tortures of an indifferent world.

"I felt let down at school."

"They weren't there for me."

"I've never had a chance."

"Not one."

"I would have taken it."

"I know I would."

"I work at a job."

"Got married, kids."

"I have adequate accommodation."

"A saloon car…"

"Drink too much."

"Cry sometimes in the bathroom."

"For what life could have been."

There was an awful lot of money in the sou'wester. What seemed to me like plenty anyway – though I would admit I am not used to handling it in large amounts. Our visitors mostly chipped in notes. Barbara stuck in forty quid all on her lonesome.

Forty quid. Bloody hell.

Each visit took maybe 20 minutes and we'd hit the low teens, I'd guess, when Love announced to me with a stretch and grimace that he was done for the day.

"The surgery," he said with the falling intonation of finality, "is now closed."

I wanted to know what to do about the others outside – a pile of them still – as many again as had been dealt with, then a few more who'd turned up while he had been at work.

I gave him a thunderous frown and a brutal nod in the direction of the door. You tend to overdo the body English in my position, it's not conducive to nuance.

"Tell 'em," he said fondly, "they should present themselves tomorrow."

He clearly hadn't grasped the full implications of the whole mute thing.

I opened the door and held my hand up like a lollypop man as the next woman in the queue muscled towards me tits first in a thin waft of White Linen.

"S'up love?" she wanted to know.

They were calmer now, more at peace with the waiting. A pall of fag smoke and the chill breath of winter afternoon hung over them as they steamed and stamped like the shaggy ponies which paused in the shabby field behind the retained fire station, patiently waiting for nothing to happen.

I shook my head sadly – shrugged my shoulders.

"Is he finished today then love?"

Well that was easy enough.

She turned to her pals.

"He's shut for lunch, girls."

"Aw – bollocks. After hanging about freezing my arse off n'all."

Tap on her back. Me waving my head about like a terrier with a rag.

They got it in the end. It doesn't take people long usually to work out that communicating with me is that game where you get twenty questions but the answer can only be yes or no.

Back in the warmth of my den, my nose rich with book dust and the ghost of yesterday's baked beans on toast, I found Love had counted the loot from the hat and shuffled it into two piles – a fat one and a skinny one. They lay on the table like dinner, which reminded me I hadn't had any. Or breakfast.

Love had hooked one of my books out of the foot locker and appeared lost in the thing.

I perched across the tan Formica from him and waited. He raised his eyes from the reading, dropped the book down beside him and swept both piles of money across the table to me.

"The small one's rent. The other's wages for your work today," he said. "By the by. You couldn't lend me a fiver could you?"

Without waiting for a response he picked the book up again. It was Italio Calvino's *If on a Winter's Night A Traveller*.

"I have just begun to read this book," he said. "And it occurs to me that it must be for something. All of them. All the books. They must be here for a reason, beyond just your need to reach the light switch. I mean – have you ever considered a set of steps?"

Tossed him my poker face. I wasn't about to help him out. As a matter of personal habit I kept my data gathered close. For what's the point in hoarding treasures if you don't keep them guarded and what could be more precious to a person than the sacred secrets of the heart?

"You read," Love opined, bluntly. "And, if you read, then it stands to reason, and please feel at liberty to chip in if I'm wrong, that you must also be able to write."

Poker, poker. But a big diamond gone there. A rare and precious jewel. I knew there was a reason I didn't hold many dinner parties.

Absently he was squinting at Signor Calvino's work but the reader in him was distracted by the thinker. He was deep into something he knew – though still not getting any tells from me.

But he had it anyway, I realised, as slender sunlight striped his face through a crack in the floral curtain.

"Why hide the books?"

He regarded me minutely as if, against the odds, I would provide him with a reply.

"It's no crime to read. Not yet anyway. It can only be that they don't know. Do they? They believe you are too simple to read and write."

His hissing chuckle of shared secrets – of being impressed.

"I bet they don't even realise you register what's being said to you. Not in the normal way they expect from each other. You listen don't you?" he demanded. "You listen and you record and you could write it all down for me on a piece of paper and they would have no notion where the knowledge came from."

He'd just had away with the crown jewels. He was an emotional Raffles. I had to admire his technique. He watched. He saw what there was to see.

"You listen and you read. Don't you? Come on, tell me." His voice full of excitement and sparkle.

Despite myself, my instinct, my precious poise, I felt myself nod.

Just the once mind – but there are times when once is a feast.

He woofed with laughter and slapped his ruddy boatman's hands on the table.

"You grifter. The things you must know. The things we'll soon know together. What we did today is nothing. With proper information there is no horizon. None at all. And they would never suspect. They know you too well. They know everything there is to know about you. You are an idiot. And how would you tell me, you see? Even if you knew?"

I saw.

He ratched around in his trouser pocket and found at length a green ballpoint of significant vintage, then the remnants of some crumpled handbill promising a second income of 'Pounds, Pounds, Pounds (OTE)'. Stuffing the distressed paper and masticated biro towards me across the slick surface he commanded me to write something down.

I pondered. Not just what to write – the whole situation, in the round. What was he asking? What was I capable of giving him? Then I wrote, in my generous, mannered copperplate: "What do you want to know?"

IV

Listen.

There's always more to people than you think – and less.

That's what John Love says.

The beauty of people lies in their plurality. Every last one of us is as different as a new day. How do you suppose that happened? It's quite remarkable when you think about it. It's quite a trick.

Want to know something else remarkable?

How similar we all are.

For unique things we are very mass produced. Bashed out on a press, eliminating the obtuse quirk.

We respond the same way as each other to a broad range of stimuli – that is our tragedy.

Our hope makes us forlorn; our innocence vulnerable. We want to believe in the same concepts which we consider 'good.' We are programmed like robot dogs. The way we think of ourselves, the way we see the world and our relationship with others, it is all in our common coding.

We are blessed, and cursed, with more similarities to one another than there are differences between us.

How easy that makes us to read. How simple to punish and reward.

Many of us believe that people are like bunny rabbits – that, if you take us apart and learn from what's inside then we are never the same bunny again. But perhaps people are like motor cars. A skilled mechanic can disassemble the human machine, examine it, then put it back together – and it will work as well as it did before, maybe even better.

See our patterns.

How full we are of watchfulness and need. How desperate for something to fill the emptiness which has no name, which cannot be expressed. That longing.

Love talked as we headed in the direction of the parade of shops. We were hungry and my caravan was a carbohydrate desert. It was a protein wilderness: a sugar tundra.

"What do you eat? Books?" pondered Love before we headed off in search of brunch.

I had an uneasy, left-out feeling, knowing Love was examining my island for the first time. It was as if an estate agent had sent him as a prospective purchaser.

"Cold running drizzle, note how the roofs glisten in a wet anti-rainbow from dove grey to dun."

I was anxious for him to like it – but indignant too. What did I care what he thought? These were my things – my patched tarmac, my sooty bricks.

I needed him to approve and yet I was equipped for bitterness if he did not.

This was the only place I had known – though I think it's better to know one place well than lots of spots not very well at all.

With Love I saw my world through strangers' eyes.

My chalet park was on a squat rise, flogged by constant wind. It was as though its founder had hunted hard for the most bone stupid place to build it then thought: "Yes – this is it! The very place for us. Right up here where we can get bollocked daft by the elements every moment of the day and night."

There was a view though. Under the troubled clouds, over the bothered sky, was the psychotic sea. It was schizophrenic scenery. Even the gulls had issues. They raged and drilled a shrill air-show which had no end.

There was one road down from the park towards the grit-pocked terraces and craning concrete streetlamps. Blokes saying 'morning', kids giving out cheek as we passed. Sort of street scene which could have been anyone's but was mine.

I stepped in dog shit. Love laughed. I believe that if someone steps in shit and you don't at least smirk it indicates you're not wired right. I once knew someone so unlucky she slipped in dog-shit and split her head open. Really. So think on.

Down the hill we promenaded on smashed paving slabs like toffee hit with a hammer. An odd couple; little and large – like a dad taking his tot for a stroll. At length we reached a square with shops round it.

The shops aren't much, if honesty's called for. They're humdrum, slightly shabby examples of the ones near where you live.

If you saw them you'd think "Hey – they're like our shops! Except crap."

There's a Chinese takeaway and a dry cleaners which nobody seems to use. There's an open not many hours mini-supermarket and the sort of hardware store which shouldn't still be here given the delights to be had over the bridge and out on the ring road.

There's a shop selling the most delicious cakes.

There's a shop selling the most delicious lager.

That's about it for shops really. But tell me – what else do you need?

In the approximate centre of our more or less square we have a sort of statue.

It's the only one on the island – in fact, we've nothing else you could even call art – unless you count bus shelter graffiti.

Our statue is called Mother and Child. It was bequeathed to the island in 1928 by Morgan H Stanhope of whom you may have heard.

Okay then, suit yourself. He was a modernist sculptor of some small renown who visited the island to do a spot of bird watching. We have sea-birds on the island. You can watch them. If you want.

Stanhope mooched around for a week or two in his plus fours. Watching terns and getting coated in guano. Then he headed back down to the Smoke.

He wasn't very much of a sculptor if you ask me. An over-rated plunderer of the primitive artists he pilfered from churches, the third world, his own ancient history – but, instead of adding to it, he somehow managed to subtract.

Claiming some vague Eastern European ancestry he was allowed to get away with dressing in purple robes. He grew a beard down to his nipples and convinced the chattering classes he was something of a prophet.

Some months after his visit to our island a letter arrived addressed to the parish council which said: "Shoo-be-doo-be-doo, I can't get your simple rural idyll out of my nut, I am charmed by your honest peasantry, would you please accept a small token?"

The letter is preserved, wizened and yellow as a smoker's fingers, in a glass case at the reference library. It shares the space with a few other bits and pieces forgotten by Stanhope when he left our island: a soiled handkerchief, an ivory handled cut throat razor, about half a deck of playing cards. But prize exhibit is the letter. Many a tramp, come in for a warm, has stared rhumely at it over a lukewarm can of Tenants Extra.

It contains some choice phrases.

"To see is one thing," it contends obliquely. "To go there is another." "A force of change is blowing," And um… "Purity cannot be established without bloodshed."

It also promised us the statue, which arrived some months later at the mainland railway station.

A grainy sepia photograph from the time shows that the arrival of the statue was a grand affair. There was the island's brass band, the borough mayor and his consort in full ceremonial robes and chains, along with a gaggle of local dignitaries in glistening bowlers and wing collars.

One senses they were expecting Stanhope to show up – perhaps give a short speech, that kind of thing. Yet Mother and Child arrived unchaperoned. Friendless, they were heaved onto the platform by a labouring crane and the train pulled away. Reversing out of the station to the strains of Elgar.

There must have been deep disappointment. Ours is a community accustomed to knock-backs. Yet I believe I can see on the photograph the let-down in the men's faces: washed out, moustached, prematurely aged.

But no. This was the age of stoicism, of making the best of things. These people had been given a gift – for the first time ever, and they were not at home to Mr Ingratitude.

So the band serenaded the ungainly lump of rock which must have been a bugger to get onto the island.

How the tiny ferry survived the statue's desperate weight in the winter tides is a tribute to the skill of those who piloted its precarious, Plimsoll line busting course across the canescent channel.

So here it is today. Our statue.

It is eight feet tall and made of some kind of soft limestone. The stone is beautiful under the grime, the colour of honey mixed with snow.

If you saw the Mother and Child in an art gallery, walked around it, paused for reflection, you would come to this conclusion:

"It is shit."

You wouldn't have to be any kind of trained art critic to decide that; it would just come to you anyway – a lump of brutal logic.

The statue is clumsy, disproportionate, crude and ill-fangled. It is also ours.

We were gifted it by someone the world deemed fit to be called an artist. He flattered us with his attention and we were an ugly girl asked to dance. It roosts now in the centre of our square on a mini-roundabout. Scrubbed clean of spray paint semi-annually by the council, otherwise it is neglected and unloved.

Mostly it is ignored. We found we could phase it out after a while, like an irritating hum. Today though a decent sized crowd had gathered around the thing. For decades it had been considered dull but today a sudden knot of people all at once found it fascinating. They loitered. They gazed. I'd not go so far as to say they gawped.

I gawped perhaps, at the sight of them gazing.

There was pointing and discussion in the group as if they were Japanese tourists being shown curious western treasures.

"Let's take a look – why not?" decided John Love. "There's nothing to be lost by looking."

I couldn't see anything of the statue until I had wriggled and elbowed my way past the collection of crotches which obscured the view. Eventually I forged my path to the front and looked properly at the statue for the first time in many years.

It was worth looking at, I saw now. It was monumental in its ugliness.

A lumpen larger figure clutching a blocky smaller one, as if it were a sack of refuse on the way out to the wheelie bin, slung under one beefy arm. Curiously, pointlessly, mum's other arm was stretched out to the sky – like an infant asking permission to go to the toilet.

The child's face was an essay on congenital idiocy; distorted and vacant, the mother, only vaguely female in appearance, seemed to be suffering some kind of mid-range discomfort – as though she had stood on a drawing pin maybe or her piles were playing up. Yet at the same time she looked oafish and ignominious so's you couldn't find it in your soul to care much about the petty nature of her suffering.

It was an indisputably naff piece of work, and it was judged by those critics who could bring themselves to care, to be one of Stanhope's best.

There was something else though. A fresh element in the ill thought out composition of the piece.

There was a rent in the thing, a tear stretching from the mother's raised arm down across the baby's abdomen so the damp flannel grey of the sky filtered through.

"How would something like this happen?" wondered Love out loud. Those closest to him tuned in and paid attention. He must have seemed all the more impressive after their recent diet of unrefined squalor.

Paul Repton Glazier, a car mechanic, spoke up: "It was the storm last night we think, the lightning had her. That arm stuck up in the air acted as a conductor."

"No," said Love. "How did a thing like this come to be created?"

Love had a good look up and down the statue. People moved back a little to give him room and he paced round it with his hands clasped behind his back as though he was conducting a royal visit.

Reaching out he ran his fingers over the spangly roughness of the stone.

"So what happens now?" He wanted to know.

"Call the council," shrugged Glazier. "They'll fix it one way or another. Stick a bolt through her neck like Frankenstein and pull it together maybe."

Chuckle at this from the crowd – it was about the only thing you could do to the statue to make it more monstrous than it currently was.

"Why wait?" Love wanted to know. "Why rely on others to take your decisions? You've lived with it – it's yours. You need to ask what will make you happy – what do you want for yourselves? Look at the thing and ask if that is all you're worth."

"What the hell," Glazier wanted to know, "has this thing got to do with what we are worth?"

He knew what he was worth did Paul.

He was one of the few black people on the island. Well, okay, he was the only one. I just didn't want us to seem too provincial, but, in truth, it's a pointless conceit.

Ours is not one of those cosmopolitan children's TV islands which are like a melting pot for all the nations. It's more like the gene pool stalled with the Vikings, who were the last people to visit in significant numbers. When they turned up a thousand years ago we weren't entirely keen on them so, at the risk of appearing standoffish, we discouraged inward migration thereafter.

Glazier was a determined one-track sort of bloke who refused to be cowed by difference. These days he was ugly too, like so many of those who are not the same; he was oppressed by the figures of beauty. I suppose that's why he had liked the Mother and Child statue the way it was.

John Love is heading for the hardware shop.

It is called R Bakers. But the white plastic B broke off some time ago, leaving only its ghost on a faded blue ground. There is no apostrophe. And why should there be? It is a dying tort, working its way inwards from the fringes of our society towards the centre, like a receding hairline. On the periphery it has all but disappeared. Soon the semi-colon will follow it; soon the colon.

We are living in the wild west frontiersland of grammatical shift. R Bakers is one of the pilgrims of that new age.

Love claps his hands together, making people start. He shouts: "I'm off over to Rakers to procure the things we're going to need – who's with me?"

It's too little information for anyone to know whether they are with him or without him. Yet the certainty of his voice, his use of the word procure, are enough to make up the minds of those in the crowd who are more impressionable.

Perhaps a quarter of the crew bunches off in his wake, rattled out of their inertia, unsure of where they are going or why. They look stunned, like people shaken from sleep-walking.

Some perhaps are regretting it already – they don't know where Rakers is. It could be miles away. They've shaken off their comfortable role as observers and become active in whatever is going on here today.

It isn't what you say.

Nobody listens to what you say.

It is how you say it is all that counts.

Love storms Rakers like it's civilization and he's the Hun.

Those following shuffle on after, bobbling in his wake, then find themselves suddenly released as he enters the shop and tarry there like buoys at the harbour mouth.

The rest of us, still huddled around the cracked statue, are tiptoeing pointlessly for a better view, though the door swung back after him and we can't see what's going on inside the shop.

The window displays are simply sheets of hardboard with holes drilled through it at regular intervals. The board is painted a sallow flaking magnolia and there are plastic hooks poking out of some of the holes. From these are slung a representative selection of the items for sale.

I want to say 'stuff'. Rakers sells 'stuff.'

Socket sets and garden forks, rotavators, car vacs. There are curiously fangled chrome things for I don't know what and plastic mats to stop you fouling the footwell of your car.

I imagine Love in there, behind the hardboard curtain, ferreting obscurely through the tics and nik-naks of puzzled ironmongery and brassware they hoard behind the counter. Old man Baker, hairless as a mole, regarding him through dazzled specs. Love has the trays and boxes and jars of base metal gew-gaws on the floor and is elaborately fumbling his way through items more numerous than pebbles on the beach – each destined for some slender purpose. He is looking for something to heal our statue. I had figured this out. A series of lofted, pendulous screws perhaps or a fistful of cute clamps like shellfish which would butterfly stitch the rent in our work of imagination.

Perhaps he was going down the glue route? That was certainly a possibility. He was poring over the limitless variety of fixatives and adhesives, the tiny phials of micro-engineered silicates and acetates capable of bonding dense intractable masses with a magical colourless blob the size of a teardrop. Or the great raw canisters which, once primed, pump out pints of porridge oats or viscous snot.

I envisaged him weighing tubes in each hand taking the sage council of the whey and bifocal Baker, his frayed head nodding. Two tubes, one black, the other yellow each inert on its own but, when mixed together with a plastic spatula provided for the purpose, the supernatural power of their bonding was unleashed. Quick, get that spatula out of there before it sets like a lollypop. Start smearing before it goes off. I was primed for gumming duty.

There was a medium-range wait then the shop door swung open. I think we were all expecting a dramatic re-emergence – a triumphal charge back to the statue – but instead, Love appeared arse first, bent over and slowly dragging a canvas sack full of something weighty.

He paused on the pavement for a spot of rest.

"You could give me a hand if you like," he advised the nearest of the onlookers chippily.

A handful of his chumps leapt guiltily into action and soon enough they had the bag slung between them and wrestled it over to us.

It hit the floor with a high bright 'clack.'

Love undid the bag and showed off his hoard.

"Hammers?" said someone, as if it was a question.

"All the sledges they had in the shop," Love confirmed. "Got them on trial. I'm surprised they went for that to be honest – there's not much you can do with a hammer, except the one thing."

They were remarkable looking sledgehammers. All of a job lot. They had glittering chrome heads and fluorescent yellow handles – if hammering were required in a pop video then these were what would be used. I was surprised Rakers had decided to go that fancy. There must have been an offer on – it's not everyone who wants to draw attention to themselves as they go about a job of work.

"Now," barked Love playfully. "Who fancies helping me transform this monstrosity into aggregate?"

He hauled a hammer out of the sack by its day-glo handle. It dangled, pendulous in his mitt. Then, swiftly and without pause, he swung the fluid arcing thing over his shoulder and into the body of the Mother and Child.

We all reared back like 'what the hell' as if we'd seen a snake and there were real live gasps – more or less oohs and aahs. It seemed such a shocking act of destruction. So unlicensed.

There was no visible damage to the statue but the ping of the collision echoed through us.

And he was at it again. Click, baff, clock. There were chips coming away from the thing now. Someone else leant into the bag and dragged out another of the hammers, stood there with it in his hands, watching Love lay into the statue. A second, then a third person armed themselves and at that point it seemed a balance had been tipped so there were enough people doing it for it to become acceptable. Those who already had sledgehammers began hauling them at the limestone mass with abandon while others moved in swiftly to join them.

All the rattle and frap. Things went unsaid. They threw themselves into the physical effort of the task. There was a leaping adhesive energy to the effort, whether you agreed with it or not. It went deeper than your point of view – than your morals even. There was rock to hit and hammers lying idle. I felt my muscles twitch and tendons tighten. Without questioning myself I found I was in there too. Scrapping for a place, taking my turn. Smashing at the work of art which was now barely recognisable as the statue it had once been.

Under the grime the stone was clean and new. It was as though we had exposed something pure which had been hidden. The pale rocks glistened, splendid and newly discovered as eggs.

We all joined in, all the men in the square took a turn, and a fair few of the women. All except Glazier, who stood apart from our dusty mob. Not hostile, yet not engaged either. He observed, as Stanhope must have done; squinting through binoculars at his Eider Ducks and Sand Pipers.

All was rage and forgetting, then suddenly it stopped.

Everything which could be wrecked had been, all that remained was that which had been destroyed. It didn't take us long. Within ten minutes the thing was parables and grit.

The pile was four feet high and spread out a little at the edges. As we watched, Love scrambled up the heap, leaning on the preposterous handle of his hammer for balance.

He looked a little precarious up there, a little 'unaccustomed as I am'.

Nevertheless he gave us quite a good talk.

"The way to happiness," he yelled out – so they could hear him over by the offey, "is not to get your hopes up. But everyone does nowadays. Throughout childhood we are conditioned to believe anything is possible for us – even though virtually nothing is. We are told we can achieve whatever we desire, yet we go away and fail.

So whose fault is that? It can only be our own. Before long we come to feel that, whatever we do we are still losers. Wherever we go we should be somewhere else. Whoever we are it's always the wrong person to be. It's no way to live. No way at all."

"What's that to do with breaking statues?" muttered a bloke next to me.

"He should chuck in a couple of jokes," said another.

But they seemed pleased with it, by and large. It seemed to chime with them the same way smashing stone had done.

We went for sandwiches. They were resting in the window of the baker's shop twinkling like fish in their clingfilm sleeves.

I passed. I don't eat sandwiches wrapped in clingfilm as I am convinced they will contaminate me. I have a profound belief that clingfilm gives you cancer. I possess no evidence for this. Yet I have a deep seated psychological need to trust it is so.

Nothing in nature is as sheer yet tensile as clingfilm. So transparent, so strong. These are magic, unconventional powers. I don't believe man made it. I think it was aliens.

It comes from the million year old ghosts of rotting vegetation yet it is glittering and modern – and that can't be right.

Love sees me eyeing his butties with distaste. He proffers one. I grimace. Somehow he knows what the issue is.

"It's very hygienic," he insists, snapping at the curled corner of the packaging.

I shake my head with vigour. He shrugs back to his lunch. You have to learn to pick your battles I suppose.

I had a pie.

You can't go wrong with a pie.

After that I craved my lunchtime pint – that usually lasted me until nap time and then the evening session. I was all for heading off to the King Alfred to spend some of Love's mind-reading money but it was apparent he had other ideas.

"We need to visit my boat," he told me.

I could feel the icy iron-rich tang of Guinness on my tongue like blood.

"My things are in there. You tie your life to things. What there is of me is on that boat – unless it's all out at sea by now."

People were hanging about watching us. Some were pretending they had chores which involved loitering, others just gawped. New people who hadn't been around for the hammering turned up and mulled over the pile of stones. There was a lot of low level milling-about going on and Love would have had no shortage of volunteers to help with his errand yet Glazier was still here surprisingly – and Love asked him if he would give us a hand.

Glazier didn't find that strange. People on the island often proffered hands or asked for them. It was an accepted aspect of our life and explained the local saw: 'Never buy a pick-up truck.'

We headed towards the shore, speaking only obliquely of what had gone on in the square, the clack of hammers still echoing in our heads.

"I'm not big on dreams," Glazier confessed. I suppose Love must have asked him something to elicit this but I missed it – day-dreaming of stout.

"When I was a kid I used to dream I could fly – but I don't know if that counts. It wasn't something I wanted."

"Are you saying that the desire for the thing is what makes it a dream? The need to have a wish satiated?"

"I'm saying I didn't want to fly. I just found I could do it. And everyone else could too if they only listened to me and copied my method. It was a question of good technique, like fixing white goods."

"So you believe that to truly have a dream one needs to share it as widely as possible – a kind of wish evangelism?"

"I mean that you can fix a leaking washer if you have studied the manual. There are ways of doing things, protocols which allow you to understand machines."

As we crossed the rough grasses on the foreshore I collected plants in my pocket for Love to heal the wounded, loaded, ladies whom he had promised succour during his morning surgery. Like an animal grazing I stooped to pick and prod, then ambled gamely after my long-legged companions, my trousers verdant and bulging.

"So you believe there is a natural record, a kind of harmony which we feel compelled to obey? Look, there's my boat."

And there it was, anchor weighted down with a few rocks – which Love must have found time to sort out before heroically rescuing me.

"I mean I used to dream it was possible to fly. But I was mistaken."

The tide was out like it had never been in and the little craft was landlocked – pointless on the edge of pebbles, swaddled in grey sand so you wondered how it got there. Puzzling as a mushroom.

We set about landing the cargo. Love travelled light – small trunk and a couple of cases. I took the suitcases while they wrestled the trunk between them across the curiously tamed and symmetrical stones.

The trunk had a name embossed on it in faded gilt.

It said John Lovell – only the last two letters had peeled off.

"That you?" asked Glazier. "John Love."

Can't remember whether he nodded, whether anything was said. I was thinking of porter.

Still, that was his name and there was no further mention of how he came by it. No steward's inquiry into the whereabouts of the missing ells or analysis of the questions they might have raised in enquiring minds.

It took us perhaps half an hour to get back to the van.

I was not a little knackered, carrying both cases. They didn't seem to mind. Anyway, it wasn't like they were carrying nothing; they were sharing a chest like a coffin that could have carried the remains of John Lovell, whoever he had been in the world before John Love.

Somehow I had it in my head that, when we got back to the van, we were all going to crack open the trunk and the cases and root through them like kids in a dressing up box, flinging treasures back over our shoulders as we dug deeper. I was Christmas Eve keen to ratch through Love's belongings. I wanted to scour his stuff like a forensic scientist picking at every tick of lint with tweezers.

But it didn't happen that way.

Instead he took his things into what I suppose was now his bedroom and stowed them in the corner, locks still snapped.

I emptied my pockets full of weeds onto the bed. He thanked me absently, sweeping them into a pile with big ruddy outdoor hands.

What was the greenery for? Glazier wanted to know.

"I'm thinking of getting a pet rabbit," answered John Love.

I made tea, though I was still without milk or sugar. The trip to the shops had been too atypical to allow for groceries. We stood around drinking the tea black and feeling a touch self-conscious. Glazier and Love were giants who loomed in my little van like I had the bailiffs in. It felt as though they'd soon be carting out the TV set.

Glazier spotted a book of oriental poetry poking out of one of the cabin lockers.

"Who's the culture vulture?" he wanted to know.

"S'mine," said John Love. "But here, take this."

He handed Glazier a cute buff envelope, about the size of a birthday card.

"What's in it?" Glazier asked, grasping it grudgingly.

"I need you not to ask," said Love. "Can you do that for me? Just forget it exists for now."

Glazier grimaced but pocketed it anyway.

"No weirder than owt else today I suppose," was all he said.

Glazier finished his tea and left. There was something he didn't like about Love but he didn't know what it was yet. He had the urge to complain but, infuriatingly for him, he had no justification for doing so.

When we were alone Love got busy at the kitchen stove – as animated and energetic as a TV chef.

He located my saucepan – thankfully bigger than it needed to be. I'd been gifted it, as I am so many things, by one of the people I listen to – a woman whose kids had left home and who found she had more cooking capacity than she could handle.

He put a pan of tap water on the ring to boil then dashed off to the bedroom, returning with fistfuls of my freshly gathered botanicals.

"Nothing in here which could actually kill anyone is there?" he queried, ripping them roughly into the pan.

How the hell would I know? I'm at two with nature; I exist despite not being in harmony with it. It is possible to be somewhere and know nothing about the place. I was in that state of grace.

While the pot was bubbling away I watched Love greedily as he teased open the lock of his trunk with a cute key he conjured. The lid flapped open and he fumbled behind it like a Jack Russell with its head down a rabbit hole, flinging odds and sods onto the bed.

With a conspiratorial tinkle he produced a handful of small glass bottles, then another and one more until there were about a dozen of the things on the bed. They had child proof tops and looked like the ones they hand out at pharmacies, though less official – more quaintly fangled in their design. Next he produced what looked like old spice jars.

We ferried this peculiar glassware back to the stove where Love stirred his concoction, which didn't smell bad, just green.

"Don't suppose you have such a thing as a sieve?"

Nope.

"Or some muslin?"

He obviously had me down as branch chairman of the WI.

A pause as he cogitated.

"Old socks then."

Now those I had in abundance.

The ones I donated, grey, misshapen and ancient, made a passable sieve and he squeezed the liquor from the pan through the less threadbare of the pair into my cereal bowl before decanting it with much missing and cursing, into the medicine bottles. The resulting brew was not unpleasant to the eye. Emerald and glittering in the cloudy glass, it looked almost tempting.

The bolos was not wasted. Love slopped it out of the sock into the bowl and mashed it to puree with my fork before dispersing it between his jars.

This mixture was a more earthy green and looked as though it might taste disgusting, yet still be good for you.

We surveyed the row of bottles and jars perched on the draining board.

"These," Love allowed, "should do fine."

There's always plenty happening elsewhere and that's a fact. There's a whole lot of where you're not. A world of it – smaller than you can see and bigger than you can fight.

Consider my own little island at the moment when Love and I were manufacturing his amazing panacea, glittering and verdant, bursting with health; a mood was growing in the community, accords were being reached.

This is not the sort of place where people get together in a cub scout hut and hold a parish meeting to decide what they think of a thing. Here the process is holistic. The meeting is going on all around you in a perpetual state of any other business. We are like ants in a nest.

Jeff Barnes, who was standing towards the back of the crowd in the square, might pop in on his mother Rene, who had been towards the bedraggled end of the unsuccessful queue to get her bumps read by Love. And Jeff might tell her he was impressed by Love in a way he hadn't often been by anyone. While Rene's already been chatting to her mate Lauren who actually saw Love for a consultation and testified to his supernatural ability to divine her thoughts and relay messages to her from dear departed Trevor, a golden retriever.

So Jeff's a little one-upped by this, a tad sneeped, so he says he saw something much better – he saw the man smash the statue with his bare hands, in fact he's not even sure if he touched it at all, his hands just seemed to be hovering there and the thing crumbled like a peppermint creme purely due to the force of Love's personality.

It was a miracle, that's what it was.

Which is maybe the first time that word is used, though it won't be the last, as the same verbal share dealing is going up and down the estates and terraces, in the shops and public bars, in the library, in the doctor's waiting room, at the toddler groups. People are becoming aware of Love's presence here – or at least the presence of someone they are creating who will bear his name.

Those who have snagged the threads of Love, those who wish they had, they are sharing him and sharing the word. Miracle.

After it has passed enough lips it becomes a truth.

And the scuffed and grubby sledges, back on the shelf at Rakers, are discounted. Those who wielded them will soon be among the keenest to claim that the thing happened some other way, some better way, because of the glow it casts on those who were there. They were part of the thing. A vagueness overcomes them as to the details. They would rather speak of feelings, of the change that has been wrought in their lives.

There will have been plenty who mocked on that first afternoon as Love drank my tea and the story did its work. There will have been many who chose to combat the word miracle with mirth – others who got narked, more still who were indifferent.

But there were also those who chose to believe something had happened in the square which was precious and rare, a thing which could not be explained away by reason and by cleverness and so was theirs to treasure.

They had faith. Something even the poorest people on the earth have access to.

As our islanders went about their business that afternoon: worked at jobs, picked up benefits, cashed pension cheques, a miracle was born.

The statue had smashed itself, or rather Love had smashed it just by decreeing it done. They had all witnessed the rubble.

The details were a little blurred. I later heard half a dozen versions of the thing, some replete with incident, others rough palette knife strokes at the generality.

Each tale ended with a pile of rubble in the square where the statue had been.

And, know what? When the curious went to look – there was a pile of rubble in the square. Which proved it. Whatever it was.

V

I was prince of the pub that night, and for many evenings after. I was boozer royalty.

I'd asked Love if he wanted to come along but he'd had a hard day. He said he'd snuggle up in bed with a good read and trawled a tousled copy of *The Golden Bough* from one of his cases.

I burned his invitation note on the gas ring and set off for my regular evening session in The Vengeance.

I'd always had a fondness for the pub just for its name, which was after some old navy frigate – they had jaundiced boat-porn pics behind the bar to prove it. The reason for the name was prosaic and I wished they hadn't been so leaden about it. There's lots of people, well, blokes really, who'd go to a pub called The Vengeance simply for what they felt it lent them.

It was the sort of pub one felt ought to exist here. It had caved in and given up. It didn't care anymore about its appearance as it was sure nobody loved it anyway. What could fade had done so, what there was to peel was flaking away. It greeted its care-worn clientele, familiar as the shaving mirror.

There was no economic reason, such as tourists, students or a slot on the Saturday night pub run to make it worth tarting up. 'Sides, us regulars liked it the way it was. We settled the ripped arse of our jeans down on its torn benches and were content.

There were never that many of us in there, just enough to keep it going, except at Karaoke on a Friday, and this was Tuesday so I was baffled to find the lounge bar crammed with new faces.

Perhaps stale ale and a disturbing musty smell were suddenly all the go. There was Babs, who never left the 'fun' pubs, and Audrey who never came in pubs. There was Glazier, who did pop in sometimes sure and then would sit with me, sharing his fears at my confessional, as I silently supped my deep unsleeping pint of best.

There were many people here now I had seen earlier in the day – at the statue, around the van. Perhaps they had gathered in the hope I would bring John Love out with me. In which case they copped a disenchantment as I bundled through the door on my Jack Jones.

My gurn of puzzlement was greeted with a whole lot of cheery and expectant kites all peering back at me like Bambi until everyone got self-conscious and went about their business.

I went to Glazier's table – which was traditionally my own. There was a pint of Hartley's perched on its mat waiting for me like a cat.

Audrey eyed my gloves as I took them off and put them on the table.

"I'm frightened of men wearing black leather gloves. They look like gorilla hands."

Glazier said: "I'm frightened of you 'cos you're clearly a mental."

He put on my gloves, best he could, and chased her round the table with them while she screeched.

I grinned but said nowt. They know the rules. I don't engage in conversation. If I want something I point at it. If there are greetings, farewells or thanks to be got through I stare for a moment at the intended recipient. That's as far as it goes.

Audrey sat hot and bothered, saw her arse for a while. The others talked round me – including me in the conversation with sparse glances and oblique remarks, without expecting anything die-cast back.

They knew the pluses of this arrangement, most of them. There can be advantages in talking to someone who is prepared to listen, mute and uncomplaining, without response.

Many of them used this service which I offered without tariff. Every community, I think, should have a listener. There are so many talkers out there who have to be heard.

Barbara's on about her anorexia again.

"… it helps me is the thing. It makes me pure and feel good about myself, the sacrifice."

Way I see it, anorexia's just being rude at dinner parties – put in that bit of extra effort and gear up to bulimia, then everyone's happy.

But I stare and look innocent and her needs are met.

Audrey and Glazier are at the bar, she wouldn't be talking like this if they were here. She's telling me what she intends to say to Love next time she can grab a slice of his attention. That's going to become increasingly tricky.

These people are only sharing a table with me because of the links we have somehow formed with him, stronger than anyone else has yet managed. But there will be competition I know. From people who talk; who assert themselves; who are attractive.

Glazier and Audrey are back with drinks for which they didn't have to pay. Audrey never comes out for drinks. What's she doing here in the Vengeance with a gin and grapefruit clutched in her self-conscious claw? She's trying to be nice to people and they are trying to be nice to her, which is a first.

They smile and seek to make eye contact as she edges past them to her seat – one or two try to engage her in cheery banter.

"She's loving this, I reckon," says Barbara who is as well.

Glazier's grumbling to Audrey as she arrives.

"Every time I buy you a drink you test it with your date rape drug kit – just for once I'd like to see you sup something without sticking an eyedropper in it first."

"You can't be too careful."

"It shows an unsettling lack of trust."

We're bonding. Me too. I'm included. My peculiarities, though extreme, are accepted along with those of the others.

We may be the odd-squad but we're still a squad.

Ken Naylor, who's a colleague of Glazier's from the garage, comes over with his missus and usually that would be a cue for Glazier to drift off with them but he sticks around and Kenny seems happy enough to be here with the four of us – delighted even, sharing his fruity round Spanish-Main of a laugh, his wife's answering falsetto whinny. Everything that gets said makes them laugh, even the thin gruel of Audrey's forced smalltalk. Small? It's fucking sub-atomic.

"Well, I shall be getting tiddly if I have any more of these!"

"Uh haw haw haw haw haw!"

"Yaw yaw yaw yaw!"

Before long, sure enough, they want to hear all about John Love.

Like most people on this island, they've never set eyes on him but they've heard all sorts – a congealed lump of information tricked out with mind-reading and miracles and more to come.

I realise how little we know – collectively, and the most part of that is what I know which stays sealed inside as I sit, squat and inscrutable as a Russian doll.

Barbara goes big on how he looks, he smells nice too apparently. I'd not consciously noticed that, though I know the huge bite it takes out of the way people perceive you.

I have always laboured under the wan and musty odour of stale chips.

Audrey enthuses: "He's so intelligent. I'm not joking, he must be ten times as intelligent as anyone here."

Ken Naylor takes the hump despite himself. "Ten times – ooh, that's impressive, he must be just a big brain in a jar of gloop. Since he's such an intellectual powerhouse I'm surprised he's not applying his mind to something a bit more constructive than party tricks for the yokels. Shouldn't he be sorting out cold fusion or finding a cure for cancer?"

Audrey huffs. Perhaps it serves her right for showing off.

Barbara is uneasy and hesitant when she speaks, as if she's drunk already.

"He made me think about gods. The possibility I mean. I hadn't thought about that in years."

"I don't know much about gods," said Glazier. "But I know the sea. When I think about how a boat engine works, I know what each little component does. No-one can say that about the sea. But we go out to sea in a boat."

Another time Audrey might have had a fragile snigger at this, but not today.

"It's strange what he doesn't know. I was telling him about filling the ATM at the bank. I had to explain them. Not just the term, the whole idea of a cash machine, the card, the number, money coming out."

Glazier, who gets more intense the more he drinks, talks about energy, how the guy makes him feel. He wants us to know that he's never felt like that, not for years.

"There was this English teacher when I was at school – he made us believe in the stuff they had us read – the power of the poetry, like it was for something – even Shakespeare, when he told us about it – it seemed precious," Glazier enthuses all damp-eyed, with flecks of spit in the corners of his mouth.

"This Love's like that. You can't believe it 'til you meet him, he's like a self-help book with legs."

"What makes you think he can help you?" Ken Naylor wanted to know.

"You know me Kenny, how I am. I get frustrated, pissed off. Sometimes I wake up at three am in a fury over dreams that people from my past are mocking me because I'm a failure. This bloke might not help but he surely can't make it any worse."

Ken's nodding. "You should have gone for the foreman's job when I did. You might not have got it but it would have shown the management you had drive."

I knew how he felt. I felt that way too. Maybe a little less cheery. I mull over old bitterness, stir hatreds like dark potions. I'm a tangle of petty concerns and prickly as a voodoo doll with slights, behind-backs, outrages.

We should be happy, us human beings, yet we are all so sad. Why is that d'you think?

The four of us could not buy a drink that night in The Vengeance – we were forever having them pressed into our hands by people who wanted whatever we could give them of John Love – which was near on nothing. But just being close to someone who had been close to him was enough for them.

I pondered what it all meant but came up blank, so I had another jar. What I like to do on occasions like these is some blue sky drinking. Things seem clearer and more focused when you're paralytic.

When I ventured to the bar Frank the barman grabbed my cheeks between his meaty digits and held me there pouting like an undignified fish.

"Look at his little face," he exhorted. "The things he could tell us, the stuff he must know. But he sez nowt. What a waste."

He let me go with a couple of skin reddening slaps and an oafish chuckle, then set me up another pint – on the house.

He didn't seem to give a stale drip tray for what John Love was about – which is why, when I hauled myself to the caravan door the following lunchtime with a rat's nest for a consciousness I was dazed to find him at the front of the queue.

Not that today we could call it a queue – it was a pointy crowd, perhaps seventy strong, with Franky at the arrow tip grinning at me like a trained Macaque.

"Is he up?"

I went to see.

I'd heard nothing from Love, but then I'd been tumbling feverishly in and out of the land of nod.

He was sitting on the bed reading his tattered wedge of paperback, just as he had been when I'd left him the night before.

It was as if he had been perched there all through the night reading. He could have done for all I knew – I'd been in no state in the early hours to do more than fumble my way in through the caravan door and pass out. I awoke to find I'd wet myself. People don't usually buy me that much to drink.

Love looked up.

"Are there many here?"

They must have been waiting a while. Banging on the door, milling about. I'd taken some waking. But Love seemed to have been content to hang on for me to perform my function as usher.

I scribbled on my palm: "Too many," showed him, rubbed my hands together. He nodded.

"So – different format today then. We'll go down to the shore. I have a feeling there will be a show today. An unforgettable event."

He bent down to fuss his face a bit in my mirror but frankly there was no point. Whatever he looked like suited him somehow. Contexts such as sleepy, dishevelled, grumpy, baffled; they all seemed like settings for a rare stone.

He followed me out – I had to push through the bustle.

There was a desperate cackle of excitement when he appeared – same as I'd heard only once before when a chubby blonde girl who used to be a bar-maid in one of the less popular soaps came to reopen the island branch of Easyways after refurbishment.

Love appeared – so the people clapped their hands. There's times when you're just not sure what reaction is the right one. New times. So you fall back on something you know. They greeted John Love like a gameshow host, or a politician who finds himself popular for a moment. And Love lapped up on that daft crest of applause and awarded it a rich good humoured smile – which made us chipper, each and every one. Even those of us, like me, who'd discovered an exotic new variety of hangover which would henceforth be named in our honour.

"I'm here," Love began, then trailed off in the wake of the continued ripple, as though too bashful a customer to tread on folks' well meant applause.

"I am here to speak with you," he said. "I am here so that we can have a conversation."

Suddenly it seemed nobody had anything to say. It was as though they had been switched to listening mode and now only wanted to respond as a group: quiet, loud, nothing much in-between. Individuality, when there are a lot of you, can be confusing. They were focused on John Love; he was all the individual they needed for now.

But I saw their faces out there. The people who had held hammers, the ones who'd heard home truths, others who had done nothing bar listen to a voice on the phone, or strain to hear something carried on pub smoke or the island's bitter breeze.

He lead us out of the caravan site, past its buggered together boundary wall of beach pebbles and chips of brick, slap dashed with eczemic mortar. He led us onto the tousled bouncy turf of the foreshore with its 'so what?' clumps of green stuff, too mongrel and various to have been given a name.

Love stood before us, back to the sea. He looked like he was going to give us another talk – might even have cleared his throat ready, but then he came over all distracted – hand on his frowning forehead, bit like Columbo used to on the telly.

And he yelled out: "You there. Marcus Riley. You have something to tell me do you not?"

And he was pointing to a guy in the crowd who quite clearly was not Marcus Riley – Riley being shorter, mousier, paler complected, and having just the one leg.

Riley, laughing from the back of the crowd: "Over here mate – you've got the wrong bloke."

"No," said John Love. "Marcus Riley here before me sitting in a bath chair, looking at me with his pretty grey eyes. He has something to tell me."

Riley cried out: "Dad!" And hastened over to Love's patch of nothing.

"My dad. Is he here? He can't be? Dad, is it you? Can you hear me?"

He seemed genuinely cut up. Tearful and that, you know. But the weirdest thing was that he had started to limp. I'd known Riley ten years. He'd always had a false leg and I'd never seen him carry it like he was amongst this igniting crowd of people, who knew him personally but were watching him like he was a programme on the television.

He hobbled over to Love's scrap of nowt and wrestled with it for a while as if there was a corporeal thing there he could hug and comfort; if only he focused hard enough and believed.

Real warmth, real flesh, the wicker on the bath chair, the wrinkles on the old boy's grizzled kite.

"He says," Love said softly, "you are to look after Harry."

"Harry?"

Love, squinting into an afterlife somewhere off the coast where the seagulls wheeled.

"Not Harry. Not a name I have heard before. You are to look after Hennie."

"Hennie! Henrietta, that's what he called the bike. The one that took his legs and one of mine."

"You can't have been more than twelve years old."

"I was eleven."

"You had your whole life in front of you like the motorway."

"And what sort of a life has it been? What sort Dad? A cripple. A freak. What sort of a person am I now thanks to you and your fucking motorbike?"

"Too fast round the bend."

"Too fucking fast your whole life. You were doing it to impress those birds in the Beetle you were following. Mucking about and taking risks – with me on the seat behind you, clinging on in the cold wind. So frightened I nearly wet myself."

"The road was greasy."

"How could you do it? How could you live with it after you did that to me?"

"Did to both."

"You made your own hell."

"I certainly was a low down bum. I liked that one. Low down bum."

"But what had I done dad? What had I done to deserve that at eleven years old? Nowt. I was just your son that's all. Just your son."

"He will always be your dad," stage whispered John Love. "Know that he is telling me he will always be your father."

Riley bent at the one knee, tumbled slowly to the springy turf and sat there dazed as a cider drunk school kid.

"Right." John Love clapped his hands. "Who's next?"

"Mavis Johannes," screamed Mavis from the front row.

"He never has, he never will. Give up on him. He's not worthy of you – try Riley."

Love dealt in falling cadences, dismissively.

"Now where's Neil. I'm getting Neil?"

He jolted to a halt as though somebody had called out his name.

"What?" he hollered at adjacent sky. "Can't hear you! What do you say?"

Then turned his pretty face calmly back to the waiting pack.

"It is what you make of this world."

He was nodding so we found our heads tilting softly too.

"Your life may not be like other people's, but that does not mean that it can't be a success in its own terms."

He was right, I had to concur, in a fortune cookie kind of way.

Pepin the Short, king of the Franks from 751 to 768 AD, was four feet six inches tall – just an inch taller than me. The short arse.

I've never had a fortune cookie. What's a fortune cookie taste like?

"Where is Neil? Understand that Neil is required to speak with me."

I've had plenty of budget choc-chip cookies from the Easyways – but they didn't make me feel all that fortunate, just fat.

"Neil, Nail, Noel – yeah, no. Niall."

"Niall," yelled Jello Blakeley. "My brother who was stillborn was called Niall."

"Your twin brother Niall. Your twin – beside you all these years. Your perfect other half."

Having a bird shit on you is supposed to be lucky too. A seagull shat on me the other day but I haven't noticed any particular fucking upturn in my fortunes.

Barbara shouts out from the crowd: "This is wonderful. You must be telepathic."

"No," gives back Love jovially. "I'm homeopathic. Rub a little of me on your elbow and you'll never have hiccups again."

Big laugh for that – he was on a winner for sure.

I was expecting him to push our new grog like Happy Hour down the Vengeance but it appeared I was under-estimating him.

There was simply a quiet moment when he did the rounds among the crowd, looking concerned – touching shoulders, forearms, the crowns of heads. Staring at the punters like a particularly keen and concerned GP. Straight out of medical school, desperate to prove himself god's gift to the Hippocratic oath.

To those lucky few, flattered by his attention, tickled to be picked, he murmurs that they are to know they may join him for private meditation after the gathering disperses.

They all figure in the island's upper income bracket I note. He guesses well and learns swiftly. He listens to what I tell him.

Then he drew us down to the shore. We went together, as though we'd jointly decided the thing rather than simply following him – which, I suppose is what we were doing.

"There are things it's worth tuning in for," Love was yelling as the wind clouted us. "Things it is worth acknowledging even though they fall outside of your normal experience."

Steady on, I thought, that's treason round here.

We were further north from the spot where I had first seen Love's boat. Down past the end of the golf course. We forged towards the beach across a long loping string of sand dunes undulating and organic like insect nests.

For a while we were lost among them, hulking lumps of grit-eyed blankness prickling with spartina grass.

Then Love strode panting up the side of one of the dunes, wallowing in sand up to his ankles, back sliding slightly, like Michael Jackson doing the moonwalk.

We all followed him in an undignified scrat and scramble, mine least dignified of all because, though life isn't too short for climbing a sand-dune, I am.

At the top of the dune we were gasping for breath which wasn't wind and didn't have grit in it.

Our reward was a dull view over the mottled grey shore and the open plain of the tide.

We looked at Love.

He peered back at our faces as though startled to find us staring at him.

"Wait," he instructed.

So we did.

Hanging on somewhere in anticipation of an event takes longer than just mooching about for no reason – as you'll know if you've ever stood waiting for a kettle.

We all looked out over the ocean. There wasn't much to see. Grey sky, a line indicating the horizon, then grey sea. We could have made it into the Guinness Book of Records for the world's shortest game of I-Spy.

I don't know how long we stood there, the wind blown bunch of us, performing a slow motion tap dance to keep from sinking into the softness.

But at length someone, maybe Barbara, shouted out excitedly.

"There's something out there."

The rest of us squinted out over the featureless ocean and agreed that no there wasn't and her imagination was having her a laugh.

Yet, by the time we'd all decided that, a few more people were sure they saw something too – a yellow patch out on the water – like an oil slick maybe, yet not that at all.

And so began a pissed-up, heads down, tipple-over charge as we Jack and Jilled it down the ankle-grabbing slope towards the sea, ungainly circus tumblers like I've seen once or twice on TV about cheese-rolling. One or two needed medical treatment later on for sprains, which can be painful.

I slid all the way down on my arse. I wasn't going to get caught like that again.

What was it? The yellowness, the artificiality, had us giddy. Like we'd never seen the plastic bags the sea gifted us; drinks bottles, canisters, floats. Stuff that might have had chemicals inside, stuff that might have had gas. Like we'd never shared in the sea's flotsam and jetsam; the dead whales, a leather backed turtle once, big as a coffee table. The dead bodies even, now and then, stranded in sleep with water trickling lazily from silent terracotta mouths.

We were seeing for the first time the ocean's unwanted bounty. The cat-like way it brought you presents you didn't much care for. A dividend you didn't want but could not return.

"I think," yelled Eunace, squinting through her opera glasses, "it's ducks."

"She thinks it's ducks," people told each other without asking any of the obvious questions re colour and consistency. Why none of them were flying. Why we weren't trying to kill and eat them like usual.

"Look!"

An excited yelp as Eunace had the thunder mugged from her. The very far away thing, which only she had a grip on, had lost out in favour of a much closer up thing which all of us could see. There, bounced up on the pebbles by the last feeble can't-be-arsed of a spent wave, was a sulphur yellow plastic duck.

It bobbed, like they do, it had an orange beak. It appeared to be smiling.

"It *is* ducks. It's ducks."

It was like they'd all been hoping for ducks.

Secretly, without daring to say it out loud.

John Love arrived around then. He'd been picking his rather prissy way down the side of the sand dune so's not to get sandy. He had a big pearly grin all over his kite as if to say: "You asked for ducks – I got you ducks."

Another couple of early adopters washed up on a breaker, bumbling over with the same ungainly kinetic energy as our lot had exhibited just now coming down the slope.

Love bent down and picked up a duck. Held it aloft with one arm so everyone who'd never had a bath before could see what it looked like.

"Sometimes," he said, "the world throws things at us which we could not possibly expect. The trick is to anticipate it. Glazier – have you the letter I gave you yesterday?"

Glazier stepped up to the mark.

"Got it here somewhere, yeah."

You could tell he was genuinely puzzled as he held the thing out – as grubby and crumpled as you could get a small buff envelope with only 18 hours to work at it.

He was a little put out too I sensed – that a secret something just between the pair of them, turned out to be in the public domain.

"Open it."

He did.

More ducks kept arriving in a spastic forward advance. We weren't even in the maw of the main duck invasion just yet.

"Read it out if you would – nice and loud of course so our friends at the back can hear us over this unusual breeze."

There was nowt special about that breeze. I thought so then and I'll say it now. That was your standard breeze.

"When God had finished the stars and whirl of coloured suns, he turned his mind from big things to fashion little ones; beautiful tiny things (like daisies) he made, and then He made the comical ones in case the minds of men should stiffen and become dull, humourless and glum…"

"That's beautiful that is."

"It's from that poem."

"We did it at school."

"It's called…"

Ducks.

Within half an hour they were washing up deep and thick – drifting along the edge of the shore as far as we could see one way and until the island swept a curve behind the dunes in the other.

They tripped over each other in the surf, piling up their splash of brilliance against nature.

No-one wondered where they were from. It seemed we all believed they were a gift to us.

Pointless, useless, but a gift nonetheless. And our island has always had a soft spot for a prezzie, however crap. It's the thought that counts. And this one was no less welcome than the statue of the Mother and Child.

Those among the crowd who felt moved to, began gathering up armfuls of ducks, stuffing them into pockets of macs, taking off their coats to use as improvised bags. It seemed important somehow to possess the ducks – there were plenty to go round.

It wasn't as though we were likely to run out at any point soon – or even feel the threat of a duck shortage. We could hold the world hot bath championships here on the island and we'd run out of soap on a rope and fresh towels well before we found ourselves having to send out for more ducks.

Love helped people load the things into handbags and hats. He laughed, shared his mirth – he wanted this event to bring us joy, I think, and indeed it did.

It brought wonder, it brought strangeness. These can be things you don't realise you need until you get them. Then you find out you have been yearning for them all along.

Our shoreline and the sea beyond it was a yellow plastic blanket now the full impact had hit. It lasted for a whole hour – that's a lot of ducks. People had chance to take their haul away home and come back for more – this time with suitcases, shopping baskets, wheelbarrows. They brought more people with them too, giddy with childlike excitement.

These people did not come for John Love, they came for the incredible sight of the ducks – but word soon went round that Love was at the core of it. That he had predicted it at least, maybe even caused it somehow in a way which none could fathom.

Here's what nobody said:

"The ducks are a cargo lost at sea."

"He passed through them at dawn as his lonely boat drifted."

"Heard of them through the distant mist of the short-wave frequency."

No-one, it seemed to me, was rooting for empiricism.

Hunting out that rational explanation which, however stretched, should automatically have been preferred to an irrational one.

What about Occam's razor?

We clearly weren't doing rational today. Massed bath ducks can do that to a person.

Love was up to his knees in froth, scooping up prizes for people as though we'd all hooked them at the fair. His eagerness gave the impression these things were his to give, that were we enjoying his largesse.

"Come on now, you can fit more in those trousers, over here with that plant pot – there's a huge drift just come in."

I picked up a duck.

It was green with weed round the base from being in the water a while. Orange beak with a hint of a smile, slightly mad painted eyes which stared back at me unfazed.

There was no mark on the thing to suggest where it was from, stamped out on a press in China or Taiwan. They all seemed similar; they may well have been identical. A vast cloned mass of sameness, good for nothing.

It was some gift. A thing to make you laugh at the audacity of it.

We stayed there gathering ducks throughout the whole long afternoon.

We certainly shifted some. Almost as though we had a use for them – though we didn't and they were of no cash value, the bottom having dropped right out of the plastic duck market in these parts.

When the light went there were still plenty more to take. Though oddly, when we went back out there to look the next morning the whole damn lot of them was gone.

Don't ask me whether it was a trick of the tide, or the winds, or whether some fanatically keen duck hunters had been out there on the back shift. But on that whole stretch of shore, not one speck of yellow remained. We might have thought we'd made it up if we didn't have cupboards, lofts, spare rooms, garages stuffed to bursting with ducks.

Even if he had seen them, or heard of them somehow, on the airwaves, on the breeze, it was still a remarkable guess, the timing of it, the place – his certainty that they would be here on our dot of habitation rather than miles north of the island or several leagues south. It could only have been chance that we were blessed with this arrival rather than some other unknown souls, full of wonder.

The afternoon of the ducks, when we had gathered all we could carry – all we felt that we needed, John Love spoke to us. He gave us the little talk we might have expected at the top of the day – like he didn't want us to miss out or anything, just because something big and showy had come along.

Glazier and a couple of the others were giving a wedding reception chant of "speech, speech" and Babs was trying to quiet folk down, in that coquettish way of hers, like she was promising them something of herself if they could just stay hushed.

"There is nothing I can tell you," Love shouted above the waves, "that you have not heard before. And nothing that you don't already know. You may believe yourself to be stupid – why not? You've been told you are often enough right? You've been told it by school teachers and bosses, by your parents maybe. Even by those people who have called themselves your friends. They've all been at it at one time or another. Running you down, telling you that you know nothing or that you don't understand.

"Well I'm telling you that is rubbish. It's the worst kind of evil because it's not just wrong but it's dragging you down with it into the darkness like a rock that's chained to you.

"I say again – there is nothing I can tell you. You know it already. You know it. You do. The communication of the dead is tongued with fire beyond the language of the living."

And he turned for the shore and headed briskly back up into the sand dunes. They're a place where a person can get lost. I don't know where he went. He wasn't at the van later.

Someone at the pub said they'd seen the cold light of a camp fire winking out there over the north end but I don't know if that's true. I suppose he must have been somewhere, everybody is.

In the boozer someone had the idea that we should all pay for our drinks with ducks. It was a popular notion and received enthusiastic grassroots support. But it was vetoed by Jarvis, the landlord, who said he preferred that we settle up in the time-honoured way – there being no great call for ducks as a unit of exchange.

"He could have brought us barrels of beer," objected someone from the smoky bowels of the boozer.

"Beer barrels would have been of more practical use."

So the notion seeded itself that we might approach Love and ask him if his largesse extended any further than plastic wildfowl – did he do requests? Something that we could eat maybe, or sell? I couldn't help thinking they were missing the spiritual and metaphorical resonance of the thing, but then I wasn't sure there was any – and besides, round here we've never gone very big on anything we can't eat, shag or spend. Perhaps that's no bad thing.

Glazier wasn't on such great form that night. He was morose and distant. Even further away it seemed than the fire in the dunes.

See, Glazier used to be married. But not anymore. He had kids, but he rarely sees them; he's had women but doesn't seem to care for them all that much. That personal closeness seems to be the first casualty of whatever it is that's ailing us.

I know how he feels: angry all of the time – impotent. Like he could smash something big outside in the world, or something small inside himself.

"Look round the pub," he told me. "We're all in the same mess. We all used to be better looking – we used to have more chances in life. That's one of the tragedies I think – that you can remember what you've lost, but there's no chance to get it back. And you have to ask yourself: What's it all for?"

He said that as though it was a question never asked by anyone else in the whole empty world.

We all ask. But there is no answer.

At least there was none. Now it seems there might be. That's what John Love has offered us perhaps – without ever putting it in words.

An answer to our longing.

Yes, we need answers – we fucking well demand them – why should we be left to play blind man's buff with our lives like this?

All of us deserve our answers – even the most dribbling drunk of our men, the hairiest chinned and most snaggle-toothed of our grotesque old women.

We hide behind booze and bullying, work and sex. We don't know what we're for.

Dave 'Pinocchio' Dobbs stumbles in – his huge hooter red from the cold.

"Here he is," whoops Helga – one of our hags, "Here's Pinocchio – let me sit on your face pet and you can tell me some lies."

Love has given us something. Even if it is only a gauge to measure our pain.

VI

It was curious that morning waking up in my van alone. It felt as though something had shifted.

I've been waking silent and alone for the best part of 20 years. Since mam died. That's what's normal. Then two days of company and it's odd on my own again.

It's a rum business being a human-being, particularly an adult one. I wouldn't recommend it if you find you have a choice.

I looked at the pebbles I kept by my bed – Love's bed: still moulded into his much larger foetal curl, still smelling of his curiously seductive musk.

I stared at the pebbles I had taken from the beach because they were beautiful like jewels, standing out from all the grey slate in which our shoreline specialised.

Where do pebbles come from? There are so many kinds when you examine them closely – the limestone, the flecked peach granite I had in my hand: sandstone, flint, something black, another nearly white, and lots of others filling in the spectrum.

Where do the rocks come from that make the pebbles?

Did they arrive all at once, ripped and jagged, then get smoothed together? Or did it happen over millions of years?

Where did the material come from? Huge lumps of cliff breaking off?

Does it still go on? If so then where are the jagged pieces queuing to become new pebbles? If no more are being made then why don't they erode to nothing?

I tumbled back into my usual routine. Misplaced morning in static caravan. I read my books, ate apricot jam sandwiches, lugubrious and shockingly sweet. Then I listened to the execrable local radio show from the mainland.

They'd got the idea of having a corner-shop newsagent review the morning's papers. Yes, I know – they just sell them. That's what I said. But apparently no one raised the issue at the conference where this idea got thrashed out.

It makes painful listening. A chirpy Jocasta from Radio Dull interrupting some sour tempered shopkeeper with a forty a day hack as he rifles through soiled newsprint. Pestering him as the plastic strips round the bundles poke under his nails like bamboo torture.

What does she want from him? Why won't she leave him alone? She's not from round here and would rather be in London with the real BBC.

He's behind the counter, grim and disconnected, still half-asleep and dreaming of a lie-in.

He mumbles an edgy response to her desperate breathy pleasantries, single-word answers her open questions. Just when she comes over all 'get down to business,' someone pops in for a pack of Rizlas and a *Sport*, shop bell jangling like they've got a prop man to do it for them. And he has to break off to talk about United and rattle on the till. Jocasta cheerlessly filling in with babble until he's back, grudgingly, and with bugger all to say.

And he just reads out the headlines. Slowly and badly – as if reading in itself were enough of a skill to guarantee him his moment of media exposure. He starts with the one on the paper nearest to his head, without naming it.

Words missed and mangled, syntax ground like dodgy gears.

She tries to coax him into a lame guessing game about what some of the headlines might mean. But quite frankly, he couldn't give a fuck.

"Oh, I think that might be about the Government's new plans on immigration – don't you think?"

"Mebbey."

But she's said immigration now which gives him a chance to spit some bile so he comes half to life and grumbles spitefully about stolen jobs and free houses and how we would all think differently if we could see the sights his Iris sees who works in the benefits office.

Then it's the regional papers – *The Morning Press*, which covers our general region in a half-arsed fashion, never seeming sure what its constituency is.

Can he find anything funny in it? pleads Jocasta.

There follows the longest radio silence since Apollo X.

I bang the clock radio to make sure the batteries haven't come loose.

"Okay then… anything interesting?"

Nothing.

"Just anything?"

"Says a bloke here made snakes appear."

"Pardon…snacks?"

"Says mystery surrounds claims that a chap in Dullbridge last week made a live snake appear from a bit of stick off the ground. A report first appeared in local papers. The man, who has now vacated the area, appears to have been some kind of new age traveller."

There was nothing about ducks, or any other kind of wild fowl, living or plastic, but it make me listen properly, propped up in bed and suddenly squinting through the crackly reception.

"Says the police wish to speak to him regarding possible financial fraud but that there is a groundswell of support among local people."

And that was it. Jocasta linked gratefully into the top of the hour news bulletin, which had nothing I could use.

I dragged my kegs and tee shirt on and headed down to the Easyways where the *Morning Press* bin was empty – they must have sold all three copies. I rattled it at the assistant who filled it up for me with a bunch of irrelevant local weeklies from behind the counter.

Who had bought the copies? Would more be in later? Where could I go to acquire a copy?

There's only so far an inquiring glance will get you. Besides, it wasn't politic for me to show so much interest in reading matter.

I remember when I was a kid I had a plastic snake. Articulated segments pinned together. And when you held its tail it flicked from side to side in a facsimile of reality.

Wherever I went that morning people were waiting for John Love. He was the slender bloke-shaped gap in whatever conversation I crashed. I didn't come all that close to filling it for them – but it seemed I would do.

I found Marcus Riley, the one-legged ex-biker, still convinced a man he had barely met had seen through him like a windowpane.

There were people standing around the pile of rocks by the shops like they meant something. If the statue had been hit by the bread van backing out of Easyways then no-one would have thought it represented something profound would they?

Just rocks, which had once been a crap statue.

I heard there was a commotion over at the public library on Ocean Road.

It took me a little while to get there because the bus was late. By the time I made it the crowd had been and gone.

It turned out someone had taken one of the smaller stones from the statue and used it to smash the glass case where Morgan H Stanhope's letter to the Island lay taupe and venerable, promising us something of himself.

Curious thing was, though the library staff had carefully picked out the shards of broken glass, they had left the rock where it lay. As though they acknowledged that this was something more than vandalism, an attempt not to destroy the display, but to enhance it. Complete it, I thought at the time – but that turned out not to be the case.

I don't snag on people as a rule. I never did – it wasn't as though I had a period and it quickly faded. I've always been able to walk down the street without heads turning. Even though I'm small enough to be remarkable there must be something so underwhelming about the rest of the package that it compensates.

Today though. People were glancing at me, then pretending they hadn't when I looked back at them. I wasn't sure how I felt about it. Perhaps you get used to it if it happens often enough.

BES'S CHORUS
There's the dwarf.
The little man.
What does he know?
What has he seen?
Where is he off to – wandering round?
He wanders about – that's what he does.
That and the pub.
He found our man.
Washed in from the sea.

Blown up at high tide.
Miraculously.
Enchantingly.
But he can't tell us what he has seen.
It's in his head – like a dream.

I was glad when Audrey called to me from across Central Drive.

We headed away from the library, down towards the channel side.

Audrey has her money to protect her. She tells me that it's going very well.

"People do not understand the power of compound interest," she says, animated and precise. "Say two thousand pounds, at six per cent, that's a hundred and twenty in the first year alone. Money that you didn't have to earn – so you leave that in at a competitive rate and that's where the magic of compound interest really starts – because you're calculating your next payment from the new higher sum – though you didn't put any more in – d'you see?"

She needs me to see. Confirmation is important as always – though they know I can't give it. That is for others to do.

"You know what kind of money I want?" she asked, staring round at me. "I want 'Fuck you' money."

Prim and upright, eyes swivelling round like some strange bird, like the swear police will be on her case now for sure.

Splurt of a giggle she makes: "That's what I call it when you have enough so you don't need anyone or anything – so you can tell them all where to go and live on your own terms."

Loneliness money then is what she wants. To buy a bond to protect her from the human condition – I don't believe even the most expert of financial planners could find such a product available on the market. Still, what do I know? I've not got all the answers. Though, if I keep on listening for long enough, it seems I might eventually hear all the questions.

Even if Audrey sticks to money she will always be reliant on what other people are doing to make it grow or shrink. We're interdependent us human beings – we need each other even if we don't want to at all.

Central Drive is long and wide like a Parisian boulevard, but with bungalows. The wind hurdles down it, there are weeds between receding paving slabs and the tarmac has mange, yet it has always struck me as upmarket somehow and kind of classy for around here. It seems as though it might lead somewhere, and indeed it does, down at the bottom end where it intersects with the Prom. It reaches the bridge to the mainland, and from there, obviously, you can go anywhere – eventually. So you could say that Central Drive was the main road from here to New York maybe, or Tokyo. I like to think of it in those terms. It makes me feel like I'm on my way somewhere when I walk it, connected to all which is outside.

Audrey gestures at a particular bungalow as we pass.

"That would be my ideal home if I could live anywhere in the world."

It's a tidy red brick building minus the pebbledash most of the others sport. It has been cared for: painted, re-pointed. The lawn is clipped short and the rectangular flowerbeds burst with annuals, like a council roundabout with petunias and marigolds primped by the parks department.

Small and prim, it suits Audrey perfectly – I wish her luck with it. I do not see it as an unattainable dream.

"I've walked past that house pretty much every day since I was a small girl and I've always known that one day I would live there. I thought it would be with my husband and the children – but they didn't come like they were supposed to. Still, the house is there – I suppose it could be just me and a spaniel.

"I looked around it last time it came up for sale, a few years back. It was out of my price range then, a couple in their fifties bought it – but I can wait. Perhaps I'll be an old lady before they die – maybe not a spaniel then, a bichon frise, something like that. Small. A peke. But I'll still want the house. It's a bungalow see, perfect for the retirement years.

"It was wonderful inside, frilly and pale. Somewhere that neat and ordered, it would be impossible to be too sad somewhere like that. They seem to be taking good care of it. Looking after it for me. Ready for me to be happy there."

When I got back to the van there was a queue outside it again.

Not so many this time, and I thought perhaps they hadn't heard he was gone. I shuffled towards my front door. Eyes on me. On the other hand, perhaps they were guessing he was back but that no one had let them know.

Marcus Riley was at the head of the queue.

"If he's not here – then maybe the dwarf will do?" he asked the others.

The wind popped against the walls of my caravan, rattling the tin sides so I felt I should be inside, listening. There's nothing so comforting as the sound of weather on the outside of a mobile home when you are tucked up inside with a book.

I felt hands on the side of my head as Marcus turned me to look into my eyes.

"Freak – can you help us?"

I gave him back blank. Less than nothing. The stare of a lower order animal, a reptile, a fish. You could sense the disappointment steaming off him, the thwarted hope of one who had yearned to be rewarded with the kind of eye contact one might get from a bonobo, an orangutan. He swivelled to face the crowd.

"He can do it," he told them. "He can help us."

They cheered. Not polite applause, but raw like football. Anybody might have done I thought, Love was best – he gave something back – but someone silent would do. It was my usual role, but formalised, and properly paid – they all dropped cash into my sou'wester by the door when they had finished their rambling, heartsick tales of woe.

Babs came and talked about her poor drowned sot of an intended. I've thought of a good word for her – viduous.

"I believe in everything," she said, "Except love… No. Only kidding."

You could tell she wasn't.

"I've been the one who breaks up relationships. I've left every boyfriend I ever had."

Sure, except the one who took the early bath.

Babs affected a syrupy 'come up and see me sometime' drawl.

"If you want monogamy – marry a swan."

She had a point. They are famously uxorious.

Even Audrey turned up. She hung about for ages babbling, as if to make up for all those years she'd kept her mouth shut. Eventually the next guy in the queue stuck his head round the door.

"I'll be out in a jiffy," she insisted primly.

A jiffy is an actual unit of time, equivalent to 100th of a second. Don't know whether the queuing man knew this but he waited ten thousand jiffies or so then bustled into the van to clear her out.

She went – shrill and bony.

For Glazier, I had to make a house call.

Glazier's terrace was at the far end of the council estate. He hasn't done desperately well for himself, it's true. He lives in one of those roads where every house has a rusting Cortina on the lawn, owned by a bloke with a mammoth beer gut poking out from under a string vest.

Glazier opened his door and ushered me in absently. He had a musty hall.

There was a racket in the front room.

"I've been playing the old demos from the band," he explained.

This was a punk combo in which he had been lead singer 25 years earlier. A couple of guys no longer on the island played guitar and bass, I played snare drum.

I hadn't heard the music since we made it. I was struck at once by how uniquely terrible it was – a naïve, ill-timed, sludge of inept musicianship and stolen ideas. We had thought ourselves chosen. Stars in waiting.

In truth we were musically derivative and arrived after the bandwagon had rumbled into the distance. It mattered least to me. I had not expected to 'make it'. How many dwarfish rock musicians can you name? Quite. I think there was one cropped up in a late incarnation of ABC, but I could be imagining that.

We played local pubs, never made it off the island. It seems absurd now that collectively, as a band, we believed we had a chance. But we did believe. It didn't occur to us that practical considerations mattered, like lack of talent.

"We could have made it," Glazier was repeating passionately over the reedy hiss of old cassette tape. "We could have made it if it hadn't been for the geography. What chance did we have here? We were ignored because of where we were. Look at all the crap that gets picked up just because it's from the city."

It was all a long time ago. He knows that surely?

I don't even have a copy of the tape: the only one we made, on an old four track recorder, at Glazier's dead mother's house. Wedged into the bathroom we were – for the superior acoustics.

"I want another chance," Glazier said. "We worked hard, we cared. Folk say if you want something enough you'll eventually get it."

I took the long way home along Ocean Road where I watched a sooty, needle beaked cormorant pluck a full grown eel from the sea. Within seconds a swarm of gulls appeared leaving the bigger bird battling its whiplash dinner and fighting to keep it at the same time. A simple fishing expedition had turned into war.

VII

Love's back. It's carried in the air like the saline reek of seaweed. I hear he's at the Lanes, a centre for the mentally impaired down on Millbank by the community hall.

It's low, brick built and cheery like bungalows have been breeding. The roofs have tiles red as a Noddy cartoon.

I arrive to find all is commotion. Love at the centre of the crowd, looking a bit unwashed and with a sort of beard he's embarked on, having left his Bic disposable at the van. His hair is sandy and he's ripped his kegs. Expect I'll end up sewing them.

He's pounding at the glass door of the porch with something big, black and heavy. Something three quarters his height and too cumbersome really for the job. It's a wheelie bin. He's hammering at the reinforced glass door of the centre with a wheelie bin.

And it's all he can do to bundle the thing a few inches off the ground and sway it in the right direction, where it goes 'bing,' with a less than satisfactory plastic hollowness.

I suspect, right now, he's pining for the old fashioned galvanised dustbin. That was an item designed for lobbing at things with theatrical gusto – they were easier to lift and made a more satisfying sound upon impact. The thunder, the joy of dented metal. It made more sense.

Still, Love's giving it his very best with this modern interloper. He's stripped to the waist with a shipboard tan and is strangely bereft of the cheeky little beer gut we all sport as a badge of honour on the island.

I wonder how many people here know, as I do, that the door to the centre is kept unlocked.

He's swinging away. Biff, baff, ping, of placsticised thunder. At length he's managed to puncture a melon-sized hole in the door, lozenges of glass drift on the step like pebbled windscreen. It's perhaps not the effect he'd been dreaming of but it's pretty dramatic anyway – plump with passion and useless violence – which is always the best kind, it seems to me.

He makes a show of sticking his mitt through the gap and opening the door from the inside like a TV cop.

"We're in," he yells to the crowd, who perhaps hadn't realised until then how complicit he considers them in this curiously aimed act of destruction.

"*We?*" we're thinking. "*We're* in? – And why would *we* want to be?"

A gaggle of carers is already mingling with the crowd, the green nurse's uniforms curiously formal among the jeans and donkey jackets.

After Love thumps through the door and disappears inside, more drift out and join them – they don't seem angry or in any mood to challenge this man who's bumped up against their order and discipline. Perhaps they are glad of a break from routine. Maybe they've heard of him. Or it could be that they are inured to atypical behaviour. Whatever. They accept it more or less as one would a fire alarm or a bomb scare, file out rather than man the barricades.

The manager of the unit turns out to be more of a handful – sees it as his job to police the peace. This isn't the first time there's been a disturbance: the residents themselves come and go – there have been problems with the local youth, family members sometimes.

Soon enough Love's backing out of the doorway again with this bloke shoving at his chest – a head smaller than he is with grey hair shaved short, red face, spit flying. Not enamoured then, with Love's intrusion.

The thing which surprises me isn't his reaction – it's John Love's.

Where he was hard as nails going at the window like the S.A.S. he's now come over all bashful and submissive.

Floppy as a sedated python – all give as this irascible little Scottish guy forces him back into the road with an economy pack of invective.

"What does he think?" "Who does he fucking think?" And stuff about regulations and so on.

But the second Love's espadrilles hit the pavement there's a reaction from the crowd – and it's not positive.

They're Love's mob – that's what our man with the name badge hadn't banked on – he thought he was dealing with one scruffy nutter who smelled like he'd been sleeping out in the sand dunes for a couple of days. He didn't expect other people at all, and certainly not the neighbours, folk he knows, all objecting trenchantly to him strong-arming this intruder.

There's shouts from the chorus. First a woman's voice.

"Leave him be, Stanley."

"Aye you'd fucking better."

"Right now."

A more resigned voice then – older man.

"Back off Stan. He's a good guy. You'll upset people."

A lot of racket at this. Stan was alarmed for sure. He had been 'Authority', now he was one man charging north while everyone else was heading south.

Plus – he'd been so sure. Bloke smashes the window, storms in, tries to interfere with vulnerable adults who are in your care – there's no room for grey. Yet it appeared he had been wrong – everyone was here to tell him – and this character, who had categorically been outside the rules – an invader, an outlaw – now he was the normal one.

So here's Stan – still clutching at Love's arm, though for support now more than out of anger – all the bad words he's said about him turning to ashes in his mouth.

And Love leans in towards him – intruding on his embarrassment, leans in and kisses him, on the forehead like a mother would. Then he begins speaking softly, close to Stan's ear, urgently so he has us longing to hear but we couldn't make any of it out – Stan giving a brief jerky shake of his head now and then like he was being asked questions but couldn't fathom the answers. He was sweating a bit, big bald head glistening, he seemed distressed.

Suddenly Love leant back away from him. Said one word. 'Sleep.' Moved his hand in and gently closed Stan's eyes as we do with the dead.

It was an incredible thing. Stan slumped forward still standing up there in the road but with his head lolling, his arms relaxed by his sides.

"What's happened to him?" cried someone.

"He's nodded off on the job – that's not like Stanley."

There was a deal of noise and baffled laughter but it did nothing to interrupt Stan's impromptu forty winks. He swayed slightly in an imaginary breeze. After a while a low, grumbling snore percolated from him like a car ticking over.

Love seemed to have done nothing – yet he had prevailed. And I saw that this was power.

It was something you rarely witnessed in this world which conspires to stop you getting what you desire – someone winning without trying when all the rest of us did was strive in the dirt for nothing.

It's what you do which matters. That's what I believe. Never mind what you intend or how much potential you may have.

Love went back into the centre and pretty soon a huddled confusion of stalled residents was trickling out of the door, blinking and unsure. Sheeplike they bundled together; veered in ill-chosen directions.

All shapes and sizes they were: a woman who looked old but probably wasn't, with an involuntary grimace like a Popeye mask, grey hair, cheery wrinkles; a plump childlike Down's syndrome man in unfashionable clothes, he had almond eyes, a button nose, he was sucking his thumb. There was a preternaturally tall skinny bald woman with a giraffe neck and an open mouth, a guy who cried like a toddler, held a soiled towel.

Love by the door: "The odd, the different, the unnatural. Why are they squirrelled away? Are we ashamed of ourselves – our extremes? Afraid of our own monsters? Why can't we accept and absorb that which is not the same? The chains are gone, the locks are broken. These people are among us. This place is now closed."

He slammed the door behind him. More of the glass plopped out in a pile.

There was a finality about the way he did it – we knew that door wouldn't be opening again.

The residents bunched together in the road, unsure how to proceed. The crying man spotted one of the staff he knew in the crowd, made towards her with arms outstretched but the girl shook her head at him, waved him away and slipped further back among familiar bodies.

Minimum wage, long hours, you can only buy so much love for the unlovable and it wasn't clear what was going on here, what would come next. It made sense to preserve your anonymity – to avoid standing out like Stan.

Love stalked off up the road, in the direction of my van. Pretty soon he was gone altogether.

There's an urge to hang around when things happen, in case there is excitement you might miss, but there is also the tendency of crowds to drift away like clouds.

There's probably some scientific theory of critical mass, which is the same for cattle. I dunno. I could make you one up if you like. You'd probably believe it.

Anyhoo, it turned out the individual flecks of crowd had homes to go to.

Some folk stayed to goggle at Stan until he woke up, which he did after a while. Crick necked and confused, he found he had drool like dog slobber on his tie and he seemed predisposed to cry about nothing in particular, like small children when they're all sleepy.

He moved off stiffly. Presumably he'd get round to telling his line manager what had gone on, if he remembered. It didn't seem to matter just then was the strange thing. It was as if the decision had already been taken and all the rest was tidying up – form filling for others to do.

There weren't many of us members of the general public left after a while. I was still there, for want of somewhere better to be. I regarded the little clump of residents still standing close together for support like trees in the wind. Ill made and clueless they loitered, an invisible question mark dangling above their collective heads.

But who will look after them? Who will care for them now?

Some wandered off in no particular direction. Others stayed in the cluster, waiting for a mini-bus which was never going to come.

They don't know what to do next and neither does anybody else.

Who is in charge? Who is responsible?

Not us, that's for sure.

Those residents with the foresight to worry about tea-time shed tears.

The wind shifted and sucked bad weather in after it so people stayed indoors the next day.

No doubt they were rattling on the phone, or texting, sending emails – all those modern jungle drums; so that, when I ventured down the pub in my cagoule that evening the talk was all of how Love had liberated the home.

"It was cruel the way they were kept in there," insisted Barbara as we sat in The Vengeance. "Locked up like beasts, couldn't go off up the street like decent people. It wasn't right."

"And who decides anyway?" Audrey asked. "Who says who's mad and who's not – whether they should get locked away? In another age Bes here would have been locked up wouldn't he – looking the way he does, not talking." She reached down and ruffled my hair. "Wouldn't you pet? And you're no harm are you?"

"It was a shame for them," Barbara, cut back in. "It was right what he did."

Over by the bar, support from an unexpected source.

Linus Johnson, back off the rigs or wherever he'd been. Said he'd heard the set up down there had been strange anyway. That things had gone on. Stuff the council would have taken action on if only there'd been proof.

It was vague but him saying it made it sound worth more. He was somebody was Linus. For a start he wasn't always here. Then when he was here, he was impressive – tall and fat with a resounding voice and a full beard. And we do all like to be impressed now don't we?

The Lounge Bar jury was minded to agree that all had been for the best, though no-one asked where the residents had found shelter from the cruel rain that day, or where they were spending the night. They were certainly not in here, nursing pints of mild by the fire. Red, the window cleaner, a lank raisin faced body who seemed with every glance to be casing the joint, came in, shaking the weather off his clothes.

"Unseasonable this – but welcome for farmers. Good for growing crops. It's the rain which feeds us you could say."

Everyone nodded sagaciously like he'd said something wise, though it wasn't as if we'd been burning up in a heat wave and had needed Love to come along and do us a rain dance.

Red wanted to know what had become of Stanley, the residential care manager.

"Where's he at now, the whey-faced Scottish fuck? Not that I much care like but it was weird though hey? Him dropping off for a nap like that just when Love whispered something in his ear. It was magical, it was special… it was miraculous."

Someone had pulled the juke box plug out of the wall, the pool table lay sleeping, normal business was suspended. Except for drinking thankfully, people bought me pints. My money, now I had some, turned out to be of little use.

Now I was able to get as drunk as I liked I found myself trying hard not to. In the past I had spent evenings desperate to get inebriated on meagre funds.

Since Love's arrival I had been neglecting my work. Which was to find things. My trade was to discover profit creviced in unlikely vessels. I worked the beach often, where fresh magic was summoned daily by the surf, but other places too – heath and moorland, sand dunes, long grasses – I found things then I sold them for money or traded them for what I could use. It worked well for me.

That; my disability allowance; the kindness of acquaintances.

I knew what would raise small sums of money and I had the contacts I needed, those who understand the language of commerce and required no other.

I scoured old industrial land on the derelict fringes of the island with my metal detector and eyes keen as a rook's. I grubbed up copper pipe, lead flashing to tempt scrap dealers. I rescued scores of supermarket trolleys from their temporary nests in verdant tree fringed becks. Trundled them back to the rear gate of the Easyways where I was paid a pound a piece.

I combed the high tide line for timber which I chopped and sold in bags around the village on the island's periphery where the middle classes had reverted to wood burning stoves.

It wasn't much of a living, but there were those I knew on the island who had it far worse – whose income depended solely on what they could forage from what the world discarded.

I did it for the sport, and to feed my prodigious demand for mail order paperbacks; these others hunted for their existence.

Recently I had diversified, increased my business portfolio.

I'd sold my precious hoard of gathered treasures: coins, pottery, my specks of antiquity – got good prices for them on the internet, ghosting in unregarded to use the derelict machine in the corner of the library. I made a killing this way too by selling on the junk I sifted from the island's car boot sales. There always seemed to be a demand for it on eBay, whatever it was. It proved to be a real winner.

So much so that I invested in a cheap laptop of my own and found my business buoyed to a new level.

I made my living in the gap between what one person judged a thing was worth and what another was prepared to pay. I think that's maybe the basis of all trade, all commerce. You could say I existed on other people's misjudgements. You could say that.

I had been left the money to buy my van in a small life insurance policy my mother bequeathed me. She always told me I wouldn't go short. She enjoyed a pun did mother.

I lived mortgage free, had simple tastes and a slender need for sustenance. It meant I could avoid the 'normal' daily grind of work, presumably at Remploy. So it suited me, but added to my reputation as a fringe figure in our insular community.

VIII

Salvador Dali used to keep a diary detailing his stools. He did a watercolour sketch of each one plus notes dealing with consistency, texture etc.

Peculiar bloke – and a curiously limited palette he must have used. He'd have been forever off down to W.H.Smiths for new paint sets: 'Bloody hell – the brown's run out again.'

I was given a chart by the hospital which must look similar to a page from Dali's poo diary. It was after I had recovered from my pancreatitis. It becomes important what your turds look like. You can match them to the pictures if you choose to – like a scatological take on one of those I-Spy books where kids tick off types of tree.

John Love was sitting in my breakfast nook poring over this chart when I arrived back at the van.

He looked up absently – without commenting on the peculiarity of his literature.

"Let myself in," he said. "Hope you don't mind."

I gave him a look intended as inquiring.

"Credit card," he explained. "Locks like yours slip easy. It's the only use I've ever found for them. The cards … the locks."

I rifled through my mental pile of questions – decided it was best to look forward. Showed him the pad: "What's next?"

"That's the question." He nodded. "Very perceptive. Let me know, won't you, if you come up with anything."

And he went back to looking at his pictures of shite.

Lifted his head again when I stuck a mug of tea in front of him. Black, half full.

"Yes," he said. "Just the job."

He carefully put the chart down and picked up the mug. Looked like he was going to take a gobful. Didn't do.

"Listen. I think I'm closer here than I've ever been to what I intend. There's nothing more important to me – you know."

And, somehow, I did know.

"There's no map though. And I can't be sure where I am. Not even with the help of the third realm, whatever that is. The mind, the world and it… Out there where the aliens are."

I mean, I always look pretty puzzled – it's my default expression, but I must have worn a grimace of exceptional bafflement because he offered an explanation.

"We're denied the chance to see it. Our modern minds can't cope. We're conditioned to be rational machines. Other cultures, past civilisations, accepted our world is close to another one – that the two routinely come into contact."

It was a crap explanation – but he had made the effort. I felt honoured.

"Yes, okay – don't look at me like that. I know what's going on in your head. You think you do a pretty good job of hiding it. You aren't so much smarter than everyone else. Even people here aren't as easy to fool as you might believe. It takes special mastery. You have it clearly – but what are you using it for? Sitting here in this tin can. What are you making of your craft?"

It wasn't a question I had ever addressed. I've learned to settle for what I have and to rub up as near to happiness as I can get.

It's never very near. But that's okay too in the end. People put up with worse – every day, around the world. Whatever island they happen to be on.

John Love's still talking: "It wasn't always like this for me. You need to know that."

No real chance of common ground mate, I thought, but go on – if you want to flatter me by comparing us I'm willing to suspend my disbelief.

"This could happen for any of us – well, nearly – I could make you look good."

I could see from his earnest expression he meant it. But there was no way I could ever 'look good.' Still, perhaps he didn't mean 'look' literally – like some daytime TV makeover show. And if he did manage to alter people's perception of me then may be I might feel better? He had me I knew.

"I've been hunting a lot of years, without knowing what the fox looked like. Now I've found the raw stink of it here on this island.

But now I have it I'm less sure what I want it for. Is that strange?"

It was a rhetorical question.

"I don't doubt what I can do. But what is it for? We have an opportunity here to create something you don't see often in this world. That is the truth. It's an amazing thing. Now we can be whatever we want. We can build it from nothing. It will last for ever. So what shall we be?"

Then suddenly he bounced off at a tangent – he wasn't talking about concepts now but mechanics.

"I'm thinking already that maybe I made a mistake with the residents from the centre." Head shaking and all solemn. "I don't believe they are going to be of much use to me as a workforce. They're physically strong but I can't reach them. This afternoon I went out looking, found a few under a road bridge by the shops. They're brave to be camping out in this weather if you ask me."

He's right. It's rainy season on the island. That lasts for eight months of the year, during which time nature chucks needles of sleet, hurls cruel winds and occasional hail. Then, for the other four months – it's winter.

"I had them perform a few tasks for me – for chocolate bars. Just simple stuff, fetch the seaweed, get a hat full of water and chuck it over her that's crying – you know." He shook his head. "Beyond useless. Wanted everything doing for them. What kind of an attitude is that?

"I expected they'd be grateful. Is that naïve? Of course you need to know what's going on to feel gratitude. I'm forever over-estimating people. Usually that stands me in good stead. I need workers from somewhere. People I can use: who will invest in me because they are not otherwise encumbered."

He looked to where I sat across the table, nursing my mug of Earl Grey.

"They will do as I ask if it's easier than not doing it," he said quietly. "I can make them love me. It's a powerful thing and I have the capacity to do it."

I nodded. I knew he could do it – he had already worked his deep felt sympathetic magic on many people across the island. Why didn't he just use them for whatever this work was? I felt sure he would find plenty of volunteers.

I wrote him a note.

"You have people."

"Oh yes." He smiled eagerly. "And many of them have skills I need too. But for what I want I'll need far more – an infantry – foot soldiers."

I told him I would give it some thought.

"Meanwhile – there's something more pressing."

He paused mid-sentence and disappeared off to the loo. Came back wiping his hands on his jeans.

"Um – pressing yeah? It's not something which has happened, it's something I know from experience is about to occur. I've stirred up the silt see? Even a cul de sac like this is still part of the world. With its order and pattern, its authority. You smash statues, you break down doors, sooner or later those who control things want to know what you're up to. As far as the normal world is concerned I'm a virus attacking it. There are protocols for dealing with people like me, as there are for any other type of disruption. As far as authority is concerned I'm no different from a drunk in the street. They'll send a police – or someone in a suit, works for the council. That's the way these things work – I'm only surprised it's not happened already. But it will happen – unless there's something we can do."

Most places, I saw, there would not be. Here, on the other hand, there just might be. Here we were semi-detached. We had to obey the same rules as everyone else, but there was a degree of latitude as to how they were enforced.

It wasn't that anyone had written us a dispensation. Simply that no one much cared what we got up to. And that's licence is that. An opportunity to do just as you please.

Confidently I wrote him another note.

"I'll sort it."

He was delighted. He knew I wouldn't let him down – I was a stand up guy, a marine, and all the rest of it. Despite myself I was flattered again – bloated on the rich meat of approval which I so seldom tasted.

I wasn't promising him much. It boiled down to the fact that figures of authority here are more a part of the island than they are of the outside world. They were unlikely to take against the prevailing mood and go stealing across the bridge to side against us. A few plump members of the Old Bill and parish councillors with vested interests to protect. There wasn't anyone here who wanted outside interference in island life.

It was none of their business.

It was any of ours.

The police presence here amounted to one small satellite station on the Prom which was staffed by a couple of probationers and one fat grey haired sergeant called Bob Stafford who spent his evenings playing snooker in the back room of the golf club.

So I knew where to find him. I also knew, crucially, that for the last three years he had enjoyed occasional sex with Barbara – sometimes on the very snooker table I have mentioned. Naturally Linda and the kids were unaware of this state of affairs. Most of the rest of us tried to pretend it wasn't happening. The thought of Bob's ample arse piling up and down on the baize, pallid and yellow under the table light – it wasn't something you were wise to dwell on for the good of your mental health.

Still if any man ought to be grateful it was Bob Stafford. And now Barbara had a use for his gratitude.

It didn't take long to sort out.

Once we had Barbara on board that is. The tricky part turned out to be contacting her. It seemed the telephone was an alien instrument for both Love and myself.

Love appeared briefly baffled when I told him I didn't have one in the van – then got a bit grumpy because he'd made himself look foolish.

There was a payphone down the hill and we ventured out without our pullies on to find it. It sat scruffy and loitering on the corner. There was gaggle of disreputable looking youths smoking fags outside it.

Love shoved past them to a chorus of fuck-yous and clattered through the heavy scarlet door with me in tow. We made an odd couple crammed in there. The tiny windows were misted like someone had been at them with a Brillo pad. There was a general ambience of stale wee.

It became clear Love hadn't the first clue how to use the phone. I'd like to say he held the receiver upside down. It wasn't quite that bad, but pretty close.

He got flustered stuffing in the coins I gave him and doled out an earful to the directory inquiries woman when she couldn't find a number for just "Barbara."

How had he manufactured such unworldliness? I had not managed it in my divorced and silent land.

I had to write down the address for him – which I was loath to do with the gobby bunch of teens still hanging about outside swigging White Lightning and flegging on the glass.

For all his undoubted face to face charisma John Love turned out to give terrible phone.

He'd scribbled the number down on the back of his hand but dialled it wrong and emerged as one of those who believe that, when you get a wrong number it must be the other person's fault.

"Hello? Barbara?"

Man's puzzled voice on the other end: "No… there is no Barbara at this number I'm afraid."

"Oh?" says Love, sounding like he knows the bloke's up to something and doesn't believe him for a moment. "Where is she then?"

"Pardon? I think you have a wrong number."

"But I dialled the right number."

Love's clearly itching to give the guy a bollocking for getting something or other wrong. But it's technology that's done the damage. It rules a tangled strand of fate which snags the ankles of the ill-prepared.

When we finally got it right, Barbara picked up quickly and I could hear her yelling down the line in gauche delight that it was him.

She was tripping over herself eager to get down the golf club right now and sort out that bastard Stafford. She'd threaten to tell his missus, put an ad in the freesheet with a picture of Bob's arse, and all the rest of it.

Love gave her to understand less was more and asked her to clear the way for him to put in a personal appearance – say around half nine.

She said she could do this small thing.

Near as I could make out she must have done it too as, when we tooled up at the nineteenth some hours later we were nodded through by Charlie Butler, the irascible crimson-nosed door turd who usually told me to 'sod off – no shortarses allowed.'

I stuck a quid in his contributions box. Just to burn him up. I am not above a little petty revenge. It is, I believe, a perk of whatever my job is now.

Snooker room was men only. So Barbara even being there was breaching a big rule. She'd had to walk over the carpet to get there too. Carpet was men only. The whole situation was a huge breach of regulations, etiquette, whatever. There was kind of a carnival, world turned upside down, atmosphere in there when we arrived.

Barbara was sitting across a round pub table from Bob Stafford; two or three of his mates from the golf were around the snooker table. They were chortling away all red faced and over the top – like they were expecting an entertainment, a turn.

They were all teasing Barbara about her job as a freelance aromatherapy masseuse. She was very good at it by all accounts. Charged sixty quid a session and was much in demand for sports injuries and the like. A lot of the golfers took their bad backs to her.

"You still on the game Babs?" asked one of Stafford's cronies.

"I'm college trained in aromatherapy," Barbara bit. She didn't like being called a hooker, and took pride in her work.

"Babs would never take money for it," Stafford interjected sternly, rubbing her knee. "She's more of a gifted amateur, aren't you love?"

There was a guffaw and Barbara managed to join in too, well practiced at laughing with the boys.

There were a few other folk drifting in and out of the snooker room – checking the availability of the table, making their way through to the locker room – but we had it fairly cosy.

"The dwarf's here now," bellowed Stafford heaving with laughter. "Throw in a couple of fucking stilt walkers and you'd think the circus had come to town."

Aye – and we've already got a clown, I thought.

My patter's wasted really – a great loss to the world I always think.

Babs was trying to initiate them into the wonderful world of Love.

"He gives advice and that."

"What on?" Stafford wanted to know.

"Personal issues."

"I've got this enormous dong and it ain't half giving me a bad back – p'raps he could tell me what to do about that?"

"Matters of the heart and such."

"Every time I get a what-not I go faint 'cos of all the blood that's needed."

"That's disrespectful. The man does miracles. He is a miracle." Babs was struggling to remain coquettish.

Stafford's chums were chortling but John Love wasn't laughing. He was funeral faced and dour – suited him, lent an air of gravitas.

Stafford saw him and shut up more or less, just chuckled a little under his breath to show he wasn't intimidated or anything.

"Barbara says you want to see me?"

Love said nothing, leant against the snooker table which looked as though it had been abandoned half way through a game. Balls scattered like the map of some distant solar system.

"That's good," Stafford filled in. "Because I'd have been coming to have a word in your ear soon enough. You don't serve a community this close without knowing what's going on at the grassroots."

Barbara was nodding away like one of those dashboard dogs.

"You're a fox Bob – people underestimate you."

"At their peril Bar – it's a mistake they only make the once."

The steward came over with a pint of Guinness for him which he received as his due.

"Truth is," he said after he'd taken the top third off it, "this isn't a place where we like a lot of excitement. Which is good. Because we don't get it. But then the last few days we've been getting what the Chinese might call interesting times. You heard that old proverb?"

No discernable response from Love.

"Well anyhoo. We're living in them all of a sudden. Cars that smash into statues and then disappear without trace, surprising movements involving large numbers of people, that business of residents checking out of the Centre, which we haven't had any complaint over as such, but seems the sort of thing I might just put someone on to have a look into anyway – just as a matter of good community policing you know?"

Love still didn't say anything, brushed a few strands of hair out of his eye.

Stafford all of a sudden lost patience.

"You wanted to see me," he snapped. "Take up some of my time when I'm supposed to be winding down after work. What is it you want? Let's hear it – or I've got a game to get on with."

Love leant forward without moving his backside from where it was perched on the table.

"I have something to show you. You need to see it – it will make things clearer for you."

"Well okay then," allowed Stafford – because it had seemed like an okay then kind of offer.

Love twisted round and picked up a couple of balls from the table.

A red and the black.

"Hey," protested one of Stafford's pals – Eric North it was. Lardy. Balding. "There's a couple of lads playing a game here – game in progress like."

It was as though Love hadn't heard him.

Stafford seemed nervous, the other blokes did too. This was their place. They owed Love nothing. And he hadn't even done anything much. Just come in and perched his arse on a table. So why would they worry about him staring at them and picking up a couple of snooker balls?

It was a funny thing, but not without precedent. Even just the people I've seen, some of them seem more potent than others – they appear to be playing a stronger hand. There's something about them you can't touch. But you feel it and it's there. It makes people wary. They behave as though they have something to fear.

It was a way of being special I knew I would never experience – though I also knew John Love would never know the comfort of being ignored.

Love took the two snooker balls, one in each hand like eggs. Held them in front of his face, at arm's length.

He looked over towards the far left of the room, where Eric North sat waiting to take his shot with an arse cheek hanging over either side of his stool and a tee shirt which read: *Every time I shagged your wife she gave me a biscuit.*

"See this red?" said Love. "That's you."

Then he moved his attention over to Stafford on the right hand side. Lounging there in a bogus Chesterfield with Barbara's knee nestled like a walnut in his clenched hand.

"I supposed the other one's me – is that it? Stafford guffawed. "I'm the nigger ball, that's it?"

Love said nothing. He held up the black ball and stared directly back at Stafford, so he couldn't escape the look.

Then his attention drifted away from either man – he held the balls in front of him – but he wasn't even focused on them truly, just on nothing – out where the fag smoke crawled up the spare space in the empty centre of the room.

Stafford began to say something – I can't remember what. It was in a lazy, patronising voice, as though he couldn't be bothered with any of this and was about to go for a piss.

Then Love slammed the two snooker balls together.

I can't believe that he intended it to be as severe as it was. Sometimes things in this real world have a tendency to outdo what we plan on the blurry wide-screen telly of our mind.

John Love lifted those two men out of their seats and slammed their heads together like crash test dummies. Punch and Judy. Hammered into each other.

They stumbled forward, each as though they had got up and tripped, with too much daft forward momentum to avoid an excuse-me.

They scrambled across the beer sticky maroon of the carpet and locked horns. Smashed together, 'clack' – the snap of the balls and the clap of the skulls.

Then they sat down on their backsides.

Eric slumped back with his knees in the air like sunbathing, his head lolled and he was clearly somewhere far off.

Stafford sat up rubbing his dazed head with a distracted look on his face: a toddler who's just woken up. It was clear from this singular experiment which of the two had the harder head.

It was theatre certainly – and, from the bar steward to the snooker room loungers, it had a marked and devastating effect.

"How the hell did you do that?" yelled one, high pitched and unconcerned with sounding odd. "That wasn't a normal thing."

"Who decides," John Love asked, level and in good spirits, "what passes for normal? We are what we believe – that's the truth. When Mr Stafford is feeling more himself tell him he can come and see me – after noon tomorrow where I'm lodging. We have a few things to talk about, the pair of us. I expect he might want to listen to me, it's only natural."

The steward found his voice.

"Can I get you a drink of something?" Hesitant as if it were an odd question for a barman and needed glossing. "It's cold out…"

"Something for my friends," Love shrugged. "It's not an indulgence I allow."

And he left us there, Barbara and I, with a free pint each and plenty of questions for her to field.

IX

Glazier has something on his mind.

"They should tell you in school how miserable being an adult is most of the time."

Love's listening but not saying anything. We're lying on the grass by the chalet park wall, making the most of a weak sun.

"It would prepare you better than all that helium they puff into kids about how it's all out there for you – how you can be anything you want to become. Seems to me that an awful lump of human misery is caused by you striving for something in hope, and then being disappointed when you get it. You might always dream of owning a fruit shop – then when you do you realise you're just selling apples to people." He reached back to scratch his arse, reflectively.

"At least when you're young you've got a future. Sat in your bedsit – dreaming how great it will all be later on. But when you get there it's just another empty room."

"You believe," John Love asked, "that we would be better to abandon hope? That we would find peace in being less deceived?"

"I believe in what I have experienced."

"Your vision of this world is one which builds up expectations it cannot deliver – that takes liberties with our credulity."

"I believe we are all disappointed."

Love's nodding at this. "I can help with that," he says eagerly. "If I find the support I need then we can work together to create something which will not disappoint."

Sometimes outsiders refer to this place as Tip Island – naming it after its most grand and dramatic geographical feature.

It is also the newest one, post-dating our cliffs and sand dunes by a few hundreds of thousands of years. It has the added distinction of being man-made in an area where not much is, or ever has been.

This feature is the main reason people come to see us from over the bridge. They never stop long. They come with cars stacked high, and trailers and flat beds. They come with lorries and wagons and transit vans. They visit the vast council rubbish dump at the south end of the island.

They don't tarry long. Stepping gingerly across the soiled lechate seeping ground they open their boots, drop their tailgates, unhitch their wagons. Then, like stevedores they unload into space. Unburden themselves of the things they do not want and cannot use.

It is a kind of physical confession. Afterwards they feel relieved and grateful, perhaps a little guilty.

They creep their empty vehicles out of the compound then head down the road and off our island as quickly as they can make it.

Tip Island. We should wear the name with pride I think. It is the main reason the world wants us. And it is always nice to be wanted.

I knew the time would come eventually when John Love would wish to visit the rubbish dump.

It is not on every tourist's to-do list, true. But John Love was not your average tourist. I knew he would be drawn there as surely as Stanhope had been to the birds on our cliffs all those years before.

It was not the landfill Love would want to see; he was no aficionado of refuse heaps. He would want to get to know the people. Not the visitors who came and went, blind to the others among them. He would want to meet the ones who lived with the piles of spoil and worked them for treasure.

John Love would want to meet the Tip Rats.

It would be his idea of course, rather than mine. I had no brief either way. I'd rather not go up there where it stank and always seemed to be raining. I'd also rather not have anything to do with the Rats who fascinated me only a little yet scared and appalled me a lot.

I could probably have got away without going. All I needed to do was keep my comfortable and accustomed silence. But, dangerously, I found I wanted to please John Love.

That was what he had I think, that more than anything. If you could put it in a bottle you could make yourself rich.

So I got up from where I lay on the damp grass and shambled off up the slope to my van. I hunted through the locker under my bed where I kept my treasures until I found a small tarnished golden brooch in the shape of a tiger leaping. It had a single green glass eye and orange glass spots, some of which were missing.

I took it outside and dropped it on Glazier's chest.

He started from his half-sleep, staring down at himself, somewhat put out. It took a little while before he worked out what it was I had thrown at him.

Then he didn't know why I had done so.

Love was standing up to look out over the sea. There was a view past the low wall where you could see down onto the beach, though I'd never seen it personally. All I saw was wall – which suited me because I could pretend, when I needed to, that I lived somewhere else.

Love was fretting over one of his favourite hobbyhorses again. The unsuitability of the centre residents for whatever purpose he had in mind.

"They found one dead the other day. On the rocks under the bridge to the mainland. Probably gone there to keep out of the rain – but still caught hypothermia anyway. I can't use people with that little horse sense. It isn't going to play. I need people who are able; capable; useful; but will support me unswervingly without all these complicating matters of the will. It's for the greater good. I have such things I will show you. But every army needs foot soldiers."

Glazier squinted down at the brooch again, then lay his head back as if he were planning on another nap. I caught him a crack in the temple with my Doc Marten.

"Fuck."

"Sorry?" Love inquired, absently, like a lecturer put off his stride by an unexpected question.

Glazier plucked the brooch from his chest and tossed it languidly through the air at him. Love caught it, examined it.

"Seems to be of no great worth, glass, gold plate, base metal. There's no value here I don't think. Except," he said, looking at me knowingly, "sentimental."

As so often, he was half right. He had assumed I inherited it from my mother. In fact it just looked like the one she used to have.

She left me nothing but ideas. It was her idea, for example, that she educate me at home. She realised a sprat like me would be bait for sharks if I was released into the pool too soon. I don't recall who told anyone I was deaf, or an idiot – it certainly wasn't me, but, by the time I ventured out to the pub, in adolescence, the island knew what it thought of me.

"Where it came from," explained Glazier, "is important."

Love turned it over. "Malaysia," he said.

"Where on the Island," Glazier cut in patiently. "That's salvage that is. That's Tip Rat treasure."

It wasn't the look of the thing – there's no way you can tell, like some oddly fangled antiques dealer, that something has been grubbed out of landfill. Things are just things. Even the smell of must and decay leaves them in the end.

Glazier knew because he had been with me when I bought it. He had bargained for me in the pub when the Rat came in one evening those few years ago with his tray full of sifted gewgaws.

It had come to him in the end. I knew it would when he saw the cat. On the night I bought the brooch he had been curious as to why I might want something so ugly and useless.

But keepsakes, even second hand, can be precious.

Now, watching it glint in Love's hand, he offered: "Maybe there are some people who could help you. If it's labour you need. So long as it's nothing skilled."

"We have skills," shrugged Love. "We can find as many tradesmen as we need – but what I have in mind requires brute strength and force of numbers if we are to get things done quickly, which I think we must."

"There's some families," Glazier allowed, grudgingly, "a community you might say, who live off the rubbish dump. They scavenge what they can use or sell and somehow manage to live off that. It's hard and dirty work. The sort of thing that makes a body cry out for a change."

"They are strong?"

"They get sick, they don't live long. It's no life for their kids. But they have their own kind of strength I suppose. Like weeds you see growing in cracks in the masonry high up in buildings and you'd wonder how they survive."

"Sounds promising," allowed Love. "Can we catch a lift?"

"Bus goes somewhere near," said Glazier. "Then there's a walk, if you think it's worth it. They aren't much these people. Not much at all."

It was a grim sort of sight I suppose, all those acres of everything we've disowned, tumbled in piles: the low foothills of our dissolution.

The tip had gaudiness about it, an artificial quality – perhaps because these man-made things had been pressed into feigning a natural landscape, though they were not quite up to the task.

These hills and vales of refuse were too obviously fake – like a tinsel Christmas tree.

White was the predominant colour here: the wet glitter of plastic bags, the rusty sheen of soiled electrical goods. There was plenty of black too because of all the bin bags, then a speckle of other, unnaturally bright hues: the reds, the blues, the rusty browns.

The place was busy, it is never still. There were cars and vans ferrying fresh loads of junk. Arriving, unloading, leaving. There was always someone who wanted to get rid of something.

There was movement among the mounds of refuse too as the gulls fussed across them – hovering, roosting or squabbling over scraps.

I scanned the piles of rubbish, hunting for a different kind of tip dweller. Then, I saw one – fidgeting uniquely, mid-way up one of the mounds. A Rat. Soon I spotted another and when my eyes became accustomed there were more, dotted across the unlikely landscape. I counted about twenty, grazing like goats.

When someone had dropped off a load of refuse, the moment the boot banged shut, two or three of these figures would be down on the spot like crows on fresh road kill, swiftly assessing the strength of the haul.

If there was treasure there then perhaps they would soundlessly summon others to give the fresh waste a more thorough sifting.

They moved slowly for the most part, wore dark clothes and stooped to their task. They made no eye contact and there was nothing to pick them out from the mass of junk. It was easy to edit them out all together, as though they did not exist.

They carried sacks which they filled with this or that – they were engrossed in a task which was outside the ken of the off-loaders, and so they were disregarded by them.

How long did we stand there – Love, Glazier and I? It was one of those occasions when time defines its own pace and an hour somehow crowbars itself into ten minutes.

I looked up to see Love laughing with an incredulous shake of his head.

"They're amazing. Look at them here, clinging on. Like strange odds and sods of life in an ocean trench. Who do you suppose we speak to with people like these?" he wondered. "Do they have leaders? Have they a head?"

"They have a home," Glazier offered. "Well, shacks. You know. Down in the shelter of the next hollow past the tip. It's a hell of a place."

"We'll go there then," Love insisted, brightly.

Glazier looked glum. "They'll have dogs. There's bound to be dogs."

"Are you not an animal lover?"

We made our way across the valley bottom.

Everything stank. The ground, the scenery. The air itself was ripe with the reek of decay. And the place was alive with gulls and flies plus the smoke and surprise of spontaneous fires.

Gulls, flies, people – all scavengers, all subsisting on what the world says won't sustain it.

"Hey there!" cried Love to a Rat, who ignored him and continued, poking holes in a pile of rubbish with a stick.

Love sounded quite American – needlessly upbeat and cheery, like he was making a point about the squalor being someone else's fault – someone who hadn't pulled themselves up by their bootstraps, who had failed in life by not being positive enough.

I couldn't help thinking it might have been the wrong tack – but what do I know, and it was only two words after all.

Love tried small-talk instead.

"S'windy."

Rat said nowt. Looked a bit sullen. Well, a bit *more* sullen. He found a tin can and added it to his sack full of tin cans.

"I see you collect tin cans."

Rat ignored this impressive conversational gambit and continued his never-ending search.

It looked like this whole thing might be a big round shiny waste of time.

But then Love did a thing he so often did in the period I knew him.

He did the right thing.

He scrambled up the mound of desiccated crap to where the Rat was scavenging. He got down on his hands and knees. He started looking for tin cans.

The guy was sharp. I don't care what anyone says.

All of a sudden Glazier and I found ourselves feeling mean and ungracious because we weren't crawling round on all fours shifting through junk.

You could tell the Rat was impressed too. He said nothing but greased out the occasional glance sideways through his matted dreadlocks.

Pretty soon Love found a can. He said nothing – just flicked it into the sack and went on looking for another.

Soon enough he found one – and added it to the hoard.

He was finding more than the Rat. Had it been a can finding competition then Love would have won. To be fair, he was entered in the tin can sprint while his opponent was a marathon man.

I pretended to look for cans while still standing up. Kicked a few bits of rubbish around. Glazier didn't even pretend to look for cans. Looking for cans was beneath his dignity.

Love found a couple more, Rat found three, thus more or less catching up. I accidentally found one, got all excited despite myself, added it to the bag. Love said well done, I felt gratified, Glazier gave a little snort.

We covered a fair bit of smelly ground I suppose between us. Even in the wind the place got up your nostrils. The exercise made you hungry too in a stomach churning, couldn't possibly, kind of way. Bending over gave you a bad back.

Eventually though the sack was full.

"Now," said Love, all patience. "Where do we take this then?"

Rat sighed.

"Just leave us alone."

"We've helped you out here," Love reasoned. "P'haps you could do something for us?"

"Leave us alone."

"I don't mean you any harm."

"I don't mean me – I mean us." Rat looked at Love directly. "I know who you are. We're on the same small island you know. We talk the same. We know about you – and we don't see how you could come to any good."

Glazier looked horrified. I think he genuinely was too. It was perhaps the first time the notion that John Love could bring anything but good had crossed his path.

"This man has done more of worth than you will ever know," he spat. "This man has plans – he means to show us another way to do things – to rescue us."

Rat shrugged.

"Well we could do with rescuing that's for sure. But there's life rafts, and there's sharks."

Glazier was mad suddenly.

"And what the fuck do you know then? What makes you so smart sitting on a heap of shit all your life?"

And I swear he'd have over and thumped him if Love hadn't broken in.

"We don't want to cause any pain here. Quite the opposite. I need to talk to you all to see if there's anything I can do. To make your lives easier. Things must be hard."

He was nodding 'must be hard' and the Rat was nodding back.

"I know, I know," murmured Love. "I know how hard."

"There's harder lives," muttered Glazier, sulking.

"Yeah?" The Rat wanted to know. "Like what?"

Glazier had one ready: "You could have been a pure scavenger in 17th century London. Their job was to pick up dog shit off the streets and attempt to sell it to the tanning industry as an astringent."

The Rat thought it over as he hoisted his bag over his shoulder.

"That does seem to be the bottom end of the market," he allowed.

Then to Love. "You can come along to the camp if you like – though what you want us for I don't know – we have it hard enough already from fate it seems to me. Last thing we need is another force of nature."

We edged across the tundra of flapping bin bags and newsprint tumbleweed. Our trainers slapped wetly in the sour puddles.

A few hundred yards through vales in the undulating landscape we found the earth bund which separated this world from the sea and the Rat took us out through a gap, uselessly pushing the wind bothered hair from his eyes.

It was a shock to see the sea, our sea, from this little elsewhere.

I've been in this tight place all my life and yet I've still not been everywhere. I'd never come out of the back of the tip and seen the ocean like that. And what a sight it was this blustery day.

The brutal, breath-grabbing wind had whipped up the sea into suds on the stony shore like the froth on a cappuccino, gathered globes of lather into the air and hurled them. I grabbed at the froth and it disappeared like a cloud.

The wind, how it steals your balance and punishes distraction. How its cold becomes part of you so's you can't remember what it was to be warm.

The camp, it turned out, was in a hollow on the springy grass foreshore. It was protected from the elements by the dip, and huddled behind the earth wall which had been bulldozed up around the tip to keep that world separate from ours. It was like an encampment without a city wall. A medieval notion, which suited the place.

Glazier got his dogs. As whipped up as the ocean; raging like poltergeists; they came down on us in a pack as we crossed the grass.

"Shite," mouthed Glazier, resigned to his fear. "Fuckers."

I saw him scanning the ground for a stick or a rock, a charm to protect himself, but there was no time and the slavering things were bellowing at us in rage. All sorts of dogs – mixed together. They weren't a particular breed yet seemed related somehow. Big ones, medium sized ones, all rangy and lean. They were a muddy sand colour mostly, bits of ridgeback in there, lumps of mastiff, a touch of husky in some of the more wolflike ones perhaps.

"Go on with you – fuck off now," the tip rat commanded waving them away, and though they didn't move off entirely, they did step back a little, grumpy and ill at ease.

One or two came back at us with even more of a row like there was something in them which couldn't be told what to do and fuck the consequences.

I glanced at Glazier – he was shuddering – angry about being frightened. He stayed like that all the way into camp, with the dogs, still hollering and slavering, backing up in front of us.

It was a strange enough damn place when we got there. And somewhere else on the island I'd never been. Can't remember the last time that happened twice in the one day.

It appeared to have been there centuries – rooted deep as the land itself.

It was a shantytown of sorts, thrown together out of whatever odds and sods had come up on the grubby lottery of the tip.

There were a few geriatric caravans making up the core of the architecture. They looked like they'd been in a fight – like someone had taken to them with a sledge hammer then crapped on what was left.

Around them things got quickly worse. The tents and lean-tos were made of chunks of plastic sheet, driftwood, lengths of aluminium and rusty iron rods. There was canvas, nylon, other fabrics, which appeared to have been rendered waterproof by smearing them with some sort of melted plastic.

There had been no stab at town planning. The dwellings grew organically from the centre like mould or weeds, until they more or less filled the hollow.

An architectural motif of the place was its use of rotting hulks of long abandoned cars. They hunkered in twos and threes, skewed at odd angles with their windscreens missing, bonnets torn off and innards in bits across the rocks and mud of the site.

There were some old touring caravans which cannot have been habitable at all – but had simply been cannibalised for what could be used then left as shells. One had the whole left side missing in a vast gaping hole with jagged edges so you could see what was left of the cosy domesticity inside. It was like one of those cutaway drawings they have in encyclopaedias.

There were used gas bottles everywhere too, and rickety bits of furniture – chairs and tables for alfresco dining.

Over by the nearest lean-to someone had strung a heavy punch bag from the branches of a stunted elm.

The floor of the site was hardly any less free of rubbish than the tip – where at least a bulldozer came through occasionally and shovelled the stuff up into heaps. All of this mess was what someone had plans for – but then got distracted. There were car parts, the innards of long dead computers, there was something that looked like it might once have been a generator, something else which resembled the crude fibreglass carcass of a boat.

There was more organised chaos too – a huge hopper constructed of wood and wire – filled with the findings from the tip. There were glass bottles, newspapers, ragged clothes and shoes. There was a smaller box filled with mobile phones, one with tattered electrical apparatus – it went on.

Our Rat hauled his sack over the lip of the can bank and added his haul to the hoard with a light-weight, apologetic rattle.

The place, I saw, had grown from the tip and been nurtured by it. It was an extension of the dump but tamed somewhat by the intervention of man. Like a junk garden.

Love, Glazier and I stood around among the other spare parts watching the Rat busy himself with his hopper full of cans. We'd invited ourselves to the party and now we felt a bit out of place. I did anyway, I don't think Love knew emotions like embarrassment. It wasn't in him.

"This place, is fantastic," he enthused looking around. "It exists completely outside the straight world – it doesn't ask permission to be here, it just is. There's a power in that. A force..."

People were coming; gravitating towards us. One or two heads popped out of a shelter towards the rear of the compound – another couple of folk who were trailing back from the tip hauled up and stopped when they saw strangers in the camp.

Those who began to gather around were not like us. They seemed a race apart. Sinewed and skittish – an entirely different genus.

But then, what is us?

Are John Love and I so much alike we form a single species? Only in as much a Doberman and a pug are both dogs.

They didn't attempt to communicate with us at first – just sneaked glances, first at us then at each other.

Then a slight, chimp-haired girl in a Dennis the Menace mohair jumper challenged us.

"Want to buy stuff? We have all sorts. Metals, textiles, mobile phones – good prices, 'specially if you buy in bulk."

The others nodded as she warmed to her sales pitch.

She grimaced slyly at Love; I think she was aiming for coquettish.

"We have other stuff to sell too."

Drugs? Herself?

"No" Love stopped her – holding up a hand like a smiley traffic cop. "No, that's not why we're here. We don't want anything from you – in fact we want to give you something – we have a gift for you."

They're not happy. You can see that right off – there's only one relationship they want with the straight world and that's the one where they hand over the treasure they've sifted and receive hard currency in return. They're not pleased, but I'm not worried.

I know how this goes. First they're hostile, then they're curious, then they're hooked.

Pretty soon, and without them realising how, John Love has become the most significant person in their lives.

"What's the matter with that girl?" asked Glazier. I followed his gaze.

It was easy to spot the one he referred to. She was thin and whey, hutched up in an improvised wheelchair with pram wheels like a kid's go-cart.

A small tousled thing like a starling broken by a cat.

She'd be pretty I supposed if she was less ill, better fed. So much comes down to looks – we even like our charity cases to be easy on the eye. It makes them more deserving of our pity and our time.

"She's chilled inside," answered Doctor Love evenly, though the question hadn't been for him. He began to examine her with his slightly distracted bedside manner, staring keenly past the person to the body itself – then beyond that even. Weighing her up like a mechanic surveying a faulty engine.

"What are you doing?" Our guide wanted to know.

It seemed rude of him to ask somehow – throwing back a favour.

"She's broken," Love said absently. "You want to see me fix her?"

"Hey," the girl demanded. "I'm here y'know. You can talk to me and everything."

Love's gaze faded back in so that he could see her – rather than just what was going on inside.

"How long have you had this problem with your spine?"

"Too long. The doctor says it's spurs. Too close to my nervous system to operate. I'm a cripple basically – can't walk more than a few steps."

She was resigned it seemed, rather than angry or sorry for herself. All the sorts of things I'd have been.

"They say it's only going to get worse. I'm in a chair – they want me to become one of them. They'll give me a flat to live in – someone to look in on me, a kitchen where I can make a cup of tea without having to get up."

It seemed like a pretty good offer to me, but the few other rats around were shaking their heads horrified at the cruel audacity of it.

Love was nodding as though he understood something only he could hear.

"You're not in this place because you want to be – but you're damned if they're going to tell you who you are. When you've got nothing at all then all you have left is what you are. That's the thing."

He turned to the girl.

"D'you want to walk again?"

She nodded – it was a yes kind of question. "What d'you think?" she murmured – bitterness at last.

"Then walk," he said simply. And dragged her roughly to her feet, kicking the chair away from under her.

"Fucking hell," yelled Glazier.

There was one of those empty moments when you feel horror at what someone's done but also smug that they're in trouble and you're not – like being tucked up in bed when there's a storm outside.

"Fred…" wailed the girl incongruously.

A string bean in a tattered yellow hoodie bundled towards her out of the crowd – ready to catch her as she fell.

But she didn't fall.

Love had let her go and she was standing unaided – swaying slightly, but in control.

Love grabbed the rat while he was making his run towards her and dragged at his rag of a top so he sat down sharply on his arse in the mud.

"Now walk," Love commanded. "Never mind these people. Show me you can walk. Your back is not an issue. It is whole. You are whole."

He was not asking.

Then she's sure suddenly it seems – his knowing has rubbed off on her – and she takes a few humble, apologetic steps forward.

Towards Love, who has his arms out like waiting for a toddler; baby's first steps.

"That's good," he tells her as she totters into his clasp, "that's fine, you're doing great."

"Aye, fine pet, you're fine," choruses Fred from his seat on the ground.

Then: "I can…walk – I can walk again!"

And Freddy Rat hugging her – bouncing both of them so their straggly dreads leap and tangle.

"Frankie," he's singing to her, "Frankie – you're well darlin' – you're well."

And I'm thinking: she could walk before – after a fashion. She never said she couldn't walk at all.

A glance over at Glazier convinced me he was thinking something similar, despite his best intentions. Yet we seemed to be the only ones entertaining any kind of doubt about this remarkable thing – this miracle, which had taken hold of everyone in the camp and enthused them with the high-proof spirit of hope.

It was chilly out here in the hollow, surrounded by the corpses of dead motor cars and smashed consumer durables, but the rats didn't seem to feel it – they were deeply excited.

Overwhelmed by her cure, the girl sank back into her chair for a rest.

She looked up at Love with real tears right there in her little sparrow eyes, tippling down her yellow cheeks.

"Thank you – thank you so much."

Love waved it away humbly.

"I'm only a channel – it's not me you should thank – I couldn't have arrived here by boat if there was no sea."

She'd brightened up considerably had Frankie – anyone could see that – she looked alert and perky sitting there, happy and connected with the rest of us, whereas before she had seemed detached and far away.

"What I feel like," she laughed, "what I really could use – is a fag."

One of the rats noodled about in his pants and began the laborious procedure of manufacturing a remarkably skinny roll-up from tobacco rescued from the butts of dead cigarettes bequeathed by the tip.

"I can help you all," Love told them. "It's not always obvious when someone is sick – even to them. I can give you what you need."

One or two of the guys were nodding along with him by now – they already wanted a bottle of whatever he was selling. I could see I'd have to get picking more weeds.

Others in the group would require more work.

But Love found patience when he had need of it. Like a fisherman – for whom the willingness to hang around uncomplainingly is the greatest virtue.

"I am trained," he told them, smiling welcomingly, "in shamanistic ecstasy."

He said it as though he was telling them he was a member of the local Rotary club and did a lot of good works for charity.

"I had an experience many would consider traumatic. I fell from a plane. The parachute I was relying on for a soft landing failed to function in the way described on the packet."

He looked around the group, seeking out eye contact, finding it. This was a lot from him. This was more revelation than we were accustomed to – and I knew that many of his friends further up the island would be jealous it had not been saved for them.

"I could easily have died," Love told his rats. "But instead I was chosen – I experienced a call. An election."

There was some sniggering. But not as much as you might imagine. And it was quite embarrassed with itself, as though the double entendre merchants knew they were not worthy.

Frankie spoke up – from where she rested in her chair – still letting the miracle soak through her bones.

"It must have been one hell of a bang. There can't have been much of you left. How did you get better?"

"I healed myself. I found I had the power. The entire process of my learning took place in a dream state. And when it was done I found I had knowledge of other realms of being and consciousness – worlds which border ours. I found the borders had become suddenly blurred."

On the whole he couldn't have found a more receptive group. They tend to have open minds on the fringes of society, if only because they have to find something they can own.

He didn't have them all though, not yet.

"Sounds like cobblers to me."

"We just collect bottles and cans and such."

"We'd heard you were an odd customer – they weren't fucking wrong."

Love nodded as if it were all as he had expected.

"There was a fire in my head. There still is. I do not seek your understanding. It is not necessary that you approve of me."

They nodded at this. That was a basis for agreement I suppose – that you could exist without the say so of the normal world.

"I'm a lot like you," Love said, managing not to sound disingenuous. He was a sleek Burmese cat next to these mangy, undernourished vermin. They were all mammals. That was it for similar. Yet, in common with the rest of us, they wanted to be like him. And they cleaved to him, as a toddler does unquestioningly to its mum.

They were a strange mix it seemed to me. On the one hand deeply practical – able to use everything we discarded and even take electricity from the air itself with a groaning overworked windmill, standing lanky and self-conscious at the far end of their compound, yet they were eager to suck comfort from the bones Love threw them.

Were they vulnerable people with no other means of survival, or proud with an off kilter identity of their own? I couldn't work them out.

They're people. What do we think of people?'

Then suddenly Love's leaping around all agitated as if the fire in his head just got stoked up. He's racing towards the rat who made us a sales pitch and he grabs her head in his hands – stares into her eyes.

He's squashing her cheeks up so she looks quite comical but it doesn't detract much from the moment.

"I see your fear," Love yells, spit flying out – "Let that fear be gone."

And he's away off to the next one with her shaking her head dazed like she's banged it on a low doorway.

He slaps a tanned and manly hand on the next chap's forehead and simply pushes him gently backwards saying "Be at peace."

Incredibly the bloke crumples like his bones have disappeared – curls up foetal and asleep in the cold mud.

Love does three or four like this guy in quick succession.

"Be at peace...be at peace..."

They're lying all around us – children playing a game of sleeping lions.

Then he's urging those who are still standing: "Come to me – if you need me come to me, I know what you need, I can give you what you need."

Today it seems, nobody gets to be a spectator, except perhaps myself and Glazier. We watch, is what we do. As, in twos and threes and then an untidy gaggle, like sheep being harried by a dog, they come to John Love. Who receives them with open hands.

Some he merely touches, dismisses with the slightest brush of his fingertips – others he grasps as though he is dragging them from the ocean, he hauls them towards him by the head or the shoulders, hugs the breath out of them leaving them sobbing and weak with gratitude.

Afterwards each is drained. They wander somnambulistic or slump down on their arses and sit where they've landed, like their strings have been cut.

When he's through with them he stands over them and commands:

"You will come with me. You will come back to live with us – we have places to live, we have food. We owe it to you as part of our oneness."

They perk up a bit at this, particularly the news about the free grub.

Leap for joy, we're all going to live together like one of those big 21st century step-families where everybody wrestles to make the best of it.

There's a surprising lot of these people when they all come out of their holes: scabrous blokes and straggly birds, snotty kids thin as weasels with empty eyes.

Where are they all going to stop?

Fuck 'em really, they aren't my problem – they aren't my people.

There's this thing you get into if you aren't smart where the whole world is a matter for you.

It's best avoided really. We all have our island.

"The caravan site where I am staying has plenty of empty space," Love tells them joyfully. "There is room for all of us – you can bring your vehicles – your shelters, and we will help you build more."

Pardon me? The site? My site?

This is not a good thing.

Perhaps he's got the nature of the place wrong. This isn't America. We aren't trailer park trash, we're owner-occupiers. We're a community, of overweight single mums and geriatric widowers who crash their Fiestas into the gateposts.

It's true we represent the lowest rung on the housing ladder but to live on the site you have to be solvent enough to buy one of the vans.

There are not many prospective residents who could have brought down the tone of the neighbourhood, yet here some are, managing it.

I'm hoping they won't be persuaded – that they'd rather continue to live here – uniquely, surprisingly – than become an adjunct to us.

But they are persuaded.

They don't gather round for a parish meeting on the subject. But first a few go to see if they can jump-start their vans. Then a few more start packing up their assortment of rags and engine parts, until soon we find they've reached a critical mass where the ones who thought it would be odd to go now find that they're taking an extreme stance by insisting on staying. And, since all they'd ever wanted in the first place was to go with the flow, soon they're push starting their shit-heaps too and we're off.

They're chuntering to each other as they pack their socks and undies.

What the rats say:

"How could it be worse – what we got here?"

"Our freedom."

"Freedom to shit in a bush."

"I like him. He's handsome."

"Imagine what he'd be like if he hadn't fallen out of a plane on his face."

"I'll miss this place – it's been home."

"You'll still have us."

"Us might change."

"Is change that bad? He makes it seem natural."

"He makes it seem like the tide coming in."

Soon our convoy of bangers was stalling and kangaroo hopping up the road like the Rio carnival had hit grim times.

Glazier's sent on ahead in a car which works to massage public opinion back at base, while Love and I catch a lift in one of the least tragic lumps of available transport – an old double-decker bus which has been stripped of all but the first couple of rows of downstairs seats.

The rest of the dingy interior is a mess of stained sleeping bags and dog crap, empty fag cartons and limp plastic flagons of loony lightning strong cider.

As the engine chunders into some kind of agony-wracked life the whole metal and glass mass of the bus shudders like a broken heroin addict. There's a noise like kicking an oil-drum down a flight of stairs.

We're all going on a summer holiday.

Our driver today will be Flange, a curiously named wee turd with a Jerry Garcia beard and small round glasses with purple lenses.

He has stuff to say on the route – which takes us a good hour despite being just a 20 minute drive as we have to keep stopping for breakdowns further up the convoy.

Flange, unfortunately, appears to be camp mechanic, so when we stop he has to hand crank the bus door open and shuffle on up to where the action is so he can spray WD40 on the leads and supervise the swearing.

He's clearly not as conversationally challenged as some of the rest of them mind you and he treats us to his life story – though we didn't ask.

"I used to be a taxi driver – had a share in a proper black cab and all that. I was pretty successful, didn't mind the hours, the money was fairly good and it suited me. Then one night these three guys got in, asked to go into town and it seemed legit but then one of them sitting behind me poked a carving knife in my throat and they took me right out on the motorway – hundred or so miles to nowhere much.

"Had all my takings, the car, my jacket even. A couple of them beat the shit out of me just for a laugh and left me in a lay-by. I could just about walk and one of them told me to head for some bushes across a field. I started walking. I could hear him following behind.

"I was shitting myself – I thought he was going to kill me. No, I knew he was. It wasn't a time for doubt.

"He said to go for the bushes and if I stopped he'd slash my throat and if I came back he would – so I hobbled over to those bushes and I stayed there in all the wet and freezing cold until it stopped being dark.

"Since then I just haven't been right – my head doesn't work like it should. I get drunk a lot and take smack and that. I can't feel anything but fear. At the tip you don't need to feel afraid. You don't need to feel anything much and that's the way I like it. I was withdrawn into myself before I met these people and started living this life, now I don't have to be. There's a family of people as messed up as I am."

We drive in silence for a while. My piles are itching and I'm trying to rub my arse on the seat like a little dog without making too much of a three ring circus of it.

Then we rattle to another halt and tumble out grumbling onto the grass verge. During this bout of hanging around Love takes our man by the hand and draws him round into the thin sunlight and tips his specs up to look in his yellow eyes.

"You have no need of fear – it offers you nothing you can use. Be free of it."

Our new pal Flange is shaking his billy goat head: "That's easy to say – I have to live with this big dog chasing us every day. There's no way free of the thing. I know, I've taken everything a man can take – snorted it, drunk it, injected it. I've stuffed things up my back passage that vets use to knock out farm animals. None of it works. The fear's always with me."

Love grabs him roughly by the shoulders and stares into him. When he lets go Flange flings himself backwards like he's had an electric shock. The poor old sod's left sitting in a pile of marran grass on the verge. Floppy as a ventriloquist's dummy.

"There's nothing you need to fear. There's no dog – never was. You are free of it now. So get up and drive us home."

Bewildered, he does as he's told. Gets back on the bus and behind the wheel. He doesn't refer to what's happened and soon starts chattering away again but there is a change which gathers pace like a swelling breeze. He's more confident, less prone to twine on about what a tough time he's had of it.

He's subtly different – and significantly less irritating, which is a major bonus as far as I'm concerned. He starts laughing suddenly – loud and long like he doesn't care who hears him cackling away there.

"This is fantastic!" – he whoops, banging the steering wheel and giving the bus's asthmatic horn a bit of a workout. "I feel as though part of me that has been missing for years is back again – bits of my jigsaw..."

While he put together his mental picture of a couple of kittens frolicking in a basket of knitting I wondered how we were going to slip this parade of weird past the site steward. Also wondered whether, now that Love's got himself into the healing business, perhaps he can do something about my farmers.

I suppose I'm glad Flange has got his head better – though I don't really give a shit. One might have thought I'd have more empathy with these people. After all, Flange and I are both salvors – it's what we do.

Yet I feel I'm above them socially. Which feeling I relish as I don't often get it.

As we drive through the gates of the park I'm expecting an angry mob with pitchforks but instead it's low key. Mike, our site steward swings the gate open himself and as we pass between the rows of vans one or two people wave as they would at any new arrival.

Glazier has carried out his mission well. A few of our followers wait in welcome at the Green which sits at the centre of my mobile village.

Green's going it some I'll allow – it's more of a Yellow – a receding patch of scraggy grass mined with dog turds which has wind howling across it day and night. I'd like to say my community gathers here on balmy summer evenings for barbecues but the only time you see a crowd gather is if a couple of the single mums are having a drunken scrap on the way back from the boozer.

We have perhaps a dozen vehicles in our convoy: clapped out camper vans, worn and rusted mobile homes towed by geriatric Land-Rovers. There's our bus, a couple of ex-removal vans with gaudy emulsion swirls hand painted on the bodywork. When we arrive most of the other vehicles have already pulled up on the Green but no one has got out. There's a curious impasse with rats in cabs pretending nobody can see them through the windows and our pals on the turf more or less refusing to notice the vans for now.

Our bus pulls up and Love takes charge, cranking open the door and jumping down like the first big suit on the moon. Audrey shuffles up and clasps him in a too familiar hug. "I've missed you," she stage whispers in his lug.

Not 'we' I notice. She alone has done the missing, as though there is something which gives her a right. What though? I'm not really good at this stuff; it's not my subject.

Once Love's set foot on the saggy turf the rest of our intrepid team of travellers disembarks from the fleet, motley as pirates. I survey them in all their grubby dog-eared glory and am briefly thrilled to be among their number. There's something gratifying to be associated with such a dissolute bunch of customers. Part of me has always yearned to run with a bad crowd and this lot were indisputably that.

They were happy to be here, you could see. Flange gave a few whoops and hollers, other voices joined him. There was some rudimentary dancing, with even Frankie clambering gingerly from her chair to shuffle a few crooked steps. One of the rats slipped in mud and fell on his backside, all of us laughed uproariously, like you do when that happens.

The few islanders who had gathered as our welcome party were looking frankly baffled. They stood round the fringes of our unlikely gathering: mute and uncomprehending.

And the rats bounced about in curious celebration of a new home which was little different from the one they'd left – a sodden and wind blasted patch of grass on our lost and disregarded island at the far stretched fringes of whatever was happening on the rest of the planet.

What had Love done for them by bringing them here? What was there to celebrate with such noisy gusto? They had become part of something – even if that something wasn't very much at all.

Love was up on the bonnet of one of the Land Rovers motioning for calm. The rats gathered round, shoving good-naturedly, shouting stuff at him like he's making a speech at a stag do.

"I brought you here for a reason," he told them. "And there's all sorts of things we have to do – I can't begin to tell you. But that is for another day. Tomorrow we can save the world. Tonight we party."

X

It can be extraordinarily hard work having fun.

The preparation, the doing of it, the recovery time after. It's a lot of tough graft is having a laugh.

Our first chore was to fetch a vast quantity of wood. Many of us were skilled at sourcing raw materials for nothing and the beach nearby was rich with salt slaked timber. But it was still a righteous pain in the arse.

Scrambling over slick stones gathering each bleached plank and branch, lumping the load up the hill back to the park and across to the Green. The rats approached the work with brash good humour. This put me in a foul mood.

Curious residents peered from the windows of their lonesome vans.

They knew the news headlines thanks to Glazier's vanguard and the island drums but the reality of having a bunch of scrappy ne'er-do-wells tramping across your petunias trailing lumps of driftwood behind them defies advance billing.

Glazier was very much with the programme, he took on the role of head foreman for the whole wood gathering enterprise – Audrey and Barbara were well to the fore as well. It was as if the hierarchy had been established already and the islanders accepted it, even these new ones who we'd barely acknowledged as existing before they came to live outside my bedroom window.

Love sat on the bus bonnet with a book. Leaning back on the windscreen, oblivious to the wind, except that it kept flipping his pages over – which didn't seem to irritate him as much as it would have done me. He was wrapped up in the same tousled copy of the *Golden Bough* I'd seen him studying earlier.

I suppose I could have hopped up and sat next to him; perched on the radiator like an ill-considered hood ornament. In the role of his familiar I would have been allowed this latitude I think. But instead I gathered wood with the rest. Don't know why, I was busy doing it before I thought it through and then there didn't seem the right opportunity to stop. Not until we had finally finished and a pile the size of a double garage was stacked up in the centre of the Green.

Barbara went off to the shop down the hill to get matches and whatever accelerant was readily available.

She came back with a crowd. The committed, the curious. Those who had been desperate to find out what Love would reappear with, those who had hardly noticed he'd gone, and those who frankly didn't know who the hell he was but had heard there was going to be a party in this grey place where even the slightly unusual was to be celebrated.

The people bought food and alcohol. The booze was mostly cans of lager with some bottles of wine, spirits left over from Christmas and so on – whatever they'd been able to lay hands on swiftly. The food was bread rolls, cans of hotdogs, burgers from the freezer.

We lit one vast fire in the centre of the Green, then several other smaller ones around the outskirts. The big one was just for show – plus what it afforded us in heat and light, the smaller ones were more use for cooking the barbecue people were obviously expecting.

It was like a big community fête, only held in a scrap yard with the corpses of rotting motor transport towering sourly over the bunting.

The islanders and the rats were both on their best behaviour – making small talk, scoffing chicken wings. As getting to know you gatherings went it couldn't be better.

But, as night muscled in the fire grew brighter. Some of the blokes ferried down to the offy and one of the pubs for more booze and came back with plenty. There were other things too, for those who wanted them, and you couldn't just blame the rats for that either. They were among the island's more enthusiastic users of non-prescription drugs but they had to get them from somewhere and their suppliers were all here among the gathering throng.

Fact was we'd had a closer relationship with the rats than we would admit. We weren't here meeting for the first time, we were forging an alliance with a neighbouring tribe – one we had co-existed with for years without ever getting close enough to swap oral poetry or interbreed.

Love passed through the crowds sharing himself with everyone – letting them bask in his wide white grin and enjoy his physical presence. Audrey and Barbara were beside him, introducing him to those he had not yet met – easing him further into our world. They encouraged those who were angry about the rats being here to see it as a joke, a carnival which did not much matter as it would all be gone soon. Besides, how could anyone blame Love for the movement of so many people and so much transport?

He was just one man – if anything he had helped to keep things civilised – the rats had done no harm had they?

I was standing close when the three of them were approached brusquely by Douggie Yale, the grocer.

"How the hell's this mess going to affect the community?" he wanted to know. "There'll be glue-sniffing and hopheads all round my store. Pissing in the gutters and scrapping. Trade will suffer."

"Cheer up pet – think of all these new customers," twinkled Audrey – but he wouldn't be assuaged.

"It's not on – and if that idle sod Stafford doesn't do something about this then I'll speak to his superiors on the mainland."

"But he's here," soothed Audrey. "He's over there with a drink, keeping an eye on things, look."

And there he was too. Bob Stafford. Propped up against his squad car – pissed already, with a hotdog hanging out of his gob.

Love didn't bother to answer Douggie – he just ignored the man as though he wasn't there – and pretty soon he wasn't.

He was not the only unwelcome visitor to our fire that evening. Around the edges of the group some of the former residents of the Centre began to gather – attracted by the warmth and the need for human company.

Some of the lucky ones had been taken in by locals when the Centre unexpectedly closed its doors, but these last few – the ugliest and least loved – were still subsisting on scraps and finding shelter from the elements where they could. It had been over a week since their world collapsed and who knew how much they understood of their predicament? They knew certainly that there were burgers here, and laughter, and the chance perhaps to make much-needed friends.

But the young men on the fringes of our party – rowdy after too much beer, chased them away from the fire hollering and aiming kicks at the stragglers.

Most got the message eventually. All of them left, except for Walter. A bald, toothless imbecile, he was like a little old man – though who knew his real age? Tiny he was, only a few inches taller than me. He had always been a waif but now, after a week of little to eat, he was skinny as a shipyard cat.

He wandered grinning and gurning among the crowd where he was tolerated for now as he was on his own and one of the less unpleasant looking of his fellows.

One or two of the drunken women even mothered him a little. He was given a kebab and someone put a baseball cap backwards on his head, to the sound of exaggerated merrymaking.

The fire rose high above our party on the Green, sending flecks and fraps of flame into the night sky. Every so often a belt of wind would hurtle through and the blaze would veer, giddy as a drunken man, sending a cloud of sparks into one or other section of the crowd. Folk scattered with a cackle and a slither on the mud.

The rats rigged up a decrepit public address system hauled from the rear of one of their vans and powered it up by running a line from the toilet block. It had woofers the size of dustbins. Soon music, with a thunderous looping bassline, hammered all around us and through us so we could feel it more than hear it. What it felt like was something we had generated inside ourselves. A collective heartbeat, rendered gigantic and grotesque.

"This is wired," yelled Glazier, standing next to me. I couldn't hear him. I could hardly read his lips in the murk.

This wasn't the best forum for communicating anything – other than perhaps a general energy and power. Most people got that. And the ones nearest to the fire began to dance.

It wasn't the rats and it wasn't the islanders, it was a mixture of both acting in unison.

Shambling and shuffling along to the music, leaping into the air repeatedly like seals after fish, as I remembered we used to do in my former incarnation as a punk rocker.

They were enjoying it, got caught up in the passion of the thing and soon others joined them. The time for trying to talk was over –

there was drink, there was dancing, there were drugs if you wanted them, which various of the younger people seemed to. I saw them sidling over behind the vans to carry out their transactions in the shadows. Some I wouldn't have expected to indulge, nice kids, quiet and kind and obedient. But this evening was a time when the normal rules which bound us had been suspended for a while.

I've never been much of a dancer, too self-conscious to shake an efficient shoe. But I indulged in bouncing up and down a little. For old times' sake.

Glazier didn't dance, he want and sat over on the step of the bus and watched us all leaping about to the cavernous rumbling of the drums.

There weren't any lyrics to the music but there seemed to be whoops and whistles way back in the mix. One or two of the dancers began whooping and hollering too as they jumped and staggered with abandon – more joined them. It didn't look fun precisely but it was infectious none the less.

I hunted around for John Love. For now he was nowhere to be seen. Barbara and Audrey were dancing a little self consciously with one or two of the others who had been with Love since near the start.

The girl in the wheelchair was with them, and Flange. And Ken Naylor from the garage with his wife. Marcus Riley, dancing better than you might have figured on one leg.

Were there many islanders who stayed away this night? The elderly, the sick, those like the residents of the centre who weren't invited. Thinking of them I searched out Walter in the crowd. Someone had given him beer to drink and he was pin-balling around the dancers, crashing into them, coming of worst each time. He was falling to the ground and getting groggily to his feet. His shirt, his face, were coated with the cloying clay mud which lay underfoot where the grass had once been.

Where was Love? He should be here. Somehow all of this was for him.

Others noticed his absence too I think. He was present by not being there. It was as if my people wanted to show off for him by letting him see him how wild they could be. How unfettered by the insularity that this free creature from over the ocean might have supposed governed their lives.

They drank more. Took more drugs.

There was hemp and psilocybin, which grew natively, then more powerful things which came from outside – mongrel and unpredictable alloys. Opiates, cocaine, lab cooked pills and capsules with proper names like a poor hand at Scrabble.

All these they imbibed. Cautiously at first for the most part. But gradually less so as the dancing intensified and the heat from the fire bloomed in the frozen night.

Fights broke out. There was no real malice in them it seemed, just a rush of misdirected energy which having built up, had to escape in some direction or other, like the explosion of foam from a shaken beer bottle.

Rats fought with rats, rats fought with islanders, islanders fought each other. Men fought mostly but women fought too. They weren't any worse at it once they got into the groove. They could punch just as wildly and kick every bit as ruthlessly. Drunkenness is a great leveller anyway in the scrapping stakes. It made the combatants stronger, less pervious to pain, yet at the same time more likely to misdirect their blows.

There was still more dancing than fighting, but the dancing had become so intense and that it was sometimes hard to tell the two forms of expression apart. Dancers staggered into fighters and became fighters themselves.

I had drunk a lot. But I always drink a lot. And I had taken only hemp so I felt enough in control of myself to steer clear of the violence I knew could consume me if one of these large and brutal human beings turned their energies against me.

Picking my way through the firelight and mud, avoiding the staggering figures, I came across Barbara, straddled across an old and ugly lecher named Ken Tate. He represented one of her least successful and most regretted conquests. I thought at first they were making love as she sat astride him, undulating slightly. It seemed a poor choice of location, even given the licence of the evening. But as I got closer I realised she was throttling him.

He was struggling to speak; managed a few snatched words:

"You wept, but your soul was willing."

I watched her remove a hand from his throat and reach behind to take off her shoe.

She held it over her head then brought the heel point down, again, then again, in his face.

On an upbeat I plunged at her arm and managed to wrestle the shoe from her grasp, flinging it towards the great central fire.

Ken rolled groggily away, blood from his punctured forehead dribbling down his anguished face.

All eloquence beaten from him he still knew what he wanted to say.

"Uv you Bar. Uv you pet," he kept bleating absently as he was consumed by the crowd.

I did not know what it would all come to.

There had not been many times in my life when I could say that.

Despite the peculiar nature of my own circumstances, trapped inside my mute and dwarfish body, the world around me had always been meek and ordered.

I had nothing to fear, except perhaps the weather, which terrified me. I assumed everyone else was the same.

They had no worries beyond what they confided in me.

If you had asked me what Barbara's biggest hobby horse was for example, I would have told you that she hated anyone to change the position of the mixer tap on her kitchen sink – for fear that it would spring a leak. The fact that it had been engineered to turn through an arc meant nothing to her – as long as she held sway in her own home it would remain static. Anything so that dark water could not rise and drown her as she slept.

I assumed we were all like me. Happy in our misery.

But this.

This represented change surely.

Crashing around drunk near an unguarded fire. Unnatural substances. People hitting each other with shoes.

It could never come to any good.

More wood and petrol were hurled on the fire and the PA was banged up another couple of notches. It was impossible now to make oneself understood, even if any of us had anything worth saying.

The dancing, the fighting, became more intense so it was no longer at all possible to tell one from the other.

The very old and very young had left this place, but there was still a broad range of people here. Callow and fresh faced, saggy and grey, they hurled themselves around in the red half-light. Larded in mud, consumed by the waves of bass.

Then the music stopped. The spotlights flicked off so we were left in 3am dark but for the flicker of the fire.

And the midnight sun came out.

The mood of the place shifted. People looked up from whatever torso they were pounding or patch of earth they were stomping on. We saw a low star in the dark sky. As if the dawn had come early and white and from an unnatural direction.

The light showed us up for what we were: sickly and thin, pale and unprepossessing. Mud and blood and puffy eyes and ugly tempers. It was a bad light.

'Listen,' the light seemed to say. 'Pay attention.' So we did, tilting our heads and giving good face. We stared up towards the roof of the double decker bus.

Where we found a figure spotlit from below. And that figure I knew by instinct, before he uttered a word.

We waited for him to speak.

He didn't.

The fire made uneasy static, the frap and rattle of burnt timbers collapsing somewhere in its midst.

I don't know what we were waiting on, but by then we wanted something.

We craved a host of different things. But there was a common yearning. We did not know *what* we wanted. We only knew that we *wanted*.

John Love did not speak in words but sound came from him. A keening, wailing ululation which found its home somewhere in the heart of the crowd.

I saw him there, tall and beautiful as a Michelangelo. He seemed incredible – more than one of us, something special in the spotlight high above.

He seemed lighter than the air around him, not chained to the earth like the rest of us. Instead he seemed to be hovering some feet above the roof of the bus.

And the sound, the shape of his raised arms, morphs in my mind until I make sense at last of what I am seeing – not the John Love I know, not a man of any kind, but another creature altogether.

A gull. Wings spread wide, beak open. Calling to us from the breadth and depth of the night air which is his element.

Ripping my raw eyes away I look around and know by instinct that others see what I do. There is no shock – not even surprise. We know what is there. We see it.

I look back and the bird is gone. But still it flies in my mind. Probably always will.

John Love: beautiful, upright, proud, seeming to float almost on the cusp of something new – beyond what we can comprehend.

Love, the bird, fresh and natural, part of this place and linking us to the sky above.

"I am Taranus the Celtic god of thunder. I am Dispater, the Roman god of the dead.

"This morning I may be a curl of mist, tomorrow night a leaf, the next day rain.

"The form I take means nothing. Ignore it – it's just my spacesuit.

"I call you here tonight as I have work for you. All you who follow me. I know you look for something of yourselves which you have lost. That thing you have misplaced like childhood, yearned for, longed to find again.

"Find it through me. Use me in that way. I offer myself to you. As my servant did once here before. Together we can build something majestic, permanent and true. Something beyond anything worlds have seen. Beyond imagining.

"I don't ask you to give yourselves to me, I don't ask you to sacrifice yourselves as others have done and as I must. Don't give me more than you can each afford. I don't want to break you. Don't put yourselves to too much trouble – go about your daily lives and leave the bitterness to me.

"But I'll take your labour. If that's all you have to give then I'll take that. Your skills, your brawn. I'll let you lift yourselves up higher than you imagined a person could fly. Like free bloody birds you'll be, up there in the all comprehending sky.

"Like birds. Like me."

The light went and he was gone, our man, our beautiful bird. The light went and Love went with it – disappeared into the night sky, perhaps like the gull he had become for us uniquely, brilliantly.

The night was gorged with energy. It seemed we had a right, a duty, to kick off – and half way there already, we obliged – in celebration, in defiance of our ordinary lives, we whooped, hollered, danced and fought. Bedtime, it appeared, was for wimps.

I stuck around to see how things turned out. I couldn't go to bed since my van was within the fallout of this ear-ringing din.

But I became absorbed by the thing too, I will admit. I drank perhaps more than I usually would, danced a few ill-fangled steps and watched the show.

Our young people, gambolling like bullocks. Slipping ungainly in the luscious mud, coated in the half-light, clattering with pointless laughter.

They began then to leap the fire – which was fading surely. I don't know who first realised that, clarted in wet mud, it was possible, with a drunken run up, to clear the worst of the conflagration – flames flicking harmlessly past your face, warming you for a moment, perhaps instilling a little panic as you hung there for a fractured second in the dangerous air.

But then down safe on the other side – sparks flying as a trailing heel caught the foreshore of the fire, a glowing ember of driftwood.

They leapt the fire, one and then another, until there was a queue – young men, young women, backwards and forwards across the blazing gulf, yelping with laughter and fear. Older people tried it too, the middle-aged who would not be denied their chance to taste the sour thrill of fear in their mouths, knowing one slip could leave them flailing, wracked by agony, in the midst of the blaze.

And some decided to load the fire with timber – which dampened it at first before it blazed higher and more fiercely than before, so only the bravest of the jumpers could bear the leap, which was now fraught with peril. But still they did it, those that could, as though it meant something more than a cheap thrill and a show of bravado – to prove to others you were doing something which they could not.

It was as if they were doing it to defy death, or sin – or whatever else flame can be made to represent. They were seeking salvation.

And when the tower of flame was at last too high and wide for anyone to jump there was a commotion in the watching crowd – until through it progressed a gang of people bearing above them something small and wriggling with life. A cat. They had one of the island's strays, borne up above them for us all to see and this knot of bodies, far more than were needed to subdue so small a creature.

They moved towards the fire, holding the thing aloft, where it squirmed and mewled, sensing that things, which had not been going well for a while now, were about to take a turn for the worse.

Then they flung the tiny living thing high into the stoked and smoky air above the fire where it fell awfully, inevitably, into the turbulent core and screamed and leapt but found itself unable to get clear. An invisible cage of energy-robbing pain kept it in the heart of the heat, shivering as if cold but clothed in flame, then falling prone among the blackened logs until it resembled them. There was nothing to tell between them.

Nothing to say that it had ever been a cat.

Except it wasn't a cat.

XI

The next morning there was a sunrise worth seeing.

I glimpsed it from the window of the van as I opened the curtains then went out into the breath-stealing cold to get a better look out over the ochre sea.

Bloody and intense it was, so beautiful it seemed to have a point.

There is no need for pretty things. But it hung there as if created on purpose, this accidental quirk of light and atmospheric conditions.

Love was not in my caravan, though his bed had been slept in. I put on my parka and went in search of him. Found him at length on the charred and muddy ruin of the Green, circled by its wagon train of rat transporters. We were the only people there, though the tip-rat dogs haunted the edges of the makeshift site, grumbling.

It was strange to be here after last night. Though the place was familiar it had taken on a whole new suit of clothes. I associated it now with the pulsing music, the drunken anarchy and the heat of the fire. Everything now was odd, even daylight. And the grubby mud and charred embers seemed a downbeat setting for the momentous events which had occurred.

John Love was on his knees where once had been our main fire. He was scrabbling in the rain soaked charcoal. Hunting for something.

Soot coated him, his clothes, his hands and arms, even his face and hair. Much longer and he would be one with the black ground.

He hunted patiently and with method, sifting through the debris with forensic precision.

Scratching away at the darkness with his fingertips until finally he found what he was looking for.

He stood up then, slowly, holding it in his hands tenderly, as one would a cat.

Blackened, battered, tortured by the heat but still whole. A skull. Small like a child's. All that was left of Walter.

Love trudged from the fire and turned towards me thoughtfully, rubbing the thing on his shirt as if hoping vaguely a genie might appear.

He acknowledged me sparely as he passed me on the way back to the caravan.

I followed him to find him washing the thing in the sink. He couldn't get it clean, not the pearly white of a medical student's skeleton. It was buff and tarnished as if by age.

He dried it with a tea towel and put it on the shelf in his bedroom.

XII

I went to see Barbara.

Hers is a place of comfort. She welcomes everyone, without exception. It's purely a matter of the form the welcome takes.

Many men visit her, many people. We all need love in some way or another.

I'm her baby. The infant she doesn't have. Me and the dogs and the cats and the stray nippers of the neighbourhood.

In some ways this means I get an extraordinary welcome. If you clocked the first five minutes of me turning up you'd think we were unlikely lovers. More: she left her lovers, me she kept. And kissed me each time we met as if it was the first time for years.

It was better than being lovers because we would not part, and worse because of the way she recoiled if her flesh brushed against the wart on my cheek.

And here she is clasping me "darling" in her lovely tits with their vanilla smell. And she swings me round her small hall where we're nearly knocking off the pictures from the wall.

And crikey I feel the hot force of her love but then so does everybody, which has always been her downfall – that she gives away too little and too much at the same time.

Glazier's there; they've had a thing in the past I know. Not sure about now.

Glazier was keen for a while to sleep with any woman he could lay hands on, with the possible exception of his wife, who sat at home with the kids for as long as she could bear. Then she took the children and left the island. Glazier stayed, bereaved and uncomprehending. Unable it seemed to make the link between his earlier behaviour and the purgatory in which he now found himself mired.

Barbara provided comfort and succour. Glad to be of use.

It's a rum business this sexuality. I'm grateful at times it's left me unscathed.

Barbara's crying, which is something she does a lot.

I put the kettle on, make us tea. They accept it gratefully, this sacrament.

Barbara lights an incense stick in the hearth and we watch clots of scented smoke percolate through the air. I want to hear what they think about the night before. But they are so deep inside their own movie that, for a while at least, that's all they can talk about. Their tortured souls. What they want from Love.

Still, there are chocolate digestives, and I have no shortage of time.

Glazier's like a tortoise with its head just poked out – tentative and inquiring, a different animal now from the lion we used to know.

"People seem to have stopped noticing me," he confesses. "These past few years I mean, not just today. I pass them in the street and I'm the ghost of someone they once knew. They don't remember me too well. But when I pass they catch a breath of me and bring me back."

Unthere he is, faded muddily away. And I know how this is – it's the way I have been all my life. Barbara knows it too. As her looks have faded, the call she had on people's time has diminished.

"I could have gone anywhere," said Glazier, as though he still couldn't. "Anyplace in the whole world. Doing more or less anything. There's nothing to stop me – I'm not tied down anymore – by family, the kids, I don't see them anyway. So what's the value in hanging around here?"

He seemed to be waiting for us to supply him with some answers but I'm not big on those and Barbara was listening only vaguely, as if straining to hear something across a body of water.

"We have a bridge," Glazier supplied his own answer. "I could cross the bridge and go wherever I wanted. Meet new people I had more in common with. Ones who understood what I was about. I could get a job in the media. Be on telly say.

"Imagine the fuckers stuck here on this island turning on the set to see me there. Getting interviewed by someone famous – all deferential and laughing at my jokes."

I was still getting over the 'people he had more in common with' crack. I hadn't asked to be called insensitive and here I was – being. True, on the face of it I don't have much in common with anyone –

but I thought there were people with whom I connected on a level beyond all the gabbling. A place where it's possible to sit quietly and understand.

I thought I had that with Glazier. But what do we ever know about other people? The alliances we make are a shotgun wedding of convenience. We use people for what we want and make concessions to their needs in return. So they will like us and give us what we need. We're all just needy animals.

Neither of them mention what went on last night. The abandon, the consequences. It's hanging over us though, that big guilty secret, we all know that we went too far. But the beauty of the thing too – we know what we saw, what Love became.

Then there he is, hammering at the front door.

I can tell it's him before we even go and look. There's something in the clamour of his banging – nobody else on the island would be rattling out a confident rhythm this morning.

We let him in, Audrey slipping behind with barely a glance at Glazier or Bar.

Love's brimming with vim. It's like he's spent a month in a health spa with facials and foot massage, wheatgerm smoothies and colonic irrigation.

We're looking all duffed-up and second hand. We need aspirin, tongue scrapers and time on our own with the lights out.

Love makes a start on the agenda before he's even out of the hall. He's on fine form.

"Glad you're here. Saves me scouting round. There's lots to do – I'll need you to get some of the others together – that simpleton that runs the plod, a couple of the top rats, perhaps that bloke with one leg. Whoever you think really. We need to cover the bases as far as influence goes, create a situation where whoever you look up to, they're with us."

There's something different about him. I'm counting the buttons on his shirt before I realise what it is. He has a feather behind his ear. It's a wing feather from the island's biggest bird, the herring gull, a hulking glossy brute with cruel beak and yellow glass eyes.

It suits him. Makes him look all noble savage and last of the Mohicans, which seems appropriate for our wild west frontier, out on the edge of nowhere.

Barbara's gone to make tea. She comes back carting an enormous purple mug with Daddy written on the side, hands it to Love.

"But what do we need the people for?" she asks him. "What are we doing?"

He's nodding, like she's been providing answers rather than asking questions.

"Yes – exactly. They'll want to know all of that. And we'll have to be ready to tell them. Something at least."

He paused for a major draught of tea. Sat down on a hessian beanbag and sloshed some over his crotch.

"Heck – that's hot."

There was a scurry to relieve him of the mug and help him back to his feet. Nobody exits a beanbag with dignity – I don't care who they are.

He recovered from a bit of a coughing fit with Glazier thumping his back before carrying on.

"What we need is skilled craftsmen – good people. We have the labour now, that isn't the issue any more. But we need to make sure things are done properly – that what we build will last."

"We're going to build something?" Audrey piping up, despite herself. I expect she'd wanted us to think she knew a big heap more than us about what was going on.

Glazier ignored her, asked his own question: "What sort of trades?"

"Bricklayers," Love told him. "Plasterers, stone-masons, scaffolders welders, metal-workers, glaziers, carpenters, painters ... we need people who know how to build things."

Glazier shrugged. "There's plenty of those on the island. Builders and plant. Depends on the size of the project mind you."

Barbara, sitting back in the draylon sofa, gave a little 'got it' gasp: "You're going to build houses," she said excitedly. "For the rats – you're going to give them somewhere permanent to live."

Before we left we had a meal together. Beans on toast.

"Did you know," asked Glazier, "that the cuisine of almost every culture in the world has an equivalent of beans on toast?"

"Yes," said John Love.

How many of them gathered on that cold Spring Saturday because it was Love who had asked for them?

How many because Barbara's social housing theory had become common currency?

How many wanted to feel they had worth outside their normal lives?

How many had nothing better to do and got swept along by the ocean?

There's lots of reasons to be somewhere but we had a spectacular turnout by any measure on the spare salt-swept grasslands of the foreshore. Empty they were and common land. Ample areas of nothing, waiting to become something. It was here Love had chosen for his grand building project.

At first there were a few of us, then more arriving. People standing in knots. Banter. Laughter.

There were the young and disengaged, come along for a look-see on their way down the boozer; the elderly, huddled and chilly, bent and perplexed – yet they were there, glad to be of use.

Many of our people can do things with their hands. We islanders are more of a manual than a cerebral breed. Overwhelmingly we are trained in a craft – young and old and inbetween, we have a trade.

When Love arrived they swarmed towards him briefly until it became clear he wasn't planning any grandstanding. Instead he strode around like a site foreman with his hands behind his back, surveying the plot as Glazier gathered together the craftsmen with the most nous. Then they gaggled together consulting on the project with arm waving and bits of paper flapping from clipboards. Love stood a head taller than the rest of them, his tangled locks wafting about, intense look on his face as he nodded sagaciously in response to the advice of a pot-bellied planner. It was as if he was watching himself at work – I often thought that about him. It was as though he was seeing himself on TV – 'this is me marshalling the team at the start of the great project.'

It's a useful skill to have in some ways – one which we all possess at some level. He had a more developed superego than most though I'd say. Better than mine anyhow. I've spent all my life avoiding how I look.

While the worker bees milled around with loosely corralled purpose, a straggly line of well wishers and wanters assembled on what we must now describe as the site. One of the first things the builders had the rats do that morning was string a luminous plastic tape of exclusion around a vast area of the scrubby veldt which had previously been open to all who wished to jog across it, fly kites on it or let their dogs shit among the tussocks.

The tape was supported on metal skewers for most of its length then bamboo poles when these ran out. The bamboo bucked and shimmied in the gust.

There was a break in the so-called fence where the road widened into the grassland; it was a lay-by for cars to park so pensioners with flasks could stare vacantly out to sea. At this gap the queue formed. Cold folk huddled in duffle coats and macs.

They waited for most of the day. Love ignored them effortlessly. He was absorbed in his fag packet architecture, surrounded by courtiers. Once an orange plastic workman's hut had been erected on the edge of the site he made it his HQ, disappearing inside with a gaggle of consultants to pore over papers on a trestle table.

When I came in Love was there with four of his craftsmen. They were wrapped up in a debate over something technical and I wasn't even acknowledged. A couple of weeks ago that wouldn't have registered as unusual but now I caught myself feeling hard done by. Me, me, me.

Garrett, who was one of the island's better builders, was shaking his head at some of Love's drawings saying: "It's not physically possible, some of this. You can get maybe near if you use chicken wire as a base then build it up with concrete – more like a sculptor would than a builder. Then you could bed rocks in it for added strength – and to make it look how you wanted. You could use whatever stone we can get – plus there's the material from the beach you mentioned – there's enough down there so you could build Buckingham palace and not notice it gone."

Love was nodding, seemed satisfied. "We'll have no shortage of materials – it's important we vary them – it mustn't look uniform – it needs to be chaotic."

Garratt squinted at the drawings a while with his head tilted.

"Well, it's certainly going to be that mate – if it looks anything like this spec it will be like nowt any of us have done before."

Love nodding, animated and excited.

"That's right. Like nothing you have ever built – or anyone. It must be as though all the styles from all the countries throughout time have collided together. That they've bonded to make something new."

He looked down at his drawings, frustrated. "That's not what it looks like here, but," he tapped his head: "Up here it does – here there's all sorts of incredible things going on – we've just got to work on getting it out there so we can all share it."

He stared over at me. "Bes!" Made me jump.

I didn't think he knew I was there. But it was only a small hut so how could he not?

"We need to start stock piling – there's preliminary work to do of course – foundations and so on," he sounded vague over the detail – wafting at it like a cloud of midges. "But we'll soon need stone – all the colours, separated out. And shells, make sure you bring plenty of them. Take who you need – but no-one who's any use for the building work. Take women, the old."

It seemed many of the crew had taken advantage of the lunch break to scavenge the shore for herring gull feathers. That afternoon there was a sudden outbreak of them, like a childhood craze which sweeps the playground. By the end of that first day on the site every third person you saw sported a gull feather. Within the week more or less everyone wore one – in their hair, at a jaunty angle in their hat, or pinned to their jacket like a brooch.

There must have been some pretty bald gulls around the place. I mean, you can find these feathers fairly easily, but it struck me that to provide so many quickly some of the fishermen amongst us must have been netting the birds.

They were a tough crowd to impress, the island lot. Dour, stoic and resigned to their place in the world. There was an island face – a typical mug which we knew meant someone was from the same patch we were. Centuries of inbreeding sure – but more than that, it came from a shared burden.

It was oblong, jowly, emotionless – like a cow chewing the cud.

The prevailing mood among these parts is phlegmatic. It is an attitude a tribe adopts when it witnesses nothing faster than coastal erosion for millennia. And we realise, despite our aspirations, that nothing is likely to change much in the future as we all roost here, waiting to evolve. So we hunker down. Accept things as they are.

If islanders have a general trait it is an acceptance of their own obscurity. That path represents maturity, a strength which will stand up against the rigours of the world. Anything else is to be mocked or ignored.

Wanting to be noticed is putting on airs. Expecting change? That is to disregard the countless lessons of the waves and wind, their action on the rock.

All of this provided stony ground for John Love's seed to grow upon. But then, as any botanist will tell you, some plants thrive on stony ground.

Grape vines for example.

We couldn't drink champagne if it weren't for poor soil.

Love made time for their wants – that seemed to be the trade-off. Many hours he spent working the queue outside the site. Each feathered invalid received an audience, a lightning bolt to the brain from his hand which left them reeling, sometimes caused them to collapse or vomit, but always had them professing themselves much better thank you.

With children he was particularly intense – dandling them on his knee, caressing their crowns with the butterfly palm of his hand. Tousled they were like favourite collies. But, though they were given licence, they sensed his essential seriousness and didn't dick about too much in his presence – naturally wary perhaps of the wrap around the lug they'd been promised by their parents if they misbehaved.

Many were sick of course, their playfulness hobbled by pain or infirmity. Love healed them all – sending them sprawling and puking, swivel eyed, rising weakly to their feet in rapture and approval.

One kid I remember was Natalie. Tiny she was, as if she could have been mine, except that she had ginger hair – what there was left of it. Her blood, it turned out, was curdled by leukaemia.

She had warts on her hands and her skin was translucent as greaseproof paper.

Propped up on a bench in the queue she asked me in a pygmy shrew squeak if I wouldn't mind opening her packet of crisps. I could have half, she said, if I would open them for her.

It's not such a tough gig opening a crisp packet, a fifty per cent cut seemed kind of steep, but I'd been a sickly child myself and knew what it was to be low on bargaining power.

Love relished getting his hands on Natalie. Wafer thin sylph, you feared would blow away like a toffee wrapper in the wind as he paraded her before the gathering.

Her parents, worn with worry, fidgeting with hope, took on supporting roles.

Love chanted at her in lost languages and blew acrid smoke over her from a clay pipe. He made her tiny frame jolt south with a caress of his fingertips and yelled: "Her cells are healed, her blood is one, the malign forces are in full retreat – you'll see."

"But the doctors," stammered her dad, "they couldn't offer us any hope."

"What do they know?" demanded Love. "These dissectors of meat, creting away at a pad of adenoids. Do they think that's all there is to the mysteries? There's more ails flesh than you can cut with a knife."

And then: thank-you, thank-you. Tears of fearful thank-you as they led her away. Another triumph.

And because children when they are sick are so gossamer and needful, and because she reminded me of me, and because there are times when the world does need miracles – for a short while I hated John Love.

The gap between perception and something you could rest your beer mug on, that's the crevice people fell down.

Perhaps they were cured by what Love did for them – who am I to say? Maybe there was something more in the bottles of green gunk than I thought I put there?

Cures can be found in the strangest of natural crannies. The beaver was hunted to extinction in Britain during the 14th century due to the pain relieving properties of the secretions from its anal glands.

One would have to be in a whole world of pain, that's all I'd say.

The fabulous building grew with surprising vigour. Vital as bean sprouts. It sprung one day from dirt and within a month was preposterously large.

The craftsmen muttered grim incantations about foundations and sandy soil yet seemed to dig down deeper than any building I'd seen constructed before on the island.

Made me think they must be planning to go up a long way too.

Cautious they moved like crabs with a bird in the air, scattered over the sandy sockets in the earth then settled still as death to gauge and probe.

I wasn't party really to the blueprints. After a long day's giving directions and healing the sick Love said little to me about his plans as we sat together in the snug caravan we knew as home. He talked about nothing – about ideas and books he'd read. He pumped me for ever more detail on the island's character and history, its geography and nature. Most of all he wanted to know about the individual people – their past, their relationships with one another, those things which moved them to love or to despair.

I told him too. It seemed the thing to do. And, with all the weight of work going on, and me just gathering stones together, it was a service I could perform. Something of value to him. To show him I still mattered.

So the evenings passed in indolence but during the days we worked hard and the thing grew.

We did not work on a small scale, yet the progress was rapid. There were many hands turned to the task, and we seemed to suffer none of the incomprehensible hold ups which conspired to stall normal building projects on the island. Tools never lay idle for weeks waiting for fresh funds to arrive. The shell of our building did not hang skeletal and unfinished, shrugging its shoulders and peering at us through the empty sockets of its soulless windows as the men drank tea and talked of shagging.

We weren't for stopping. We were for pressing on.

As far as the supply of construction materials went Love did not seem to mind too much what we used. He made his specifications with a sweep of his hand and when we ran out of red brick for a while white would do. When these were in short supply then swift advances were made using breeze blocks. It looked unlovely, but, as Love told us, more would be done with plaster and render, with colour and decoration.

Work there was, and many of us were there simply to soak up the joy of doing it and the wonder of what we'd see when the toil was over.

The grass swath on which we were building was maybe two hundred feet wide and stretched out of sight either way you looked along it. One side was boarded by the silver ribbon of threadbare tarmac we called the Coast Road, the other by the stark pebble shore, shark grey under the clouds. Then there was the sea, another ribbon. Ours was a landscape made of strips; it would have been fairly easy to paint I'm sure, if you had an inclination and a box of watercolours.

In this new reality we all had roles.

My job was to marshal some of the women and the older men whose skills did not lie in construction and collect stone from the shore. There was plenty to go at.

We gathered buckets, wicker baskets, trugs for making cement and with them trailed to the shore where we pecked among rocks, carefully grading by size and colour then hauling our loads back up to the storage area marked off in boundary tape on the mud sodden site. We made piles of our strange haul alongside the stacks of more traditional requisites which had been gifted by the hardware store, the plant hire firm and by builder's yards around the island. There were sand and cement bags, breeze blocks, bricks, lintels and joists, the lengths of timber and the scaffolding poles.

Our graded piles of rock grew daily. Occasionally someone would compliment us on them. Flange maybe, who had established himself as chief Rat, would walk round them saying "That's a lot of rock there. Our lads would have been proud to scavenge them lot."

Or Audrey perhaps, in green wellies – queen, for now, of all she surveyed.

"Now – well done. I just came over to tell you how much we appreciate how well you're doing. All the jobs are important you know. So give yourselves a pat on the back."

I didn't like it when people said our piles of rock were splendid. They hadn't earned the right it seemed to me. My gang of growthy old girls and myopic codgers knew how hard it was to haul stone up the beach – we didn't need anyone to tell us 'good boy.'

Though our pebble piles grew daily the store on the island's endless shore never diminished – and I was proud of her natural bounty – that we could do our worst and make no impact. This resource made building Love's vast structure possible I think – that and the rubble the rats ferried back from the tip – then broke down forensically into its constituent parts, ready to be repurposed to our baffling ends.

A couple of weeks into the project a vast web of sandy foundations were underway; they spread out before us like first world war trenches under the silver skies of northern Europe.

John Love turned up an hour early one morning toting a carrier bag. Me tagging along behind him like a Jack Russell.

The early shift was still gathered round the grubby canvas of the mess tent having a brew.

They watched curious as, without ceremony, Love scrambled down a set of aluminium steps into the trenches.

It had rained the night before, same as every night, and water pooled brightly on the floor of the earthworks, as if to make them even more like a picture postcard from the Somme.

Love edged his particular way through the grime to a point at the heart of the imagined structure. He upended the bag and something white, smaller than a football, fell with an empty clack at his feet.

Later he supervised as concrete was poured over that bare patch of ground.

Say a meteor was to arrive now. Travelling towards our speck of earth many times faster than the fastest bullet. We would not see it until it warmed up in the earth's atmosphere, which would be about a second before it hit.

The air beneath it would be compressed so hard that the surface temperature would rise to around ten times that of the surface of the sun.

In an instant everything would be more than gone. All of us. Love, his building, the island on which it sat, the sea around us, would be flying rock and superheated gasses. Nothing more.

Sometimes I wish that would happen.

XIII

Things progressed sufficient to Love's ends – whatever his plans amounted to beyond some half-imagined scribbles on scrap paper. As far as the building work went he continued to be flexible, agreeing immediately to whatever alterations needed to be made for practical reasons.

We had been grafting for maybe five weeks. My gang assembled as we always did at seven thirty in a corner of the taped off builder's yard with its heaps of sundries and requisites hulked like farm animals, forlorn in a field.

There were eight of us and I marshalled my workforce into groups of two, manhandling them like oversized chess pieces in a pub beer garden.

To each pair I gave a rock from one of the existing piles – this was what they were foraging for that day. It was no random decision. I was making full use of my management A-level from the school of the streets, BA in personnel studies from the University of life, MSc in hard knocks, doctorate in… You get the idea.

Penina and Edna were both in their eighties. Sisters. Spinsters. They'd been keen to help – followers of Love from the start – they'd possessed what passed for a spiritual life on the island before Love's arrival – reading tea leaves, peering at palms and so on. You might have thought these mistresses of chiromancy would have been sneeped at having their clothes so comprehensively stolen but no. They were overjoyed by Love's presence in that sunny open way that old ladies have.

They weren't much cop at heavy lifting mind you, which is why I got lumbered with 'em.

They were frail it's true but Penny still had her eyes and they found themselves with more or less a full set of marbles between them. I gave them a palm sized white flint, pearlescent and pretty, which seemed to glow a little from inside.

"Oh, lovely," said Penny. "It's special is that, it's a work of nature."

It was a rare rock as far as this beach went, they would have to forage up and down a mile in either direction to gather a modest basket each – which was good as that was all they could carry.

Dora and Harris were fitter and had ten years or so on the old girls. They were on peach granite which was scattered around in relative plenty.

Black basalt: Edgar and Jimmy, the two raddled old topes from the Fisherman's – wheezing and rheumy eyed they remained curiously uncured by Love's regular attentions – though to listen to them they were fit to run a marathon these days.

They could manage the larger lumps of dense black stone which could be found in brooding isolation along the shore.

Grey rock we didn't bother with at present, having hauled a big enough pile of that off the beach already to decorate ten enormous follies.

My favourite purple stone I kept for Frankie the rat and I.

She'd been put on my team to prove her cure was holding up and she could indeed leave her chair in short bursts of wobbly energy to accompany me on spotting missions for the rich, dark lavender stone which could be found here in rare lumps, anything up to the size of a child's head.

I didn't mind the work, I thought, as we set off across the mud, which had once been grass, down towards the pebble beach for the morning's gathering. The work was curiously relaxing, the days swam by like ducks. Foraging was what I had always done and the materials I had sought were difficult to find. Now, here I was being asked to source stuff which was plentiful and obvious.

The routine we had developed was a slow, regular trudge between breaks: mid-morning, lunch, mid-afternoon, then down the pub. I could get used to this – it had its charms. I felt more a part of something constructive than I had in a long while and I think the others felt it too – not only my gang, everyone.

There's something cathartic in the process of work – no matter what you are doing or what it's for.

That day would have been much like the others, steeped in the satisfaction of our slowly growing heaps of stone, except that at elevenses I realised half way through my doughnut that I'd forgotten my sou'wester.

Bollocks. I toyed briefly with the notion of scaring up a different hat to collect Love's dosh when it came pouring in during the post lunch healing session – there would be plenty of hard hats around the place which would have greater capacity. Or, we could try a different style of cash register entirely – say a cardboard box.

But no, a pattern had been established, and the doing of things a regular and repeated way was important to John Love.

Established behaviour patterns – bursting people out of these patterns in ways which unnerved them.

So I went home to fetch the hat.

And Glazier came too. Why, if you ask me now, I'm not sure.

It's never taken two men to carry a hat – however feeble the chaps, however substantial the headgear.

You could even wear the thing on the return journey and bring something else back with you as well.

But two of us went. I think maybe Glazier was bored. While I relished the repetitive nature of my work he found his frankly dull. On the way to the caravan he confided in me his latest set of woes – which were, at least, different ones from those he had shared with me during our one-sided conversations in the past.

"Site services manager," he grumbled, "means I make sure the coffee doesn't run out and that there's enough soft bog roll available in the shithouse."

It wasn't true, he marshalled the mechanics in charge of the upkeep of plant and machinery. But he felt his star had fallen somewhat, perhaps because he lacked the necessary skillset to thrive in a construction environment.

"What it's taught me is how his attitude to you can change if you become less use to him. I used to be *for* something. I was his way of getting to know the people. But he's done that now. So what am I for?

"No one round here's that impressed that he's palled up with the black man. I stopped being black round here a long time ago. It's not an issue except to the occasional ale can at closing time. I remember when it at least used to get me the odd shag. If Love needs to show how much he cares for freaks he's got you. If he needs a way in he has

Barbara. If he's after sensible advice he's got Audrey. Muscle – the rats. So what am I for then?"

And I'm thinking: What d'you mean freak? You cheeky fucker.

I remember when Glazier was young – he and his mates, who aren't around here anymore, were the laser dot of attention for everyone we knew. Which was everyone who mattered in the whole of the world. The girls would gossip about Glazier and his boys as if they were pop stars. Where they'd been on any given night, what they were up to, who they'd shagged or chucked or fought with.

They were the subject of discussion and analysis even for those who did not know them personally – who just knew of them. In that respect, at 16 years old, Glazier was as near as you can get on this island to being famous. He was famous for round here.

His tumble to bog standard did not happen swiftly like Icarus falling, yet it happened in the end.

"It felt like being in a glider," he once told me in reflective mood over a pint at the Fisherman's. "I was in the air but after a while the ground got nearer. Then I realised I was back on the floor like everyone else."

I knew something was out of kilter the moment we arrived at the van. The curtains were closed. I left them open. The plant pot where I keep the key had been shifted slightly. Someone was at home, there were only two of us in residence and it wasn't me so you didn't have to be in the CID. I gave the door a tiny shove and it swung open.

"Hey," asked Glazier. "You leave it like that?" I didn't answer.

I made a bit of a racket going in – out of politeness; it's not hard to do in a mobile home, because every heavy tread you take sounds like the finale of Lord of the Dance.

Love popped his head round the bedroom door like a startled cat. He looked tousled and flushed as if woken from a nap.

"What are you doing here?" he said, a bit brusquely I thought, given it was my bedroom from which he was poking his kite.

"We're just picking up a couple of things," Glazier told him, sounding a tad defensive. "The little guy was heading over here and I came for the walk."

I headed over to the foot locker where I kept the sou'wester, put it on.

"Oh yeah," said Love, vaguely. "The healing – I'll be over in half an hour."

And the interview appeared to be over. That would have been it I do believe – if we hadn't heard Audrey's voice, steady and distinct from inside the bedroom.

"Tell them I'll be over too if they need a hand with sorting out the crowds."

We got her message clear enough. Love came all the way out of the room, looking as near as I'd ever seen to sheepish. She followed him out. Proud she was, glowing the way people like us, plain people, do when we have been graced by the figures of beauty.

And seeing her there with him I felt something in me I thought I was beyond. I felt the soul-decaying sting of sexual jealousy.

"What are you doing?" yelled Glazier – raw and unvarnished. It wasn't clear whether he was talking to Love, Audrey, or both of them. "Why the fuck's she here with you?" he demanded directly of John Love – stabbing a digit at Audrey. She was fazed, you could see, by the unalloyed fury.

She'd perhaps planned to be brazen – more than that. She'd had a little twinkling tiara perched on her head, her position was altered and enhanced. It wasn't fair that this was being challenged so soon and so radically. It wasn't right.

I was reeling. I was feeling feelings I didn't think I ought to feel. Ones I thought I wasn't chemically capable of.

Just when you think you have this human being business under control it comes back and nips you on the arse.

"I'm here, with John." Audrey's voice all quavery. Un-Audrey-like and intense. "We're here together – John, aren't we?"

We all looked at John.

He looked back at us blankly.

I'm not sure what I'd expected – conjuring tricks, tantrums. But whatever it was, it wasn't nothing.

His stillness defused us, made us feel silly. His iced inscrutability was unnerving – the cold black-run of his gaze would have chilled even the most experienced emotional skier.

Glazier shouted a couple more things at him about betrayal,

about knowing who your friends are; realised suddenly he probably sounded like a jilted suitor and stalked off back towards the site.

Audrey remonstrated with him too. Why hadn't he stood up for her? Why hadn't he explained about *them*?

But her accusations slid off the sheer sides of his glassy impassivity.

Still he was still. Still silent. Until she went too.

Love turned to me. Grinned.

"That one," he said, "I learned from you."

He didn't want to talk much. I suppose he might have been embarrassed. I'd hypothesise I might feel that way in a similar situation.

He seemed pleased enough with himself mind you – just quiet.

He slipped back inside my bedroom which seemed to stink of sex, now I knew. He rummaged in his trunk and came up with a book which had a photo of strangely fangled towers on the cover.

"I'll be in here recharging my batteries until it's time for the healing," he said. "The people you mentioned the other night – the ones whose problems are more of the nervous variety – I'll take them first – it gives the others hope, which is a thing to have…" his voice trailed off as he sat under the window and opened his book. I realised I was dismissed.

Near as I could tell Glazier must have rushed straight off and told Barbara without passing go or collecting his two hundred quid. Outrage doesn't seem so real unless you have someone to share it with. I was feeling angry and conflicted, betrayed and bruised – all of those American TV show things. But I couldn't tell him and he knew if he offloaded on Barbara then he'd have a pain buddy.

I found them in the planning hut at the site. The place where Love showed his fag packet dreams to the craftsmen and they wrestled to turn them into something which wouldn't fall in a big heap when the wind blew.

Barbara was crying. Glazier was pretending he had something in his eye. They didn't really notice me slip in.

She was spitting bitterness at him: "If he's lied about that, what else isn't true? How do we know what he is – or what he wants us for? It's not just this – I've had these feelings for a while. He just uses us – only Audrey's so sad and desperate, so in need of a cock."

"Are you saying you wouldn't have?"

"We're not talking about me – we're talking about him. Things here were okay before. Well weren't they? What have we really got now? Ask yourself – what value has he added to our lives? If he didn't want me then why couldn't he let me know himself? He owed me that. The things I've done for him. The support, the love."

They're stewing these two. Rocking like skiffs on a bad day at sea. They neither of them seem to know what they want.

"I don't know what I believe," Glazier admits to her and to himself. "I only know I need him – the feeling he gives me. I don't know what he wants from us, but he makes me feel like I've found something I lost a long time ago or maybe never had, no time, ever."

"What does she know? Barbara demanded. "What does she have to give him? Knotted up little spider of a woman. Wound so tight she could snap. What can she offer a man?"

Jealousy. It can do rum things to your chemical cocktail. Her words stirred me I'll admit. I had been looking for someone to hate and now I'd found 'em.

I hated her. And him. The pair of them in here plotting against the one good thing ever to happen on this guano encrusted rubbish tip, this shit-heap sitting on a silted sea, this oafery, this nothingness, this island.

"It's right what you say," Glazier admitted softly. "And if we don't believe in what he's doing then we should do something."

"We have to – there's other people at stake. People's lives – all those ones who trust him to heal them. All those giving him their money."

Glazier couldn't go this far – not yet.

"He does heal them surely? And the other things – I've seen him read minds, the thing we all saw at the party – what he became."

Doubt just made Barbara harder – it wasn't about John Love, I saw, this disenchantment. She'd had plenty of time to fill up a well of distrust in which to drown men as a group.

The cloying, groping, needy, hateful bastards. And who's to say they didn't deserve it?

I remember she told me once while drunk: "All intercourse is rape. All sex is the man raping the woman – I read that somewhere. Someone said it."

Andrea Dworkin. Though I'm not sure she really meant it.

"We have to show them what he is," she told Glazier. "Who knows otherwise what he'll do? Do you want your life dictated by his whims? You used to be so free."

Glazier shaking his head: "I was never free – I was always here, the whole of my life I was here. I thought he showed me other ways of being free."

She held him, she let him feel her softness as he had before and other men had.

"We have to question," she told him as she hugged him. "Is it real? We need to ask him. When he's with the others. Prove it."

"I hate being an adult," said Glazier. "There are so many ways to cover yourself in shame when you're a grown man. Just having a sexuality – that's enough to do it straight off."

We sat mute for a while, the three of us in the silent hut, faces turned tangerine by the battery lamp. Our closeness felt comforting. We could have been anywhere in time. Say a year ago when none of this had happened and our lives seemed predictable as a whelk's.

Later, as I sat scarfing back doughnuts at a trestle table in the mess area, Audrey found me. She'd been helping pile out steaming heaps of lunchtime comfort food onto the plates of rats and young islanders – fuelling the engine room of this vast and growing construction project. They had worked hard and wanted to fill up on nebulous mashed potato, omelettes, bacon, meat pies, thick dark gravy, mushy peas.

Theirs, it seemed to me, was an enviable life. They worked hard to develop an appetite, then satiated it. They had the self-assurance of youth to protect them from any notion that they were heading in the wrong direction. For what did it matter? When you have so much time at your disposal to turn around and try another route then why not just relish the view?

Audrey wasn't really one of the dinner ladies. She'd been helping out in the manner that a princess might feed the troops once or twice during a war – still wearing her crown and only for as long as the cameras were there. Then on to the next engagement – keeping up morale.

"You must all surely have known?" she said crossly, sitting neatly next to me with a mineral water and an apple. "He could hardly have made it any more obvious over the last few weeks – his affection for me. I've been a little embarrassed about it myself to be truthful – but when you're drawn to someone. And why shouldn't we?" she went on suddenly defensive. "I'm thirty-seven. I've worked hard all my life at my career – so much so that I might have neglected a part of myself."

I just tucked into my doughnuts. It wasn't that I was disinterested and I didn't particularly wish to appear ignorant. It's just that gathering stones together is hard work, and after you've done it you need saturated fats, sugars – all the main food groups, bar alcohol, which had to wait until clocking off time.

I didn't know who was right – perhaps they all were, or none of them at all. Audrey was only doing what the rest of the island yearned to do – she had got as close to him as one human being could get to another – in a physical sense anyway. But that was bound to make the rest of us sting – those who loved him, who had invested in him and would do whatever he asked, whatever we thought he wanted.

He knew how we felt – he'd made us feel that way. In my heart I understood this squabbling would pass, the way rough weather does. Soon we would all remember what we had together – wholesome as an apple, with Love as its core.

When Paul Repton Glazier walked south down the shore that Tuesday afternoon towards the gathering at John Love's healing I believed he had come to join us and reconcile himself with the man who had shown us a world beyond the one we inhabited.

I saw his approach as the chance to normalise a relationship which had become strained between the two of them and so had shaken us all. As if he had brushed a cobweb. As if we were flies on that web.

I can't surely say what Glazier had been feeling. I am not Glazier. But I had watched him, as I watch everyone. We all need a hobby. And I believed, that, whatever his torment, his was a soul deep and wise enough to shrug off the fleshy concerns, the cocks and tits and fannies we're all forced to care about, and see that there was something in life more interesting than sex. If I was prepared to do it, why not him?

Yet when he drew close I could see he had come to war.

I don't think the others knew. Even Love if I'm honest. All his closely observed reveals didn't help him on this one. Glazier wasn't giving tongue show or fidgeting his hands behind his back. He seemed as calm and relaxed as a bloke out for a constitutional with his dog, just before he realises he forgot the dog.

What gave me the tell was that Glazier was grinning like a variety show chimp. And this was not a grinner. I'd seen him when he met his kids off the National Express, when he was in the process of pulling a girl he'd been after for months, on his wedding day. This was not a bloke who expressed happiness with a display of National Health dentistry.

"Welcome." John Love broke off from his hands on treatment of Iris Slack's impetigo. "Join us – I'm sure your spirit can lift us higher."

There were murmurs of approval, the odd cheer and even a semi-whoop, the nearest a northern crowd is ever going to get to evangelical. We mostly liked Glazier you see – he had never done anything to us to make us not like him.

"I've come for a reason," he said grimly. "And it's not baffling little old ladies into chucking away their hearing aids."

Pulled Love up sharp did that – the acid notion of impropriety.

He turned calmly to Glazier, bathed him in a big grin.

"Don't worry," he told him. "I can feel something's troubling you – don't let it. We're here for you, all of us; we'll see you healed."

There were nods and mutters of approval.

"You've nothing to heal me with," griped Glazier. "I don't buy your shite so that's all you had. Gone."

Love seemed so calm. It shimmered from him. He seemed so pure. I know the word, the word is holy. John Love was a holy man.

It was wrong of anyone to be attacking him, dragging him down to their petty level with bitter little names and behind-backs. But here was Glazier, allowing his sordid dispute over sex to get in the way of all the good which had been going on.

"You're a fraud," said Glazier – loud and clear over the gulls and the breeze, over the distant endless rattle of the tide on the stones.

"You're a crook."

Iris Slack – his most recent patient, skinny, twin set, unfortunately marked – barked in derision.

"The things that man has done for me, and for the rest of us, have been little short of a miracle, young man," she told him, prim and steely. "He has brought back my daughter to me who I haven't seen in ten years since the cancer took her. Have you any idea what that means to me? Of course you haven't. You can't do.

"You've no right to get involved here – you don't belong here anyway – we put up with you, accept you – and this is what you give us back."

"I have proof," Glazier smiling again.

"What proof?" yelled Iris. "You mongrel. What proof?"

It was then I noticed what Glazier had in his hands. A document folder, flat and matt black – he waved it at us – goodbye, goodbye.

"I've been reading the newspapers," he said. "I've kept some cuttings."

Thinking about it now – he can't have been the only one to have read any local press – little old ladies dived head first into the stuff and they were among John Love's greatest fans.

The material he had in that folder could not have been such unexpected news. But it felt like a blade, it felt like a bullet. We knew fear and savoured the dull reek of blood at the back of our throats like animals in an abattoir.

He opened the folder and began to read.

"Magician, hounded out of Hardcastle. Police were investigating today after a near riot in the rural village of Hardcastle, which was sparked when an itinerant magician convinced locals their dead relatives had come back from the grave to visit them.

"Civic leaders spoke of a disturbing mass hallucination in which followers of a preacher, recently arrived in the area, gathered in a noisy celebration in the car park outside the Civic Hall, claiming to be communicating with loved ones who had passed away."

He thumbed over to the next shred of newsprint.

"Sea on fire claim. Coastguards have denied reports of an oil spill offshore as Beerswill residents bombarded the Herald office with claims that the ocean was ablaze on Friday night.

"Mystery surrounds reports of the conflagration which eye-witnesses said could be seen miles from the shore. They described fire which seemed to flow into the air like a tower of flame."

Glazier glanced up briefly to be sure he was marshalling our attention, carried on.

"Riddle of the missing frogs. Every frog in Boretown has disappeared overnight say alarmed naturalists. "Local residents pin the blame on a stranger to the area whose new age therapy sessions on the village green had been widely popular over the last few days..."

"He's a one man natural disaster," yelled Glazier gleefully. "Like a human oil slick. And there's other stuff too – messing with people's minds. He's ripped down the coast here causing chaos in quiet communities, places where people lived blameless lives. They didn't ask for whatever it is he's selling. Yes, selling, because, believe me, there will be a bill. Stopping clocks, communicating with the dead, turning conjuring tricks with the elements as if nature was a kids' magic set. But all of this stuff – it depends upon what you see. I'll bet if we were to leave this island now – cross the bridge and take a bus up to Boretown we'd find frogs hopping around the place like fleas on a sick dog – and there'd be no towers of flame off Beerswill either."

We looked at Love. He was doing less than nothing. His eyes half closed, his head back. Only thing moving was his hair, which had got rather long and shaggy during his time on the island, still golden though – still vibrant so you wouldn't squander your conditioner on it.

"I know you," whispered John Love.

Glazier looked taken aback. Didn't know whether to embark on a voyage on the good ship Bleeding Obvious, for fear of hidden hazards: desolate sandbanks, blind and groping, with only mussels for company.

"We have met before," said Love. "Our journeys have intersected. Not here, not now. But sometime. I know you, and that is why you fear me."

"Oh here we go," yelled Glazier, light peeping over the horizon. "Here's a new one, past lives – don't think we've heard this one before folks – though I've no doubt it crops up in the cuttings somewhere – or if not these then the others from wherever else he's been spreading his lies. Who knows where he's been over the years – those times when he's not been locked up, mind. We've never met before this, for the record – but I'm sure there's been plenty of mugs like me – empty and desperate, willing to grab any life belt that got chucked at them in the storm."

Then Love spoke. "I know you and I know your evil. It is deep and basic, it is what you are for. There is no other purpose to your being here than what we see today. And now we have a choice."

And he turned away from Glazier to address the rest of us.

"We can climb higher with the project, build and progress – see where it takes us, and believe me, that is a journey I will take with you. Or I can leave, things will return to the way they were. This creature will have won and nothing will have altered. Perhaps it's better the fellow you know?"

Resonated in our heads, that sentence. Even though he hadn't said the word. Sometimes I could see the cogs. Look closely at a Canaletto and it isn't light and water, boats and beauty at all, just paint which any of us could have applied, had we the skill.

But then all insight was gone and I felt only rage. Fury. That the only precious thing to happen here as long as I had lived was about to be snatched away thanks to some grubby scraps of newsprint and a rootless man who had no concept of what he was doing to me. To all of us.

And I swear that, when I threw my arm out towards Glazier, it was to force back his objections.

I did not know the stone was in my hand.

And that stone I did not know I'd thrown described a crippled arc through troubled air. It wasn't a big one, common blue slate, the size, the shape, the pregnant smoothness of a hen's egg.

It hit Glazier just below the left kneecap.

He let out a hollow yap of anger and surprise.

"Who fucking threw that?" he wanted to know.

Commanding he sounded, authority thwarted like a school gym master who's just had a face full of football.

"Come here and I'll stuff it down your throat."

But it had hobbled him, my rock, and he hopped about a little on his one good foot, ungainly on the shore where no-one ever looked sure footed on two.

"You fuckers," he spat, sounding suddenly less sure. "I knew I couldn't count on you when the weather turned."

Which was when the second stone hit him. Clack. A good one on the side of the head. It was larger than mine and thrown harder, with more venom, or desperation perhaps.

It spun him half a reel on his one dancing foot, thumping him drunk and baffled on his arse like a sack of spuds. Two, four, half a dozen more stones – none of which hit Glazier, just pinged off the rocks around him, flipping back up and off down the beach. Then another one caught him on the ricochet, thump up into the stomach – a confused yelp, still dazed from the shot to the head.

Then more stones and many in a rattle, most of them missed, were thrown to miss, same way soldiers on a battlefield shoot wide – hard wired to cherish human life, not destroy it. But some of those stones, like mine, found their target, straight and pure, they sought out Glazier where he lay: vincible, trembling.

At first he was angry, attacking the rocks as if to force them back with his body – still bellowing his disappointment in us; the island, this whole thing: this life which was leaving him swiftly and surprisingly soon. Next he became fearful. Blood pumped from a cut to his head, covering the marks on his face as he held his hands up uselessly against the onslaught. He ducked limp as a beaten boxer, shots wracked his torso and clattered off his arms and legs. He stumbled a little way back over the beach until, caught soundly again on the forehead, he lay, unable to move. All his defiance gone. Now when each stone hit he barely yelped, the sound he made was involuntary and without purpose – air expelled from his body.

The stones kept coming. After a while he stopped making sound, so it seemed that was the end. But then he roused himself for a moment, squirmed where he lay like a drunk starting himself awake, and shouted: "Michael…Anthony!"

A while after that the flow of the rocks slowed, the way rain does after a storm, until it was just drizzle. Then nothing.

By the time they stopped throwing the body was more or less covered. You could see what it was but only from the shape of the mound and the extremities poking out.

It was as if Glazier's children had played a trick on him, burying him in the sand on a seaside holiday.

Iris Slack emerged from the crowd, made an ungainly trip over to take a closer look. She knelt down by Glazier's head. It was twisted sideways, gory. Its blind eyes shut.

"Fucking nigger," she told it calmly.

John Love said nothing. No one else spoke either. There didn't seem much that needed saying. For once my silence made me part of the majority.

One or two folk went over to review their handiwork but most simply drifted away. They headed back to the building site; some of the more sensitive knocked off for the day.

I didn't think much about what we had done, not for a good while. I imagine other people tried the same tactic. But it kept sidling up on you anyway, at times when you weren't thinking about much. That gap in our heads on the edge of sleep say – that's where Glazier lived now.

XIV

Our building was beginning to look like something remarkable. I know there have been grander constructions: taller, better proportioned, more architecturally pleasing. But ours had a verve and off-kilter ambition. It wasn't trying to be anything except itself. And that was a thing which had never existed before.

I loved to watch John direct his workforce – central and commanding, talking while people listened. He gave instructions and sketched towers in the air while the skilled men by his side paid close attention and took notes. Because of what he said things would happen – big solid things which made a difference in the real world.

Which of us could not thrill to that?

Me particularly, I admit it. Leadership has never been part of my skill set. The most noise I ever made, as a teenager playing snare drum in a poor quality punk rock band, was made from the rear of the stage while others took the applause.

Love's fag packet plans had taken on a glorious reality. My islanders had prosecuted his vision with vigour and spirit.

The construction spread out across the muddy plain deep as we could manage and as wide as the ocean would let it. But it was into the sky where we made our grandest incursion. Pillars and totems and towers like a model village Manhattan.

There was a great emphasis on decoration. We had a whole section working on the stone carving. We were lucky to have a handful of people who were members of the art society. Most were watercolourists but some had experience of sculpting. They were serious people, if limited. They had a strong basic grasp of their trade.

Everyone on our site who had ever made a clay pot at school was on the team. Any curious lump of stone our sources managed to turn up was sent for carving.

Huge heads became the speciality, gurning and grinning, empty eyes bulging at nothing.

The sculptors carved a wooden sign reading: 'Artworks' and hung it on a pole in their domain. I found comfort in their company. There was the unmistakable clack and stone chip of work taking place. They knew the architecture of splintering stone and the maths of making beauty but their aim was to create art, and that is always pure.

The finished sculptures were scattered about the site from early on, as if to encourage the craftsmen to greater freedom and creativity. It wasn't unusual to find a section of the building which was little more than foundation or scaffold, which already had a row of leering sightless gargoyles keeping watch over it.

When a wall or tower went up, there was immediately more decoration. While my team delved into our hard won hoard of coloured pebbles to give the wall a patterned facia, the art team worked with stone or clay to construct filigree and statuary for the cornice. They worked on window arches, doorframes too, using swirls and caprices which echoed ancient cultures – the other worlds of China, Asia, the Americas.

Sometimes, at Love's direction, pillars of stone were built up against the sides of a tower and carved, once in place, into string-bean men and small breasted women with strange headgear. Unlikely serpents coiled around the shafts and spires of the building's high rise.

The towers grew tall and our work took us to the tops of them, those of us who had a head for it, tricking them out in precious stones. I would sit on the peak of the tallest, peering out like a gargoyle from the crenellations. Misplaced in my thoughts.

I remember, as a small child, I hated to be tucked up in bed. To me it was a parting – like a little death. I would rather face what horrors the night might hold, stoic and alone, than have the heartbreak of broken hugs and the memory of a kiss.

I don't know what made me think of that, up there on the tower, but it clung to me as I mulled over what we were about.

That high up, the wind made my eyes water. The tower swayed gently, and the work below seemed to matter less. I felt unconnected to the island, as if I was passing over the place in an aeroplane, on my way to somewhere posh. I would glance out of the window and see us winking grimly in the sackcloth sea. And I'd wonder what the place was and what manner of people lived there.

Sometimes, when planes pass over the island, I wave. Even though I'm a grown-up I still do that. So long as no one else is around.

From up here I can see the place taking shape. This palace or temple – whatever it is we have been pouring our soul into these weeks. I can see a shape nobody on the ground could see – it shows there must be some plan. However unique the individual buildings may be, there is order.

We seemed to be building towards a focal point at the centre, with concentric layers, broken by a garden here, a tower there, but always leading inwards to the bullseye.

Close to this central point was a white tower – a tall and imposing stylus in our empty town.

The lower buildings had walls, banks and ornamentations which were not always precise in their outline. Poured from concrete they had the look of worn stone, hounded through time by the waves and the wind.

Often there was decoration. Statues of animals perhaps, up on the walls – a lion with wings, a bull with a horned, outsized demon head.

Love had encouraged planting between the buildings. Topsoil had been brought. Back gardens, nurseries, glasshouses had been raided for greenery. Now plants poked out between the half-finished walls and strangely fangled statuary.

The planting was lush and sub-tropical: yuccas and pampas grass, tree ferns and temperate palms. Sheltered from the worst of the wind it seemed to be doing well enough.

All of our structures had internal rooms; some were linked already by squat shell lined tunnels under the ground – which seemed roomy enough for me but were giving the others cricked necks.

In the centre of our creation was a flat-topped pyramid. It's lower level was decked already with a multi-coloured facade of chipped pottery and glass from the tip. A sea of greens and blues, a fire of red and orange. Gold and yellow. Black and cream. The top three levels were pure white with glass mirrors for steps.

It was a lovely thing. Whatever it was.

A gull flapped off the pitched roof above me. Startled me. I felt daft. Fucking hell and all that.

I shifted my weight and a loose rock plapped from under the flap of my sweaty palm and trickled off the edge of the scaffold.

And as I watched it tumble, ricket and flail end over endlessly towards the people below I found myself willing it away from their helpless softness. Delighted as a final cannon pinged it high over some miniscule bloke's head and he ducked to yell baffled obscenities at me, far away.

And I was thankful, grateful, that this person, who I could not identify because of the distance and his dashing for cover, has escaped without harm. Because it is natural and it is right for us to love each other unconditionally.

That is what I believe.

Up in my eyrie I watched the shape of people moving. The way the specs gathered and converged with purpose – lines formed, huddles developed and scattered again.

Then I saw the pattern change. A drift of bodies towards the shore. A gathering around a single spec beside the sea. And something larger in the water – what was it? Couldn't see.

So I scrambled down the ad hoc scaffold with its swinging gates and mislaid planks, nearly did myself several injuries in my hasty decent to the island.

Once on the ground I tugged at the shirt of a man heading swiftly past me. Baines he was, son of Frank the alcoholic butcher, had left the island to go to college then come back, worked in the same bank as Audrey.

"Love has something to share," he told me briefly, then moved on.

There was a simple way to find out what and I found the back of the crowd. Began easing my way to the front.

I could hear his voice before I saw what was going on. He was on good form.

"There's never a good way to lose somebody you care about – someone who's part of you. It never feels right, or just, or true – and that's because it isn't.

"Paul Glazier was part of this island same way these stones are – his parting from this place was part of the plan I think, the endless tectonic shift between the day and night – the battle which is always raging around us.

"Our role in his leaving us was written – it could not be undone from the moment we were born. But that does not mean we have to lay down and accept fate without a whisper. We can't change the script – yet – but we surely can comment on it. And that I why I have brought you here today."

I scrambled finally from behind the fat backside of Sophie Ellen from the pie shop and found myself on the front row.

Love was standing on the shifting cusp where land met water. He must have had Glazier's dinghy brought down from his yard. The small, sky blue fibreglass craft which I had watched Glazier sail many times on the murky glass of the channel. Fishing forlornly for bits and pieces. Hoping to find a bit of peace.

The boat bobbed wanly a few yards off the shore – shrugged its shoulders each time a swell came. And in the boat was a sack.

"We know," said John Love, who was holding a can of petrol, "what it means to say goodbye. Here on this island people leave and we stay. That is the nature of life here. I ask you to say goodbye again. This time to someone who did not leave because he had better things to do than hang around with us. Or who found he could make more money elsewhere. Or was one of the many who tell you they feel they have 'outgrown' you. I ask you instead to say goodbye to someone who is one of us – and who we *will* see again."

With that Love turned from us to the sea and waded out, brine flapping around the tail of his shirt. He stood behind the dinghy, which bucked and kinked indifferently with the waves – three small, three large, three small.

Love unscrewed the cap from his can and upended it over the sack. From top to bottom he drenched it in accelerant until there was no more.

We gasped and muttered; it was a coup de théâtre, or would have been, had Love not forgotten his matches, hunted for them, given up eventually, and had to wade back to the shore where he managed at length to bum a pink disposable Bic from Barbara.

He barely glanced at her as he took it.

Audrey, I realised, didn't smoke.

She had as much to do with this whole Glazier business as I did, as Love did – as the rest here who'd all thrown stones. But we seemed content to forget that and instead let Love seduce us with his ceremony, which gave us succour.

Now, most people look uncomfortable when they are up to their privates in cold water. Something about the ginger way they totter on tiptoes or the lemon sucking look on their face will tell you that this is not their natural state – they are putting themselves out a bit. Even trawlermen I've seen, who spend a fair chunk of their lives thigh deep in brine – adopt a stoic look of getting the job done.

Love looked like he belonged there – beaming and beatific, moving with the swell. And I thought again of all the queer things I've seen washed up on the shore over the years: the whales and porpoises, seals and leather backed turtles, the coconuts, letter bottles and jellyfish big as dustbin lids. I thought of the seaweed draped human husks which celebrate successful suicide bids.

But this here John Love was the weirdest flotsam we'd ever had I'm sure.

Then I felt Audrey's spiky presence by my side, a bony elbow nudged my cheek, and she said, softly:

"Can you feel it? Can you feel the love that we have for him here?"

And I wasn't sure whether she meant Glazier, but then I reckoned if we'd have loved him so deeply we probably wouldn't have stoned him to death. I looked at her and she was staring at Love with a peculiar weak smile on her face – an expression which I suppose was intended to convey acceptance and joy, bliss and peace but which seemed to me to come from the part of her which wanted to send out signals, rather than from the bit which tells us what's really inside.

I turned my back on Love for a while, looked around the crowd. There were many of us, perhaps even a majority, who wore that same feeble, transported smile which seemed to speak of acquiescence.

"It's pure love," she whispered to me, excited at her realisation. And it came to me that this was one word I'd never heard John use.

He held his pink Bic aloft where it winked in the thin sun.

"Thanks," he said. "For what you meant to us. And for what you taught us, even in your necessary death. We will not forget the sacrifice you made for this people and this place."

With that he brought the lighter down and flames bloomed inside the boat. The pretty fire seemed at first unconnected with the sack but hung feathery in the air so the hessian remained unmolested. In time it scorched and blackened, became one with the conflagration. Love produced a cut throat razor he'd liberated from among Stanhope's belongings and swiftly cut the line anchoring the dinghy.

He walked the boat out a few more yards into deeper water then waited for a retreating wave before he shoved it on its way.

I've seen plenty of things launched like this come back again but he hit it about right and the sky blue boat with its pretty flame moved further away from us and nearer to wherever it was going.

"It's beautiful," cried Audrey. "Magical."

Though all I saw was Glazier's tatty snub nosed painter turning slowly from sky blue to charcoal.

Then, as we watched, one or two voices shouted out 'look' or 'what's that there?' and soon all seemed sure something was visible in the flames above the boat.

So I squinted at it, to get a glimpse of what they all saw. But I saw nothing aside from the gathering smoke, battling with the breeze.

Next, a woman's voice from the back of the crowd yelled; "He's there, I see him there – look."

And they did, more intently now; shielding their eyes from what there was of the sun.

John Love didn't join in. He'd waded his way back to shore and stood on the stones to one side of the group dripping calmly, eyes downcast.

I looked back over the tarnished silver dullness of water and sky, eyes drawn to the only bright thing out there. And as I did so, it seemed I half saw something in the smoke, examined it more closely, decided it was nothing, looked again, wasn't so sure. And all the time behind me the crowd was growing more sure of itself, more ready to accept.

"It's Glazier – just his face."

"No, I see all of him, he's walking!"

"He's holding his hand out to us, there's something in his hand."

"There's nothing in his hand; it's just a sign of friendship."

"He has with him a child."

"A babe in arms."

"A small child by his side, holding his hand."

While they were making out a case for Glazier having opened up a branch of Puddleducks in the afterlife I was still struggling to see past the smoke.

But eventually I did so – saw that yes, there was Paul Glazier, standing tall and erect as in life he always had. He was some distance away over the water but I could see that he was smiling – holding out his hand to wave to us like window-cleaners do – goodbye, goodbye.

"What is he saying?"

"His lips are moving – what has he to say to us?"

I couldn't see the lips moving – he was smiling, that was all, smiling and waving.

"He says he loves us."

"Says that he was sorry to leave."

"He says that we will see him again soon, that he will always be with us."

"Look out for us."

"Keep us in his care."

I never saw his lips move as I say – but other people did, and who am I to argue with the hundreds of words of succour and fond farewell he seems to have imparted in the slender moment when we all witnessed him rise above the boat which held his mortal remains?

I only know what I saw. It didn't change the way I had begun to feel about John Love, except perhaps a little.

I never doubted he had a guiding role in what went on. Though when I thought of all the miracles around me: the daily ta-darr of sunset, gulls, seaweed even, and all that, it didn't seem that his stacked up quite so high. What did it matter that you saw a man if you couldn't shake his hand?

The people here were very keen on Glazier now apparently – thought him a force of nature and something to be applauded.

It wasn't about him so much as the idea of him, I suppose – both now and when we'd killed him.

"Paul, Paul, come back, come back to us love…" this from Iris Slack, bleating as if she'd lost her own son out there on the ocean.

As the dinghy moved further out to sea and the light from the fire diminished, Glazier faded too. First so I couldn't make out his face. Then so his whole form became indistinct, part of the smoke again, and of the heavy air around him.

Perhaps none of us could pinpoint the moment he was gone.

XV

That night was quiet and we all went to bed as though we'd been naughty – but the next evening after work we were back in the boozer.

There's blessed relief in a pub if you ask me. Don't care who you are or what your thing is – you'll find some kind of nourishment there. Though here, in the Vengeance, you wouldn't touch the bar snacks which are many years old and for display purposes only.

Prelapsarian peanuts and antediluvian anchovies surrounded us like sacrificial offerings as we gathered there – many of us: Frank the barman, Jeff Barnes and his mother Rene, Marcus Riley, pale and monopedal.

He has something on his mind does Marcus junior.

"I've been thinking about dad a lot recently – since John talked to him for me that day on the beach – that time and all the times since. Dad wasn't one to offer up information in life, but now he's dead he seems to have turned into a proper diarrhoea gob – can't shut the fucker up. And, you know, when I think about it, a lot of what he's been telling me through John doesn't make a whole lot of honest sense. The stuff which does could have come from anyone – just general advice and such."

"But it has helped you?" asked Frank, shaking a banana Daiquiri for Rene.

"Yes," Riley had to admit. "It has brought me peace, and I needed that. But what I'm saying is…" and here he stopped a while to motion for another pint of Bull's Pizzle.

"There's a funny thing about legs. When you lose one it's still there, as far as you are concerned. Sometimes my Achilles tendon aches, or I get an itch on the calf which there's no way to scratch. Then there's mornings when I'm half asleep, I roll out of bed and put all my weight on my leg. But it's not there see? However real it was to me, I still fall on my arse."

He looked around the bar – decided on sub-titles for the hard of thinking.

"I'm saying that I don't feel entirely comfortable on this matter. I know what happened on the shore today was a beautiful thing but still – that doesn't make it real."

Barbara urged him on: "And earlier. The accident."

It was as if she couldn't bring herself to call it death. Even less killing, or something more clinical which smacked of authority and the world far away, cut off for now.

"Well maybe he had it coming." This was Frankie – the rat who could walk. Sitting bolt upright on a bench in the corner, crutches by her side.

Bitter she sounded, defensive. She'd never been big on Glazier, who hadn't liked rats it seemed to me, and she felt she had more reason than most to be in the pro-Love camp. Perhaps she was simply feeling the strong tidal pull of difference.

"Maybe he did have it coming," says one leg Riley. "Yet who's to say? Not us I think."

He pondered his beer.

"I'm glad," he said, "we have this chance to talk without… you know."

And I did know. Especially as I was supposed to make certain they didn't have the chance to talk without Love hearing every word – in fact this was just the sort of thing I should have been going back to the van and scribbling out for him.

But something in me knew I wouldn't bother – not this time. Perhaps because old Hop Along had been speaking for me where I couldn't.

How was I supposed to feel, here in this vale of beers?

"Marcus is right," insisted Barbara, slipping her arm around his waist so he blushed. "How many more accidents before we admit the destruction?"

A few people there seemed like they'd come out against Love if the rest did. While others were not for turning. Rene had that old woman's limpet grip on anything she'd invested in – an inertia which hardened her opinions to stone. She would go to the crem believing in John Love, I knew. And she wasn't alone.

But no one was prepared to stand up right there in the public bar and defend John Love amid the ashtrays. Despite all he'd done, he'd shown us, meant to us.

So I felt guilty then of course, and wanted to hurl my pretty glittering lager at the optics. I wanted to stand up on my stool and yell at them: "What are you doing? Was it better before? At least now we are building something."

Yet I realised none of us knew exactly what it was we were building. So I kept my own counsel. Foolish. Dumb.

Later when I went to the loo one of the gnarled and elderly Tip Rats was by the sinks – washing not just his hands but his face and neck as well with enthusiastic swooshes of tap water and great oily gouts of liquid soap. I'd never seen someone have such a thorough-going wash in the bogs before. His hair was wet, there were suds on his shirt, he looked like he'd been through a car wash.

Dripping, he turned and jabbed the button on the hot air drier.

Nothing happened.

"Bollocks," he intoned.

And paused for a moment to mull over the injustice of it. Then he sloshed back wetly to the bar.

Next morning we were all back on the site, chipper as little robins.

Here we are, working for nothing, and the truth's more slippery than an eel in a tub of elbow grease.

People are treating Barbara with exaggerated courtesy. They navigate around her like she's dangerous and have a unity which suggests they've all got together in a hut to fangle how to handle the situation.

Which they might actually have done, come to think.

What they say isn't what they mean, even if it's just: "Hello Barbara."

How's she suddenly become the one who's stepped outside of what's allowed?

The more I watch people the less I figure I know what they're up to. It's one complicated waltz we do out there.

Barbara doesn't seem to notice what's going on.

We're in the lunch queue and there's one last doughnut which Rene has just put on my plate when Barbara, behind me, says: "Oh damn – I was dreaming about one of those all morning while I was painting walls."

And Rene whips said piece of confectionary back off my tray saying: "We must look after Babs now, mustn't we?"

Why must we?

She's not sick – she's not even anxious – in fact she's looking great – she's taken most of her slap off and she's lost a few pounds humping rocks. She's got that healthy older woman thing going for her – a few wrinkles yes, but a bit of a tan and great knockers.

Babs flutters and protests about my doughnut not being rightfully hers, then takes it anyway. Cow.

Anyhow, I suppose one less won't hurt me.

Love's still staying at my place – a badge of his tolerance of the weak and outcast.

I wonder how long it will be before we start sticking laminate flooring and Paul Klee prints in the folly and he'll be out of my hair?

My carpet's worn thin with the feet of the pilgrims and we're running out of places to store money. Banknotes are drifting up around the place like it is a crack dealer's bedsit. Crude wads of more or less a grand bound with elastic bands. I ran out of bands and had to follow the postman round the site of a morning to harvest more.

All this dosh – we've no use for it. Love doesn't need to buy anything – people give him stuff, like he's the queen.

I pass him a message written on the back of a twenty pound note.

"Give it away?"

"Who to?" he wants to know. "What they need I can give them. Keep the money safe. In case."

I shrug and ram a few more wads of currency into a cubby-hole full of paperbacks.

As I worked at it I could hear Love umming and throat clearing behind me. He was getting ready for a heart to heart.

"Audrey," he said, "might have been an error."

I kept shuffling bank notes into the cupboard.

"It was because I could," he admitted. "But where does that end? There are others you know – all the others – where I could if I so chose. But, if I can't separate myself from what my body wants – it means I am no more or less than any other person."

So. Not much of an apology then. No recognition of betrayal or of the embarrassment caused. Just the notion that he is something more than us and that to mix with us on any base level demeans him.

It's okay with me whatever happens. How could it not be? My life hasn't changed for years, yet I have always been raw to the prospect of imminent chaos. Existence can flip inside out in a moment – like a fly hitting a windscreen. You're buzzing along without a care in the world then suddenly, the last thing to pass through your mind is your arse.

We none of us have any say in how things work out. Not any. That's what I believe.

You might think yourself king of the world then get into your car for the last time. Wake up in intensive care numb from the eyebrows down – a lump of meat to be pitied and worked around.

You can gaffer tape yourself in your flat, roll up in a duvet and then choke to death on a peanut. There is no escaping life.

Rain rattles the tin walls of the van. I make us hot chocolate.

"You and I," said Love, "we both know the power of saying less. Some people never learn that. They think the more they say the more people hear – that's not how it works."

I said nothing.

He looked at me with Bambi eyes.

"I've given you a precious thing. I've given you the gift of trust."

I tried not to smirk. If I'd known he was going to be doling out presents then personally I'd have preferred the gift of socks or the gift of underpants.

The thing about trust is that it's more of an obligation on my part than a prezzie on his.

Barbara wishes to speak with me.

We go up to the dunes, just she and I. It is a place we both have a passion for: lonely, yet comforting. It's like being alone in bed, snuggled in a rolling duvet of silky sand. There are ponds too, home to natterjack toads who are cheerful.

It's a lively place on our rare sunny days – light a fire at the end of the island, try to catch a fish, swim a little maybe, trap rabbits.

I've spent time here on my own, Barbara has too. I wonder if she's brought men down here? I hope that she's had more taste.

There are many of us here on the island who, much as we cleave to company, also yearn to be alone.

Barbara's always had a terrible fear of the weather – this was a sore affliction in a place where we had so much of the stuff. It spoiled her loneliness in the dunes I saw, always having to look over her shoulder for storm clouds.

At least out here she was free from worry about the mixer tap.

For a little while we walked. Afterwards we stood stone still with the world around us, open and endless. It felt free, as if we could have been anywhere, on our way to anywhere else.

There was a leaping sense of relief bounced up in me, broke through the crown of my head and up into the sculpted sky.

At first I did not know what it was, thought I must be unwell, high on the potent narcotic of some bustling and unspecified virus. But then I realised that what I felt was a sense of release, that for the first time in many weeks I was free of John Love and found myself outside of his orbit. I was thinking of him, but I was not in a place where he had any influence. Here the gulls wheeled and the sand blasted; there was nothing to alter this, nor had there been for millennia.

As far as we were concerned it was our place. As the whole island once had been.

"And how are you?" asked Barbara, face showing she really meant it – asking the question people asked, empty of interest, thousands of times in their lives.

I performed a barely perceptible shrug.

"Good," she said. "I'm glad. These are strange times – if you're all right in yourself..."

In yourself; my mother used to say that, I remembered – when I was ill.

"How are you in yourself?" she used to ask me.

We stood a little more, then Barbara talked. The way people always had to me and always would. She talked as she could have done alone in the dunes – but knowing someone was listening. Someone who would not interrupt.

"All the things we have done, I think they were for love," she told me. "I'm not saying that excuses evil, just because you meant it well – but it's a reason anyway, for doing things you otherwise wouldn't. I know that to be true. I've done some things I shouldn't have – you know. Well, everyone knows.

"If you had told me before he came that he would change our world this much I'd have sorted out a red carpet for him – we all would. I don't believe there was one person in this place truly happy. We all had something missing but didn't know it. He seemed to fill that hole – that's why we love him so much. Not because he's handsome or he can do things other people can't.

"But it's gone wrong now – perhaps it was never right. It can't be just me who thinks so. How could it be? We can't all have lost what we believed and trusted in before."

She paused to spit sand out of her mouth.

"I can't remember what it was that we did believe. There must have been something."

XVI

There was some kind of ceremony underway. It was one I had seen before, but didn't recognise at first, decked out as it was in unfamiliar weeds.

People were lining up outside the central compound to Love's folly, laden with heavy boxes. They were ferrying in and out of the place, walking on improvised cardboard runners so as not to spoil the newly laid turf.

I had it. It was 'Moving In.'

Barbara and I, fresh back from the otherness of the dunes, had not expected to find such a domestic scene. We had no housewarming gift, no bottle of bubbly or card or vase full of flowers.

Love saw us and waved at me. He brimmed with vigour, the joy someone always has when they move into a new place: supervising the removal men, charged with what's possible and hasn't happened yet.

"We're a long way from finished," he said excitedly. "There's mansions of room for improvement."

He was right, we were in the middle of a building site, half finished structures surrounded us, there were piles of rubble and sand everywhere, scaffolding, mortar mix.

"It's like he's bought time-share," whispered Barbara.

"Come inside," he demanded, "see the stuff."

Love's squat white temple was windowless under its flat roof. Wires snaked up the walls to light bulbs strung from the ceiling but the place was a little better than dim.

It still reeked of paint from the barely finished murals on the walls – unlikely animals and grotesques, described by Love to Tracey Etherington or one of the others who could draw a bit – fretted over in miniature then daubed on by the decorators in a pile-up of awkward hues. Love cared more about form than colour – "It's what the shapes do," he told his artists. "The spectrum's secondary – imagine you were colour-blind, there would still be a picture."

He concurred with Picasso in this respect. He was at odds with Matisse.

The 'stuff' he had referred to was tumbling out across the floor like the aftermath of a bomb blast.

Much of it was a heap of chalky rocks I recognised as the corpse of Morgan H Stanhope's lost masterpiece the Mother and Child.

One particularly large chunk of creamy limestone was being used as a table. Perched on top of it were other Love-related odds and sods – the pieces from the library display case laid out. A wizened vegetable on which someone had once traced Love's name, a blood soiled handkerchief with which he had bandaged a finger, smashed with a hammer during the early days of the construction. There was a gift of lost gold trinkets from the grateful rats, a bottle of Love's patent cure all, prepared from only the finest weeds by yours truly – which reminded me, he'd be needing another batch.

There was charcoal from the fire where Walter burned, pebbles from the beach – and I knew which ones those were.

On a bare bit of wall above the stone table was the framed picture of Stanhope's statue being greeted by our stilted ancestors in their Sunday best clothes and comedy toppers, their daft moustaches and 'what the devil's a camera?' expressions.

What would they have made of all this?

The whole set up reminded me of a shoebox I used to have under my bed as a child. In it I kept the flotsam and jetsam of my young life, bits of nothing which were jewels to me because memories snagged onto them like sheep's wool on barbed wire.

"It's looking good," breathed John Love. "It's looking how it is supposed to look."

A rat was bringing in Stanhope's letter, still in its glass library case.

"Careful, now," cautioned Love. "On that tertiary plinth to the left." Rat stuck the thing on a smaller lump of Mother and Child against the back wall.

As he was moving away he backed up into Love and the pair of them swept a few bits and pieces off the rock table – couple of stones, lump of charcoal – can't rightly remember what.

It was a fifty-fifty, what a pair of clumsy sods, kind of affair – Rat chuckled apologetically as he rescued stuff and put it back.

But Love was suddenly whipped into a righteous rage the like of which I had not seen before. He clipped the unfortunate rat under the left lug with a clenched fist with a force that sent him cannoning bewildered into the back wall.

Maybe it wasn't that hard and the guy just went down because he lost his balance but Barbara and I caught our breath. We felt sorry for the young bloke who we didn't know.

He got up and I'd have expected him to rush head down into Love and give him some back, as is the island way, but the look on his face was that of a chastened pet which needs to be loved.

"Sorry," he yelped. "You don't know how truly sorry. I would never have hurt you – or your rocks."

"Away!" bellowed Love, red and, for him, unlovely. "Get out now and if I see you again and recognise you I'll send you over the bridge!"

At this the rat looked terrified. "All I ever want is to be near you and to be part of this…"

"Idiots I don't need. There's a surfeit of them."

He made as if to get stuck into the rat again and the bloke obliged by scrambling his scrawny mess of soiled jeans and home-knit sweater out of the chamber.

Once we were alone Love's mood clicked like a fuse had tripped.

"Come over here," he motioned us towards the glass case – "Come and see the evidence, you probably haven't been through it properly before in the context, it's okay, I understand – come here the pair of you and read it."

Then a flash of remembering… "Barbara, read it."

She moved over to the case and squinted past her reflection into the age of the yellow paper and the elaborate fussy scrawl of Stanhope's hand.

Breathily, perhaps still shocked by what she'd just witnessed, she read the letter out loud.

My Dear Sirs,

I beg your indulgence to accept my humble offering – an epiphany hewn from the rock and sent to you in the simple hope that it will both gladden hearts and be an improving influence on all who have the good fortune to gaze upon it.

Mark me – in the course of human congress there will be a force of change blowing across these islands. I feel it deep within the stone I work and I know it to be the truth.

I will say before God and under the heavens that I am but a servant – 'No!' I hear you cry, yet it is true. For what I do is merely the chipping of stone and the shaping of clay.

I create statuary – yet a greater man than me will tear it down – yes – an iconoclast will come to unite the people for the greater good. I see this and I know it to be true.

To see is one thing. To go there is another.

There must be building – for the future depends on the construction of the world in His image. There must be a realignment, a return to old values of obedience when humble men knew the value of service and would doff their caps rather than scoff openly in the street at a gentleman as he makes to pass.

For the world is full of ignorance and peasantry, of those who delude themselves that one can become a person of quality simply by reading books! Or attending a place of learning! Nothing could be further to the truth. True merit is born in the blood. The purity of that blood is all which can and will count for anything.

This purity cannot be re-established without bloodshed. There will be miracles, it is true, but there will be hurt and fear also. We must be resolute – we must root out among us those who are not worthy of our congress.

You will forgive a learned man his musings on matters which must seem far beyond you – as I write I reflect that the conversation of adults must seem incomprehensible to the little mite, used only to infant chatter of the nursery!

Know only this. My Mother and Child is a gift to you and, as gratitude overwhelms you, as you muse 'how can we prove ourselves worthy of such a prize?' I urge you to remember – your tiny island home may be unsheltered and unfashionable – beset by guano, rain lashed, populated, as it seemed to me, by knaves who would issue threats to a gentleman rather than carry his bags as they were bidden. Yet it can, in its own tiny way, be a part of history.

The future does not have to be as squalid and petty as our present.

Take heed of greater men, those born to lead, respect nobility and trust like children that which you cannot hope to understand.

This way lies paradise.

Your humble servant,

Morgan H Stanhope (Gentleman)

Later on as we queued for dinner there was a commotion down at the medical tent because one of the labourers had gone face first into the window-etching acid they were using to paint pretty pictures in some of the glass panes around the project.

He'd live, said the rumours, but he was unrecognisable to everyone up to and including his dear old mam.

It was an odd one sure, but there were many accidents on site. Men fallen or crushed, spiked, sliced or dented. Flesh suddenly seemed less sturdy when it came up against metal and stone. But as for this man: it was clear none of us would see his face again.

After I went home that evening a low occluding mood gathered in me which lasted for the next several days. I wanted nothing outside of work other than to sit in the van and read under dim lamplight. I felt dull and disconnected to everything outside my tin walls.

It was a state which, in the end, I recognised as mourning.

Love stayed with me for a few of these evenings though we spoke little. My notepad was neglected as he retreated into what used to be my room and delved into his fat, rich tomes, diving headfirst into the mysteries of his appropriated truth.

"There is still work," he told himself aloud. "It might look like we're getting close – but that's just smoke. We still have much to do."

He believes, it seems, he can shuffle us around as easily as toy soldiers on a board. He knows nothing of the storm I heard rumbling in the back bar of the Vengeance.

Still it's a seductive idea and I imagine us all as minute painted figures on a 3D map of the island: its tousled council estates and the dunes made of real sand, tiny pebbles keeping out a gloss coat of sea. There I am look, even smaller than the rest of the people, here's the park where I live: well ordered silvery rows of mobile homes, like packs of chewing gum. Towards the other end of the island, before it gives way to grass and gulls, there is the man-made cavity of the tip, scattered with carefully created miniature junk. The model in my mind shows our island unique and isolated – but I know this cannot be the case. The sea on one side, the bare inviting bridge on the other; they are links with the world.

I've always been a truly dreadful painter. So awful that if say in fifty years, you saw one of my efforts decaying slowly in the stack section of some back street junk shop – where it had been saved for the frame, you would actually be offended by it.

You'd be outraged to see something so ugly and incompetent gurning out at you, appalled at the audacity of the person who had wasted paint on it then grimly held onto it in the teeth of all aesthetic merit. You'd be alarmed that someone elderly and confused might see it and believe it to be beautiful.

I used to paint quite a lot, despite the pain my finished efforts brought me. It made me wonder why I got no better at it.

Seascapes I did mostly – views of my shoreline at different times of the day. My backgrounds were okay, if I might praise myself in such lavish terms; they were mediocre.

It was when I attempted to put anything figurative in the foreground that things turned nasty – my boats and fishermen, rocks and driftwood were all the worst sort of tat, clumsy, naïve and inept.

I was sweating over the latest of my crappy little daubs as Love talked. He paused to squint over my shoulder.

"Not bad," he said, approvingly. "I like that – the little fisherman looks like he's caught something."

I scanned his face for traces of irony – but he didn't really do ironic.

I think, if everything had stayed as it was and Love's boat had blown up somewhere else, I would have liked to make my model island and present it to the library. It could have gone on display in one of the mahogany and glass cases where they had been more recently storing mouldy aubergines.

But then if our pattern had not been interrupted then maybe I wouldn't have come up with the idea.

Some nights there were no words, others they were few and functional. But occasionally John Love used me as the others always had – as a bin for storing information which had become too heavy to carry.

"I've told her," he tossed at me, late one Tuesday evening, apropos of nowt and just as I was thinking of turning in.

"I've told her there's nothing more I can do to heal her – not in that way." He lowered his eyes, his voice straining slightly under the burden of all he had to haul.

"Sometimes they ask too much."

Then, other evenings, cocooned in our home when he didn't have his snout in a tract he was mixing up weeds on my stove to replenish his bottles of magic. He knew I had my notebook, but extracting words from me was as painful and protracted an operation as pulling wisdom teeth.

So instead he sat over Su Doku. He had a book of them he'd picked up from the Easyways.

'Picked up' is not American idiom – that's what he did. He'd developed a habit of wandering in there, grazing from the shelves, trousering what he fancied, and strolling back out again with perhaps only a nod over to the manager to keep him sweet.

This relationship with the Easyways astonished me. It had always struck me as such a cosmopolitan place with its low key mood music, bold fluorescent lighting and CCTV. It was an emissary from a more sophisticated culture and made me think of abroad.

It had a section called Cuisine de France – though there tended to be only a couple of jaundiced Cornish pasties and a sausage roll in the hoppers. It was part of the thin glue which welded us to the wider world.

Yet Love wore it twinkling like a ring on his finger.

The place had the contract to provide groceries to our work camp – at no charge naturally. I wondered what the accountants were going to make of that back at Easyways head office.

It didn't seem to bother Love, so long as he had his book of puzzles.

He hunched over the rows of tiny boxes, contemplatively filling in digits and he would get through them fairly sharpish too, no matter how large the grid, or how few numbers there were to begin with. He would peck away at them like a computerised toy, jotting them off and on to the next page.

Once, when he had to go out on an emergency healing, I looked through the book and saw what he was doing. The rows and columns were filled in, of course, and each three by three box had numbers one to nine in it, But beyond that his work was entirely random. There had been no attempt to follow the rules and each one of the grids was comprehensively wrong.

I knew I could have done better myself – so I did, filling in the next puzzle on the page in tiny, tidy figures.

Next night he spotted my work and he was the nearest I've ever seen him get to bashful.

"It helps me think," he muttered, tossing the book down. "I can concentrate better. My… I was told it would help."

He didn't pick the puzzle book up again. Not ever.

I don't know what was going on there, why he felt the need for that show with only me as an audience. But I knew not to let him see me catch him out in any further deceptions.

Some mornings Love would go and stand on his white plinth at the very centre of his works and pose there with the sun behind him, watchless and serene like the best proportioned of all his statues. A triumph of art.

I can still see him towering there if I squint, shadowed face vacant, only his shaggy hair shifting in the gust to let us in on the secret of him.

Work, then sitting at home in silence. Like a married couple. It seemed nothing could interrupt our domestic bliss. Until early one evening there came a tap on the aluminium door of the van, tiny and precise. Two thin raps, unassuming and assertive, both at the same time. So I knew who's knock it was before I rattled the tin panel open.

Audrey, bony and intense.

"He's here," she told me – which was her asking a question.

She followed my eyes to the intestines of the van, where Love could be heard shouting "Where's my shirt?" Like we were married.

She had people with her, two of them, one of each gender. They weren't anyone I recognised right off, which is less odd than one might think, even here. No one knows everyone, and some folk will go out of their way to remain unknown.

"You'll remember Duke and Evelyn?" Audrey asked me.

Nope, you've got me.

Then they were through, chatting to a bemused and shirtless Love.

"We wanted to thank you," the woman said. "You couldn't save her." She had a bristle of ginger hair and the veiny pallor that goes with it.

"No one could," her old man put in. "But you gave her time and you gave us hope."

"Which is precious," added ginger.

And I knew then who they were, in a flash of red hair and frail skin.

But Love didn't – he'd kicked in autopilot – a good show though, as always.

He touched Evelyn's brow and even as she fell weak to my cushion plumped nest of a bench seat I could see he too was deeply affected by what passed between them.

His eyes flicked up into his head so you could only see the white – it was an alarming sight as if the precious blue gems had been replaced by hard-boiled eggs. Duke let out a little yelp – like the spaniel his name reminded me of. He rushed over on an instinct to support, not his swooning wife, but the magnet which was Love.

"I'm okay," gasped Love, eyes popping back peek-a-boo. "I was taken somewhere by the force of your grief – your passion. I have seen someone. That person has spoken to me."

"Who?" gasped Duke.

"Wait," motioned John, sitting. "I am weakened by forces which flowed through me – Evelyn, more importantly – needs rest. I will speak to you on the square in half an hour – with others present – it is crucial we share this. Please – please …"

One hand on his brow he motioned them to the door and Audrey hustled them out of the caravan.

The unsatisfactory crackle of a plastic door in an aluminium hole was like a starter's pistol. Love bounced to his feet, all energy.

"This," he snapped, as he headed for his trunk, "is not good."

He popped his head back out of the bedroom and glared. "Couldn't you have seen this coming? There must have been talk – that's your department."

Seeing things coming, mind you, was his, and I thought the whole business a bit off quite candidly.

"It's a mess," he yelped. "A bloody mess." I realised that this was the first time I'd heard him swear and even then it wasn't much of an effort.

He was gone again and I could hear the tinkle and clatter of a bloke hunting for small things among a tangled mess of other small things.

"I mean, if she was in a bad way," he yelled back through, "why didn't they come round to us for further treatment? I could have dealt with it then – gimmicked some way of heading it off – convinced everyone it was written – short of sunbeams or something.

"It's no real use turning up now, is the root of the matter. And I've seen this sort of thing before – it breeds discontent, raises questions which can only serve to disrupt the rich fabric of constant praise."

He was back in the break-out area again – with an armful of miscellaneous stuff.

"What are you doing sitting there like a gargoyle? Get writing. I want everything – I want to know who's thrown a double six for a kick off – then everything you know about her – they said a her didn't they? Granny most probably then…"

He ran out of wind momentarily, flopping his arms down so some bags and bottles fell to the floor.

"This is bad," he said again. "And it cannot happen this time. Not when we've got so far – built so much, and I don't just mean literally." He gave me the eye to show what a shrewd metaphysical kind of a customer he was. How he wasn't just about knocking up Alton Towers for the aesthetically challenged but wanted to be the queen of people's hearts as well.

I pulled a face and ferreted for my notebook under the cushions. I did my best for him, despite my deep doubts; when it came to it I couldn't even afford the first payment on what I owed him.

I gave him all I could, from my memory of their meeting. But this was one family I knew little about – there were cousins, in-laws, I could give him a dozen pars of fruitless local history about Falmouth Street where they lived. Semis built in the 1920s by a local builder who later went bust under the weight of drink and his wife's infidelities. How the pub at the top of the road was named after a race horse and how there used to be a kid called Hutch lived half way down who taught me as a child how to belch at will.

But there were a hundred houses in the street and I didn't have the social history of each one. I wasn't even sure what had happened to Hutch. This red-haired family and their frail little ghost of a child were an enigma to me.

"Thanks," grumbled John Love, reading my note, "for fuck all."

Which was a better effort when all's said and done.

"I imagine Audrey's done a job with the speccies by now – there's no sense putting it off – the best way is to make it look like it's *for* something." He nodded to himself. "That's always good – it's not that bad things happen, it's that they are pointless, that's what afflicts us."

He gathered up his things from the floor. One small bottle of dark liquid, about the size of an ink well, he unstopped and poured all over his head. It ran ruddy down his hair and forehead but did not stain and soon disappeared, He tossed that container aside and fumbled through others, stashing them in the pockets of an expensive slate grey suit jacket he'd accepted from one of the local councillors and wore with the shagged out jeans he'd turned up in.

"Got any matches?" he demanded of me. I didn't smoke, but I found the long stemmed Swans in the kitchenette drawer which were used for lighting the hob.

He squinted at the bulky carton with distaste: "Not very discreet."

I'd have thought, with his constant need for conflagration, he'd have invested in a box of his own.

Out in the charred circle which had once been our green but was now, I supposed, our black, the assembly Love had called for stood waiting. The islanders, at least those caught up directly in all of this, had become used to gathering at short notice for issues and proclamations either from Love or one of his appointed delegates. These could concern anything from the need to find more builder's rubble to a biographical discourse on the Persian deity Mithra. Whatever it was, it helped to pass the day.

What, I wondered, as we waited for Love to clear his throat, did those islanders who were more peripheral to our great cultural revolution make of it all?

Those who were not joiners of crowds. What did they make of castles on the shore and fires which covered their washing with ash? What of this talk of miracles and new hope? Who knows what such people ever think? It was enough that they did nothing.

Where was Love mind you? I had assumed he was following me – but now, as I scanned the circle of thirty or so faces, his was not among them. Audrey was there, Evelyn and Duke of course, Babs, the rat chiefs, a few of the major craftsmen who must have been torn away grumbling and cursing from their work. There were community leaders, the old community – Bob Stafford and so on. It was a weighty posse Audrey had assembled so swiftly – clearly not just the first gaggle of labourers and hangers on she'd stumbled across between here and the site. We regarded each other, lulled off guard in the early evening air.

Then there was the most ferocious bang, like a hundred balloons being popped, slap in the centre of the circle, with an electric lightning flash and nostril tormenting smoke in pastel shades. It was so bright we could see nothing for a moment, then just a silhouette, as if the light was still there. A single man stood in the blackened centre of the circle. John Love – but stripped to the waist and with the whole of his head glowing a brilliant scarlet – his face, his hair – like a glacé cherry.

"Bloody hell," commented somebody. "That nearly finished me off."

And Love called out, clear and high, as if he was singing. "I call upon Evelyn and Duke Chance to come forward into the circle we have made and speak to me."

You could tell they'd rather not. Duke was all for stepping backwards, Evelyn anchoring his arm where he was, but she wasn't heading forwards either until one or two of the people around them started giving them a shove, then everyone was looking and all of a sudden the easiest path was to move towards John Love rather than away from him.

"These two people have suffered a grievous loss," Love told us solemnly, a hand on top of each of their heads. "There is a gap in their lives so raw and profound that nothing any of us can do will close the wound. It will be with them as long as they are in this world."

He paused, bowing his bright red head.

"What I must do is demonstrate to them, and to you all, that tragedy happens, as night does, but that is just a passing phase."

He closed his eyes as if to meditate, but almost immediately began shivering and shaking, hands still on the summit of Evelyn and Duke – as though they had some charge passing through them and he was merely a conductor.

A high ululation began in the back of his throat and warbled alarmingly out from between his teeth, unnaturally white as he bared them between cherry lips.

And a voice came from his throat, though it was not his voice – it was the girl's. The tiny frail red-haired girl I remembered.

How could he do that? A few minutes ago he'd had her down as an old lady, yet here he was speaking as if he was a telephone receiver with her on the other end.

"Hello Mam, Dad – I can't see you very well – it's dark – but it's getting brighter, can you hear me?"

Those among the crowd who knew her nodded, in recognition.

Duke shouted out in bafflement: "Nat? How can it be you?"

"It is me Dad, don't worry. Don't ever worry – I'm okay now Mam, honest. And I'm sorry about what happened – I didn't mean to – it wasn't me."

"We know it wasn't you pet," Evelyn shook her head, paler even than usual, unsure of what was going on.

"I want you to keep my things – in my room for me, like they always were – you can remember me that way – and I want you to help Mr Love, the way he helped me. I'm in such a lovely place – I know I wouldn't be such a lucky girl if it hadn't been for what Mr Love did for us."

There was a pause, then: "Thank the tiny man. For helping me with my crisps."

"He did," gasped Evelyn. "She told us the dwarf helped her open her bag while we were waiting for our consultation."

And the crowd gasped in recognition of a direct hit.

While Love sucked in a deep draught of air before embarking on his crescendo.

"Don't be scared Mummy, don't worry Daddy. Though I've died I'm not lost to you forever. You will see me sooner than you think. I'm not lost. I am only in the next room."

Dropped head – perhaps thirty seconds of warbling – then Love snapped his red face up to great us with a grin, composure regained.

"Well – she seems fine, she's on the other side, she has pets around her, an old car, a hamster… I sense an elderly relative – name beginning with a B, a D or something – perhaps your father Evelyn? That was hard, so draining with one so young, a loss so recent. I put my health on the line in ways I will not burden you with. And I can only hope that was of some small comfort to you."

"Yes," said Duke, in a tiny puzzled voice. "It was. But … she's…"

"She's not dead," yelled Audrey, shrill with triumph.

XVII

For comfort food I go for honey. Others prefer chocolate, or packets of digestives – I have no brief against them. But bee-juice is my passion when I'm feeling low, that and alcohol of course. I often think that if I could get my hands on some mead then there would be no happier customer in all creation.

Did you know honey is the one foodstuff which never goes off? You'll never find stale honey, sour honey, mouldy honey – they do not exist.

Deep within the tombs of the Valley of the Kings jars of honey have been found, decanted into pots millennia ago for sweet toothed pharaohs. Guess what? It's still edible.

I get mine from the Easyways.

I was daubing a knifeload onto chunky white toast – thick, opaque and viscous as snot, as I sat in the van later that evening watching John Love try to scrub red dye off his head.

He stood over by the sink wetting a cloth and rubbing away – but with limited results. He'd gone streaky in places but he was still essentially scarlet in hue.

"It seemed," he said as he saw me watching, "like a good idea at the time." Pause for more scrubbing then thoughtfully: "It develops you see – like fake tan. It's an effect."

Damn sure it was, also had the added advantage of hiding his blushes given the way things had turned out.

Putting his J cloth down for a moment he admitted: "I'm not sure quite how to proceed – what is the best course?"

I scribbled 'white spirit?' on my pad and pushed it over the table to where he could read it.

"No, no – I'm talking about the big picture – but actually that's not such a bad idea – I'll have you pop over to the site later and get some – probably best if I'm not seen out again today – best to let things cool off for a bit while I sort out a retrieval strategy."

There was plenty which needed retrieving, it was true. Love had been lulled into arguing a case which was provably wrong.

What's more he had argued it in his customary mesmerising, irrefutable way – he had enveloped us in his reality so completely that it became ours. Yet this time – here were facts, hulking and bullying their way past the bouncers into our party.

And in particular the one central fact – small and frail and flame haired, lying in bed wan, weary – yet indisputably alive. For now at least Natalie was still with us.

And if she was in the box bedroom of an Edwardian semi in Falmouth Street then she could hardly be sending heart-warming, bitter-sweet missives of comfort from the other side via the John Love answering service could she?

No she bloody could not.

We didn't believe Audrey at first. Or Evelyn and Bob. Thought they must be hysterical, overcome by the emotion of the occasion – we had seen all sorts of rum things happen to people's perception once they'd been granted face time with John Love, and that's when his face was just the standard shade.

So we took our posse off down there to Falmouth Street, gatecrashed Natalie's bedroom with its Tiger wallpaper and Dora the Explorer posters. Saw her there in the bed like a baby bird. Ever such shallow breathing is breathing none the less.

"Are you all right darling?" Duke asked her softly. "Can we get anything for you love?" She didn't stir, didn't murmur. I thought of the crisps again, and wished there was something else I could do. Something practical which would inch towards making everything all right.

Love didn't come with us mind.

A few seconds after Audrey made her announcement he exited under cover of another thunder flash and was waiting for me in the van when I returned, eager to know all that had gone on.

"So why the hell didn't they wait until she was dead?" he barked at me.

I didn't know – perhaps they still hoped he could help, perhaps he was their last shot – the way they spoke about her she was already gone – but still…

It took me an hour or so sitting eating honey before I came up with the solution to his problems. I scribbled a note for him.

"Save her," it said.

I was excited by the prospect – the purity and simplicity of the plan.

If he could bring her back from the cliff's edge, even now, then everything would be as it was – better than it was. And I realised how much I wanted Natalie to be okay – to be as tough and cheeky as the island's other kids, the ones who followed me up the road, feral and ruddy, throwing stones.

But John Love barked a short bitter laugh and burned my note on the stove.

Then next morning, when we awoke, Natalie Chance was dead once more.

I don't know what we were expecting when we walked out that final morning but we were chipper enough. The storm seemed to have passed over the surface of planet Love leaving it scarred perhaps and certainly a funny colour but bathed in sunshine.

Had he slept well? I do believe he had. He was not one to worry about that which he could not control – besides, there was much that he could.

Plan and trust in your talents – what more was there to do?

He was a man who had set out on a vanishing boat into a sightless sea so far out he was lost to all but fate. He had been washed up before and would be washed up again.

So we set off at my pace down the track between the rows of vans and then onto the coastal road which would take us past council houses and golf links to the site of Love's great and growing monument.

Did we know then that Natalie Chance was dead? How could we know? Yet Love seemed prepared. Not like yesterday with fogs and dyes and thunderclaps – but with a magic more powerful and past understanding, the hex he could summon in a glance or a calmness – the thing which had drawn us to him from the start.

As usual we took a shortcut over the golf course, where no one seemed to play any more as most of them were busy building.

Usually by the time we reached the brow of the squat hill overlooking the 14th green we could hear work underway and perhaps even see movement on the scaffolds in the middle distance, shifting stone and the sweep of cranes, smoke and dust from cement mixers and tar boilers.

Today though there was silence – as if a bank holiday had been declared and everyone was down the pub for the duration.

I thought they had simply not turned up to work – lingered over the Honey Nut Loops then watched housewife telly – planning to ring in sick later on. But as we reached the compound I saw the car park full as always and there was noise too. Not the usual clatter and hum of generators, motors turning, hammers, drills and wagons shifting. Instead there was the low thrum of human discontent.

But John Love did not falter; sped up slightly in fact, so I could just see his back as I chased him into the yard, stained shirt and wave of ruddy hair.

There they were in our roped off canteen area – the workforce, the islanders, my friends. They filled every bench around each table and still there were more who had to stand at the periphery or squeeze a buttock onto one of the serving tables at the far end, where rudimentary canvas awnings formed the kitchen.

Usually when Love turned up every head swivelled. It was as if he smelled differently from the rest of us – not in some big and open way, like he'd sluiced on too much aftershave, but in a manner so subtle only dogs and little kids could know for sure. This time though it was like he'd forgotten to splash it on all over.

I went unheralded as usual – and so did he. We slipped, translucent, into the back of the gaggle and listened. I couldn't see much of what went on through the meaty foliage of buttocks.

"You say he has brought things – what's he brought?" an old man's voice demanded.

"I was happy enough here before bloody Brad Pitt turned up with his magic wand."

"You weren't happy though," said a young woman.

"Oh give o'er."

"Well you weren't. We none of us were really. I'm not saying he has all the answers."

"Well yes – he has proved that for us, has he not?" Unmistakably Audrey this, prim and precise. "He has shown us he is a liar and a fraud. All our time, our affection – our love, he has taken it for god knows what purpose, under false pretences. I am asking you now to consider the consequences of following this man further. I am asking you to think what he has done, what we have done, already."

"Maybe that's it," said the old man, resigned. "Maybe we've done too much and gone too far, so the only road now is with him."

"That is what he would have you think I'm sure if he was here. But we have a choice – we always have a choice."

Another voice now – My Barbara. And not with good news: "I agree with Audrey – we're together on this, and you know we've got as much as anyone invested in this mess."

I glanced up at Love but he remained as unassuming as a man with a big red head can be.

"I know it won't be easy going back," admitted Babs. "We've all this to explain away for a start." Heads turned to gaze over at the crazy paved lunatic's theme park taking wonky shape on the shore. "It will take us a long time to fit back into normal life," she said. "I accept that, but we have to ask ourselves what we want. And then be resolute."

"Some of us," said a voice, "have never been a part of your normal life. What way forward is there for us? For us there is only one way and that's to listen to the voice which brought us here."

A number of others brayed approval – he still had the rats then, always the rats – or some of them at least. For others even staying in the vans, having the use of the Easyways, the grudging acceptance of the ordinaries, these things I think had softened them to a world they felt they had abandoned.

"It's not that we don't want out," came a voice. "It's how we do it – we don't want any trouble."

"Don't want trouble," scoffed another. "There'll be a plateful when police get here – not Stafford and those daft sods, proper police from across the bridge. Authority, have you thought of that?"

"We can't afford to fear it, " soothed Barbara. "It's the world we're from, the one we grew up in – it's our place. And we can still stick together – more of this can be explained away than we might think, if only we stay united."

"And turn against him?"

And then a host of voices, rattling into each other and echoing off into the void, like when the gulls catch a fish.

"It's one way or the other."

"Maybe we could compromise?"

"We might want to – but it's not up to us."

"We'll end up with the biggest adventure playground in the whole north of England."

"We'll end up in jail."

"I wish we'd never started this – I knew it was wrong – I told him but he wouldn't listen."

"He helped me though, I think you're all forgetting how he helped."

"But did he though?"

"If you think he did, well then he did."

The someone yelled: "He's here."

And I took advantage of a stirring in the flanks to muscle through so I could see the rows of Formica dining tables. Yes, there he was, standing up on top of one, bang in the centre so's you would have wondered at him getting there and clambering up without being spotted earlier.

There was a commotion – at his sudden appearance, and at his general appearance – given that most of the people hadn't seen him before with his head red, and those who'd been there last night must have thought they had bigger headlines to broadcast than a change in the colour of his kite.

"He looks like a great big strawberry."

"What's he playing at?"

"Hang on, he's going to talk."

"I don't know," said John Love, so quietly and calmly so that they had to shush to listen. "I don't know, whether I am welcome here…"

If he'd been expecting a huge flurry of reassurance he was in for a disappointment.

"And those are words I never believed I would have to say in this place and to these people. Because I believed, I still believe, that you are my people – and I am yours."

He looked around at the upturned faces.

"You are thinking things through – and that's good. Nothing is achieved without thought. But show me one thing of value which has been achieved without suffering and struggle. Show me a war with no casualties or a wall that's been built without blisters."

He was calm and measured – soothing. There were nods.

Then an unexpected voice from the back of the crowd, it was Ken Naylor – Glazier's old workmate from the garage. He'd been busying himself since the building began with the upkeep of the plant and vehicles which were used on the site. He was unusual in that he was one of the few people working on the project who required payment from the funds we collected among the others.

He had said nothing, done nothing, since Glazier's death, but now it seemed he had something to say.

"Bring her back," he challenged in his fruity booming voice.

"Um sorry?"

"Or bring back my friend Glazier. Bring them back to us now if you have the magic you've been claiming – show us what you're worth. Let's have them here among us again – the idiot too, the one burned in the fire – I can't remember his name right off but he didn't deserve what happened to him any more than the others did – or any of us do. This is all a game we can only lose. The point of you is to help us win, so let's see what you've got."

Love shook his head. "And if I uncover numberless dead – all the dead of the island since it first felt human footprints – what will that achieve?"

"It will make us fear less – and we will believe you."

"Believe what?" demanded Love. "What have I ever asked you to believe? I have not offered you anything."

"Nothing specific, no. You've been very careful in that, like a politician. There's been promise rather than promises. I suppose now is the time we find out what we've been waiting for."

"But now is not the time." Love shook his head.

"Yes," rumbled Ken, "now is the time." And the crowd echoed his words, began to shift like a sea swell. Yes, now was the time and they were not to be denied.

I wonder how long we may remain here, lost in the dark depths of the sea, soft in our cringing beauty as anemones, how long we may find ourselves suspended in the air, we clouds of moisture, listless and alone?

We moved in a huddle as sheep do, fighting against each other but heading the same way in aggregate. We seemed to stray in the one direction by chance, all as surprised as each other when we arrived together in some other place. 'You got here too?' We bleated.

Anyone turning up to the canteen late would see that there we were – gone.

The flock of us drifted baffled and bleak through the curious standing stones of our half built whatever. We did not need to follow Love, most of us could not see him anyway. We were following our imagination, going our own way to the same place. The centre of things, Love's squat white house – built on several levels, each smaller than the next, perched on top of the other like layers of a cake, until you came to the flat top – all Love's things, the way he measured this world, laid out inside.

And I felt as though a dark tide had drenched us all, leaving us chill, uneasy, out of our element.

"Why are we here?" asked Barbara from within the unstill crowd. "We know how we feel about him, what are we doing letting him lead us still, as though we had no will of our own?"

But no one offered her an answer; perhaps there was none to be had. We don't always do things because there's a reason, transparent under the cold neon glare of empiricism. Sometimes we do things which are in our nature, like beasts.

We were here because Love wanted us to be. And what he wanted, he could have us want too.

There he was, perched on the highest ivory slab like a wedding cake groom: arms by his sides, shaggy hair dancing a tango with the wind. He said nothing, seemed relaxed, as if we weren't here waiting for him to act.

And I knew enough about him to be sure there would be a show. You'd have thought he'd have lost some of his passion for blousy coup de théâtre by that stage but Love's motto always seemed to be: once bitten, twice as enthusiastic the next time.

I peered up, snared by Love's expression: infinitely tender, suffering, proud.

Then he moved. His whole body shifted upwards. Smoothly, slowly, as though he was on a lift.

"His feet," yelled Barbara, "they're off the floor!"

And indeed they were – his scuffed trainers hung some six inches above the platform – he was floating in the air with nothing but the breeze to support him.

There were hollers of confusion, surprise, and, bizarrely – recognition. 'There he goes,' they seemed to be saying – 'up into the air like some free bloody bird.'

And he rose further: a foot from the platform, hovering above us – slowly he lifted his arms from his sides, stretched them out as if hanging from the air, his feet dangling. Then, from somewhere around his solar plexus, came a glow. Old gold at first, dull and insubstantial, but brightening slowly like an element warming up – spreading too, across the whole of his chest and abdomen, changing hue through pale yellow towards white light, which seemed to draw us into it so's the light became the central focus, rather than the fact that we were watching a guy paddling his feet in the empty air. Soon Love was little more than an outline in the glow – like the filament when you stare into a bulb. Still the light grew more intense, so we couldn't look at it without guarding our eyes with our hands.

Love rose higher, confounding the physical world, or lodged in a part of it which our science had yet to stumble across. We had to crane our necks to see him, glowing brilliantly above us.

Then, one by one, we cast our eyes down, so powerful was the brightness it was like staring into the sun. It was more than we were built to handle.

I cannot say for certain whether anyone witnessed the explosion or whether, like me, they simply leapt within themselves at the sharp echoless crash and looked up to find the space above the ivory platform lost in a pall of violet smoke.

We squinted through it with our mouths hanging open, people at the front started coughing. The smoke smelled wonderful, sweet perfumed and fresh, it made me think of a bunch of flowers which, as a teenager, I picked from the gardens along Central Drive on my way home from the pub, gave to my mum to celebrate mother's day.

I was lost in this for a while. It was a long time since I had thought about my mother and I wanted to remember her face when I handed over the bent stems.

Then: "He's gone!" That was Audrey, shrill and alarmed, it seemed out of place in this moment of wonder. An accusation.

But it stirred us to peer further into the smoke and we saw that it was true. Love was not on the platform, nor was he floating above it, all that was left of our man it seemed was a rapidly diminishing purple fog.

"That can't be – folk just don't go – not into the empty air. He must be up there, he must."

Several of the younger people at the front scrambled onto the bottom ledge of the structure and scaled the broad white steps towards the peak.

There was not much to explore. Waving away palmfuls of smoke they circumnavigated the platform, bumped into each other and grumbled.

"Well, he's not here," allowed someone. And one by one they looked up at the sky. Following their lead we all did. There was nothing much to see. It was late morning, there was grey cloud. Ours is the most featureless of skies. So boring during the day that it's scarcely worth moving your neck to look unless the seagulls are up to something interesting.

It was no less dull than usual, yet we found it invested now with something precious, our flat grey canvas had become a place where magic lived.

I don't know how long we all stood there silently, gawping into the firmament. The purple smoke percolated through our assembly, mixing with the air until the dilution was too thin to call it smoke – it was more the idea of smoke, then nothing. The last vestige of John Love in our world was gone, the last physical thing linking his presence to ours.

"Well," admitted Ken Naylor, all solemn. "Now there's a thing."

I found myself nodding. It was indeed a thing.

People on the edges of the group were drifting vaguely away, like the smoke. Where were they off to? Nowhere probably. Home to stare at the TV or do the ironing. They were reacting to the feeling that something is over and it's time to go. Like leaving a football match early.

But we would all be joining them soon I knew – each of us slumped in an armchair, saggy with post partum depression. Everything we had witnessed. Then a mist. Then nothing. It seemed so unresolved.

And what were we to do with this monstrosity we had constructed? The weirdest theme park in Western Europe.

People were muttering to each other in groups of three or four. There was no focus to our crowd now, no purpose. Barbara tried unsuccessfully to gird us to further research.

"We need to get over to Bes's place quickly," she said urgently, her voice just about audible over the chatter. "There must be things which could help explain this – he has a trunk."

But there was no sign of enthusiasm for the box of tricks now the conjurer had left the stage.

"You go," said one. "I'll be glad to get back to normal to be honest."

"I just want to put my feet up for a bit," concurred another. "Watch racing on the telly, have my tea."

There were cars to be cleaned and lawns to be mowed, hedges to be trimmed and Hoovers to be taken round.

The emptying site was littered with discarded gull feathers as though all the birds on the island had been at war.

I think it was a part of this drifting, rather than any positive need to explore or explain, that took a couple of folk inside the womb of the step pyramid from the pinnacle of which John Love had made his remarkable exit.

Perhaps they had it in their minds that there was something they could pinch – hoard as a souvenir against the time when all of this seemed less than real. Maybe they were after bidding some kind of weak farewell. Most probably they were simply seeking a respite from the chilly drizzle which had arrived to soak us all.

I didn't see them go in to be honest, I doubt that most people did, we all had things on our minds.

But then came a shout – of genuine excitement.

"He's here!"

No one reacted, there was general befuddlement. We were people waking from a deep sleep, troubled by confusing dreams.

Another voice came: "It's true, he's inside here, quick come see."

And we did, those nearest to the entrance of the white pyramid bustled over to have a look, got jammed in the doorway as three or four tried to get in together. I was a few yards away through the crowd and there were still enough people around me who weren't up to speed for me to wriggle between them and in through the door. There were perhaps twenty of us by then inside the dingy vault, lit by battery lamps slung from the low ceiling. Love's tokens gathered around like a museum collection dedicated to some long dead culture. In the middle the stone block of the altar, around the edges the photos, the glass case of bits and pieces, all of this was ignored. Our attention was focused on a small foetal figure curled in one corner of the room.

It was Love. And on seeing him I felt something I had not felt since the day they told me mum had died.

Loss.

So nothing else mattered or could come to any good.

Love seemed to be asleep. Flange the rat was nearest to him. Gave him a poke in the back with the toe of his boot. Love stirred, rolled over and scrambled to his feet. He turned to look at us.

"Bollocks," said John Love.

For a while nobody spoke. We all stood still, waiting for a director to say action. But no instruction came.

We looked at Love, face framed by his shaggy hair, there in the weak light. There didn't seem to be much going on. His cheeks sagged and his eyes were downcast – he did not want to engage us. Chances are he had believed he would never see any of us again – we were guests turning up to a party which had been cancelled. The whole thing was socially embarrassing. But it didn't take long for someone to remember why Love had decided to disappear in the first place.

"Let's kill him," suggested that someone with vigour.

Suddenly a switch clicked within Love and his power supply was back on.

"Right then," he announced rubbing his hands together and staring round at us with a maniac intensity. "I think – it's time for someone to give their all. Show that we're not playing around here."

He looked over at me – nodded towards the door.

I followed him as he brushed past people – who made no attempt to stop him – Love in motion wasn't someone you stopped, he was a big bundle of kinetic energy and we needed to know how it was to be spent.

He banged open the saloon door and strode into the wet chill. There was a football style gasp from what remained of the crowd outside and immediately, those on the periphery began turning back to see what they were missing.

Love scrambled up onto the first step of the pyramid, looked out over his baffled people but said nothing.

"We thought you'd gone," accused Audrey loudly. "Why are you here?"

There was a tumble of questions, accusations, pleas…

Love didn't seem to have the words to deal with any of them.

So he reached down towards me and I expected a warm palm on the top of my head, some form of benediction, but instead he clasped a meaty paw around my collar and heaved me into the air. I felt him topple as my surprising density hit him. Doubtless he wished he had not leaned so far out over the drop, but he focused his strength, readjusted his weight with a backwards stagger. The renewed momentum, propelled us up two, three steps onto the top platform. It left me scrambling up from my skinned knees, choking a little since he'd dragged me by my scruff.

He leant down to me, voice coarse: "I need you now. Follow my lead – you know what I'm capable of. It's crucial to our project."

I need not worry then. Whatever happened he would make it right. 'Our project' made a whole heap of assumptions.

Lone Ranger surrounded by a Sioux war party: "What are we going to do Tonto?" "What d'you mean 'we', white man?"

The crowd is restive, like an Elizabethan theatre audience hurling hazelnuts and abuse.

"Always knew he was snide."

"I heard he killed a girl."

"Why's his head red?"

I do not believe he will get them back.

We are too far out over choppy water – he's in dire need of a life belt and, as he hauls me closer to him, I realise I am it.

"It's time" – he's struggling to make himself heard – "for a grand impulsive gesture – for me to prove to you how serious I am about all of this."

He's moved, wow, he means it. His voice is cracking and that's real emotion – he's a crap actor and couldn't fake choking over a sob. He's on the verge of mawing – yet it's not annoying and a bit creepy like it would be if most of us did it. It's noble.

I feel for him, we all do.

"How serious I am about all of you. I realise that what has gone on has shaken you – but you need to believe in the depth of my purpose. My love for you all."

Despite his appealing to our better nature there's little let up in the hollering for his blood.

And there's clods of earth incoming. Wump – one hits me on the shoulder. The pain's more from the memory it brings.

It isn't looking good. Things escalate, I've seen it happen.

There's a smell like thunderstorms and a ringing noise which makes me giddy as a schoolgirl.

"Cry," I'm willing him. "Real tears – that would do it I believe, even now. If they could just see how deeply…"

"So I offer you Bes!" he yelled, suddenly joyous. "I offer you the nearest thing I have to a son in all of this world, the last, the next."

Wherever then, but I didn't like the sound of this. I wasn't his to offer or theirs to take. I was mine, for the little I was worth.

"I offer you his body that it may atone for the all the wrong which has descended on this place – let his stunted, silent body carry our burden. He has good heart – he is a man, he is mute – for this at least he was created."

I made a dash for it. Up on my toes and away out of Love's careless grip, leaving his fingers forming puzzled piano chords in the air.

I hurdled over the confusion inside me and down wind across the pale plateau towards the drop to the next step. I knew if I could make it off the escarpment and into the crowd I would be safe for the few confused moments it would take to wriggle beyond the throng, then away to places on this island John Love, with all the help he could muster, would never discover. This was my place, it would remain mine.

He brought me down with a clumsy rugby tackle as I reached the first drop.

I was dangling half way over and I snapped forward so my forehead caught a dizzying crack on the cold stone side.

As Love lifted me I looked down towards the crowd and saw a fearful sight.

A hideous, malformed creature in the mob, dirty and howling, it's foul hair broken over its monstrous face. It was like some ugly, snag-toothed Caliban come to pollute me so I gasped in revulsion.

Then I remembered the mirrored steps of the pyramid.

And as Love hauled me back towards the centre of the stage, a broken marionette for the islanders to gawp at, I pitied them having to look at so incomplete a creature.

"This man," bawled Love with passion, "is willing to give himself so that we may be cleansed. Pity this small and silent man. He is taking all the sorrow of the world upon his naked body."

And as he held me aloft by my neck in his right hand I saw something flash like Morse in his left. He held it up for all to see, the cut throat razor, quaint, old-fangled piece of history left by the sculptor Morgan H Stanhope in his haste to clear off back to the bright lights of anywhere else.

The wind blows a chill exhalation of damp spray. I haul in what breath I can and taste salt.

And I am thinking: "If all the salt in the world's seas were dried out it would cover the continents to the depth of five and a half feet."

And then I am thinking: "Hang on, what does he mean – naked?"

My head's fixed forward, like a kitten in its mother's mouth. I can hear the thin creak of sawn fabric.

Which sound fills me with ineluctable panic and I shimmy like a landed conger in Love's grip. He's caught unprepared. Shocked by the swift violence of my reaction, his choke hold on my scruff shifts. My feet have purchase on the floor. An undignified scramble ensues in which I realise too late he isn't trying to hold onto me.

Another ripping sound and I find myself standing alone on the chill white platform. My clothes in tatters at my feet.

Ahh.

I look down at the pebble beach of faces below. Each staring up at me, uncomprehending.

I don't know if you've ever been in a similar position? I have, in dreams. In that world I have found myself disrobed in public many times. This occasion isn't all that different. It doesn't seem real. I don't feel normal sensations, such as cold and pain. My burning concern is for my modesty.

There's nowhere to hide so I do a preposterous jig to cover myself behind invisible fans: squirming around, sideways on, sucking in my beer gut.

My dance does not get a great reception. There's bafflement. Brows are furrowed.

Then a voice from below: "He's a woman."

Others follow, hesitant and ponderous, like people waking after a nap.

"He can't be."

"Where's his thing?"

"Perhaps it's just small – it's cold out."

"I know a woman when I see one …"

"And that's one there."

"He has tits n'all."

"So have half the blokes on the island."

"But there's the other."

There was indeed the other. There was no denying the other.

I felt something was required of me – a little by way of explanation. Normal niceties were stripped away rather, and yet it seemed only … polite.

So I huffed and coughed, cleared long unused pipes and, from a long way down, produced a dreadful, timid croak.

I said …

"It's not what you think."

Eyes on me from down below. No one said anything. They had a lot on their minds.

I glanced back at John Love. Super-glued to his mark – a look of dull resignation on his face. Wishing, presumably, that he had been less specific in his recipe for the perfect sacrificial lamb – particularly with regard to gender and volume.

He threw his hands up, attempted a sort of grin.

"It is … a miracle," he offered weakly.

It was a fair effort, in the circumstances, and you had to admire his chutzpah even now. But you could tell he wasn't sold on it.

"Though I do think," he went on ponderously in the silence which surrounded us. "That a sacrifice may still be called for."

Blimey. I made to run for it again. But I saw Love was already cutting.

Cretting away at his own frayed shirtfront, until it came open and he shrugged himself out of it. Standing there with his torso tanned and tight – so that, for the first time, I was unambiguously embarrassed about my own nakedness.

Yet I had no time to fret over it as I watched John Love lift the cut-throat razor up to his chest and draw it down in a short vertical stroke. It left a shrill, scarlet shock. Then another cut – away at an angle from the first, then a third, across the two. And more below, scoring his abdomen in quick determined strokes, each producing a livid red line.

When he had finished he stood briefly before us with his arms by his sides and his face blank. It was as if he had jolted from sleepwalking to find himself in the garden.

He had carved a message into himself like the trunk of a tree. It said: '4 real.'

It was there for us to read, but transient, already the blood from his wounds was trickling down his chest and obscuring what he had written.

"They wouldn't believe me," he was saying loudly but without direction. "They thought I was in it for myself – now they'll see that it's for them, that I love them – what else can I give?"

He sounded querulous, caught up in some ill-defined torment – a teenager furious with his parents.

And he lifted the blade up to his face.

"No!" yelled a woman's voice from the silenced crowd. Audrey? Barbara? Could have been any of us.

Love laughed – adopted a mocking squeak: "Not the face, not the beautiful face."

Then he drew the razor across his left cheek, slitting it from eye socket to jaw line, roughly, so it gaped and tore.

There was gathering protest from below – the anger most of us feel at the violation of another human being – something else too maybe, the urge to preserve what is beautiful. This was not just immolation, it was vandalism.

He was slashing at his left forearm, thick deep strokes which carved chunks of flesh and left skin hanging, he must have hit a vein because suddenly there was more blood.

It seemed to cause him no pain – he was laughing, chattering to himself agitatedly, but he did not cry out when the razor bit.

Except only the once when he pulled at his left breast and sawed at it until a handful of flesh came away. He let it fall to the gory platform where it landed, nipple upwards, like some hairy sea creature from an ocean trench. It must have smarted that because he yelled out in anger – fear even, though he must have been beyond that by now.

Soon he stopped looking like John Love, and, before long, he ceased to resemble anyone I'd seen in this world. He was meat on a butcher's slab; an autopsy report; the diagrams in a medical manual, or the cold plastification carried out by the German showman I watched on television, tormenting cadavers.

He was anything bar a man and it was as if he had no further use for his mortal body, was discarding it a bit at a time, putting it out for the rubbish.

He attempted to sever a finger, failed, had a good go at his nose, managed most of that, then an ear. The bone white roof of the pyramid was red and slippery, its malformed trophies displayed with casual abandon.

Love ripped at his bottom lip with the razor, cut the link with the gash down his cheek so the whole thing gaped showing sinew and teeth white as the marble slab.

His face reminded me of meat I'd seen as a child when we used to buy pig heads and hack sustenance from them.

He was all teeth and the whites of his eyes, And the red, the red.

He carved through pale fat and groaned and glistened with the many colours of blood.

Yes, we witnessed him, before all the people, as he dissected himself there on the slab – sawing at his remaining ear, his wrists, his throat. You could not doubt he believed he did it for us.

And in the fever which fired those last moments even his most sacred self he cut, and moaned as lovers do.

Then he fell. Slipped perhaps on the uneasy footing, tried once to haul himself up onto his knees, but his weary drunken arms wouldn't hold him and he flopped down again, face first with a crack on the slab.

And I felt so many things, but sick of course mostly. Felt angry, lost – felt glad though too.

A little.

Glad.

XVIII

I don't know what I believe.

Sometimes I'll argue a thing in my head – be passionate about it, know that I am right. Then, the next day, I'll see where I went wrong.

I have always been inclined to argue the wrong thing. Perhaps I always will be.

I have an image in my head, in moving pictures, glorious technicolour. A dapperly dressed woman of middle years is being shown to her seat by the stewardess of a jumbo-jet. She has a window seat. It is not clear where she is flying to, this lady in her comfortable shoes, somewhere distant and different.

The stewardess is polite and deferential. Would she care for a drink?

"Yes please, a glass of wine. A chilled white Chardonnay would be lovely."

And as she sips her cold honey-flavoured wine the plane arcs over pale green fields. She is too high above the world to make out people or places through the window but here's the sudden grey of the sea, and then, below, an island, unlike any other.

And she looks down, does the lady, then dreams of where she is heading to.

Our speck of land has become more popular in the year since John Love left us.

There is now a more pressing reason to visit us than to tip rubbish.

Now people we don't even know come from places we have never heard of just to stand and gaze.

They want to hear about John Love. How he came to be here, the things he did and said. They want to hear what manner of man he was. Mostly though, they want to stare at John Love's tomb.

They stroll beneath the rough cut statuary, between the half finished colonnades and perch themselves on the stained white stairs of the squat step-pyramid which has become his place of rest.

Sometimes they bring sandwiches. More often they buy something from one of the stalls set up by island entrepreneurs.

What do they think about when they stand on the peak of the pyramid and stare out over the complex towards the sea?

Don't ask me.

I seldom go out there.

Bob Stafford quit the force. Just ahead of the official inquiry, which ripped through this place like a freak wind for a short while before it blew itself out.

See, the thing about inquiries is they only ask questions, and even then they have to ask the right ones. Questions depend on answers. For a while I felt like the most voluble person on the island.

After taking early retirement due to ill-health Stafford camped himself out along the coast road close to the tomb, living in one of the several stalls selling seagull feathers to the pilgrims.

He traded from his van, which had once been used to dole out hotdogs at a travelling fair, and he obtained his stock by netting at the north end of the island where the birds roosted at night.

Barbara and Audrey clung to each other with something near grief. They moved in together – bought the bungalow on Central Drive which Audrey had always fancied. She went out to work, Barbara kept house. It was like an American sitcom from the 1960s in its unlikely tableau of domestic bliss.

They had a small dog named Alan which never much cared for me. I don't know what breed it was.

Most people on the island went back to whatever they were doing before Love turned up, like characters after the end of a movie, when the cameras are switched off.

Folk here are stoic, timeless, inward looking – like limpets clinging to a rock on the ocean bed.

Here's a good word for them – salsuginous.

I stay in my caravan. If people who I know wish to call on me then I receive them with grace.

They do not want much from me. Only to hear me talk.

Which I do for them in moderation. If I am not too weary. If I have something worth saying.

Did I tell you Love had left us?

It depends on who you speak to.

For myself, I can say I have not seen him since his final act of showmanship.

But others swear they have witnessed him at dawn. Out along the long shore of the unmade day. Pale, but real. Smiling. Lips parted, as if about to speak.

And these are the stories visitors seem most keen to hear.

Some on the island have been a tad grumpy of late, suggesting life has lost its glister and they'd be happier wherever Glazier's gone.

Me, I'm going nowhere. I want to know what happens in the future and there is only one sure way I know of finding out. Our lives are a time machine, albeit a slow one. We'll reach tomorrow if we hang on tight.

The crowds who loiter outside my van eager to see and hear Love's greatest miracle are disappointed. I keep my own counsel.

I will tell you this and I'll tell you no more.

I will be my own woman. From now until the moment I die.

CPSIA information can be obtained at www.ICGtesting.com
Printed in the USA
LVOW12s2131180314

377995LV00001B/98/P